MURDER, MAESTRO, PLEASE

DELANO AMES

Also available in Perennial Library by Delano Ames

FOR OLD CRIME'S SAKE

MURDER, MAESTRO, PLEASE

DELANO AMES

PERENNIAL LIBRARY
Harper & Row, Publishers
New York, Cambridge, Philadelphia, San Francisco
London, Mexico City, São Paulo, Sydney

A hardcover edition of this book was originally published by Hodder & Stoughton, in England in 1952. It is here reprinted by arrangement with John Farquharson, Ltd.

First PERENNIAL LIBRARY edition published 1983.

LIBRARY OF CONGRESS CATALOGUE CARD NUMBER: 82-47791

ISBN: 0-06-080630-3

83 84 85 86 10 9 8 7 6 5 4 3 2 1

To Eric

Chapter 1

WHENEVER I cannot think of anything to write about, Dagobert proposes a journey. This keeps us constantly on the move.

Sometimes, indeed, it helps; but more often I come home with a notebook containing accounts of the Corsican blood feud, a recipe for *bouillabaisse*, or bits of Pyrenean topography like the following:

It is possible – though not advisable – to reach Puig d'Aze by a minor road or, rather, cart-track, which branches off Route Nationale No. 20 – the route that normal travellers take. The track twists and struggles until it reaches the cross-roads on the Col d'Aze. As we approach the signpost at the cross-roads the valley narrows. From time to time, when the mists part, there are vertiginous glimpses of the desolate gorge beneath us, where a mountain stream rushes down to join the Garonne on its long course to the sea. The upland meadows, climbing towards the Pic des Quatre Vents, are splashed with blue and gold, with gentians and buttercups and lush green grass where sheep browse. We hear the tinkle of their bells and think what a glorious sight this would be on a fine June day. It is a June day, but we are having (the natives assure us) exceptional weather....

I particularly remember the above description, because it was a few yards before the cross-roads referred to that someone shot at us.

Dagobert had just been explaining that in classical tragedy death occurs at the end of the story whereas in a thriller it comes at the beginning – propaganda aimed at reassuring me that Sophocles and I (though tackling the problem differently) were aiming at the same thing. The shot broke up the discussion rather too pointedly. We scrambled from the tandem in haste.

For about two seconds no sound, except our own bated breath, broke the mountain stillness. Then the gun fired again.

'They're getting the range,' Dagobert suggested technically.

My teeth stopped chattering long enough for me to ask:

'Whose range?'

Dagobert gulped as the third shot interrupted my query. A

boulder came unstuck from the hillside somewhere above our heads. It lumbered down, gathered speed, and crashed across the road – unfortunately missing the tandem.

'I see what you mean,' he murmured. 'Still, it's copy. . . .'

I shuddered at the word. I am fond of discussing 'copy' over a good dinner and a bottle of wine. At the moment I felt the suggestion was ill-timed.

'. . . some day you'll be able to use it.'

A fourth shot either went wild or we were no longer the target. Dagobert breathed again.

'. . . probably,' he concluded.

'Probably what?' I asked in exasperation.

He began to explain, but gave it up. Conversation lapsed. So, happily, did the gunfire. There was no fifth shot. The anti-climax was pleasant.

We were as a bird (or a bullet) flies very near the frontier of Andorra where, according to the guidebook, it is the 'inalienable right' of every adult male to carry firearms. On the slopes of the Pic des Quatre Vents they shoot the isard. It was out of season, but we had had an exquisite *civet d'isard* for dinner last night. It is a shy animal, difficult to shoot. Doubtless you stalked it in the dense fog.

Then there were smugglers. Probably the frontier people fired at smugglers from time to time. In brief, there were a dozen satisfactory explanations. I wished I could think of one.

Dagobert had been pursuing a different line of speculation. 'I was wondering,' he said, 'what mortal enemies we have made in the neighbourhood.'

'Don't . . .' my voice rose, but immediately sank to a controlled croak, 'say things like that. This is supposed to be a holiday.'

He picked me sympathetically out of the ditch and dusted me off. 'You don't like the idea of mysterious assaults on our life?'

'No.'

'Sinister attempts to make us abandon our project?'

'I wouldn't mind those so much,' I admitted.

Our 'project' was to reach Puig d'Aze on a tandem bicycle via Andorra and the less accessible regions of the Eastern Pyrenees; I was quite willing to abandon this project on the spot. It had been formed four evenings ago at the Café de la

Gare in Perpignan when the question of how to get to Puig d'Aze had first become acute.

There is, of course, a train and a regular bus service, but Dagobert had been reading a guidebook which was written before these things existed. It was full of maps showing mule paths. I had seen him gazing at the shop window next door which displayed hobnailed boots, steel-tipped sticks, campers' and cyclists' equipment. Recognizing the far-away look in his eye, I said quickly:

'There's a place down the road with motor-cars for hire.'

He nodded absently. I saw what was distracting him. It was a tiny tent which contained a plastic mattress which blew up. There was a light collapsible table in front of it covered with folding aluminium saucepans and one-piece knife, fork and spoon sets. The whole thing apparently fitted into a monstrous rucksack.

'You don't think we're getting soft and unenterprising, do you, Jane?' he said.

'Yes, let's do that,' I said. 'And besides, if you're thinking of walking to Puig d'Aze you know your feet always hurt.'

Dagobert winced. At the next table a young man who had been pretending to read a book called *Business English* also winced. I could see he was longing to tell us about methylated spirits, wearing three pair of socks and putting soap in boots. In his pale blue eyes, magnified behind steel-rimmed spectacles, there was the fanatical light of the outdoor type who is rich in such lore. He had a receding chin, but bronzed and bulging calves. He wore a beret, green shorts, and a green sweat-shirt with a large yellow badge sewn on to it. Dagobert eyed the badge with interest.

'I was thinking,' he said, 'of bicycles.'

'The Gordon-Smiths,' I mused, 'are coming in their brand new Humber Super-Snipe. I should have asked Naomi what clothes she's bringing.'

'There are, admittedly, a few hills between here and Puig d'Aze,' Dagobert went on, 'but we have five days to get there.'

Out of the corner of my eye I saw our neighbour edging relentlessly forward. *Business English* had slipped unnoticed from his fingers. I could now distinguish the legend which encircled the yellow badge. It read 'Club du Cyclisme des Pyrénées Orientales'. I murmured:

'I wonder if she still wears barbaric jewellery and bracelets with little lucky charms?'

'Bartali,' our neighbour said, 'did it in six hours, thirty-three minutes, seventeen seconds.'

'I don't seem to place Bartali,' I said.

Dagobert smiled apologetically on my behalf. While he called the waiter and ordered three Pernods I learned that Bartali was twice winner of the Tour de France, and possibly the greatest racing cyclist in the world. This was interesting, but at the time I didn't see what connexion it had with how we were to keep our rendezvous with Geoffrey and Naomi Gordon-Smith for the Puig d'Aze Musical Festival.

I let Dagobert and our new friend – his name was Jean Delattre and he was secretary of the Club du Cyclisme des Pyrénées Orientales – discuss such technicalities as Rolex gears and handlebar angles secure in the knowledge, as yet undisclosed to my husband, that I did not know how to ride a bicycle. I reserved this depressing news for the second round of Pernods, when Dagobert and Jean Delattre were deciding whether we should buy 'sports' or 'tourist' models.

'Of course, I could take lessons,' I added as Dagobert's face fell.

Dagobert had once given me driving lessons, and this suggestion failed to cheer him up. Jean Delattre, on the other hand, accepted my statement as a challenge. He began to gesticulate wildly and his 'Business English' deserted him in his excitement. By an extraordinary coincidence his *petite amie*, too, ignored how to conduct a bicycle! And yet together they had made the *cyclisme* all over France! How was this!

We waited agog.

'The tandem!'

I saw Dagobert's face clear at the word, and my heart sank. The last time I had seen that look we had ended up on a raft on the Mississippi, retracing the footsteps of La Salle – or perhaps it was Huckleberry Finn.

'Tell us about tandems,' Dagobert said softly.

The essence of tandems was that the person in front did all the brainwork. No previous experience was required of the one at the back. She had only to pedal, thrill to the exhilaration of swift movement and enjoy the scenery – chiefly, I later learned, a view of the back of her husband's neck.

What we personally needed was a lightweight racing model tandem, fitted with small saddlebags for overnight essentials like Sloan's Liniment. By an extraordinary coincidence he, Jean Delattre, had just such a machine at the moment for sale.

'But won't your – er – *petite amie*,' I said, struggling against a rising sense of unreality, 'be upset if you sell it?'

Jean Delattre slumped in his seat. He fumbled for his spectacles and wiped them on the tablecloth. He said with a catch in his voice:

'I have no *petite amie* – since last week.'

'I'm so sorry,' I murmured inadequately.

'There was a motor rally,' he added with a deep sigh, sucking the ice which remained in his glass.

'By an extraordinary coincidence,' Dagobert said, 'here's the waiter.'

I shook my head, remembering that the last train for Puig d'Aze left the station in twenty minutes. Half an hour later, when we left the café, we owned – by a final extraordinary coincidence – one lightweight racing model tandem. We were also honorary life members of the Club du Cyclisme des Pyrénées Orientales.

Bartali may have covered the distance between Perpignan and Puig d'Aze in six hours, thirty-three minutes and seventeen seconds; we took four days. The road leading up to the 'quaint Catalan village which nestles in the brooding shadow of the Pic des Quatre Vents' is said to be among the most beautiful in Europe. Some day I hope to take the bus along it and see for myself.

Less than a month ago I had never heard of Puig d'Aze. We had been living inoffensively in a small flat near the Luxembourg Gardens and our address was c/o Thomas Cook, Paris. Dagobert had been dividing his time between the Bibliothèque Nationale and fishing in the Seine, while I had a subscription at the Anglo-American library and practically nothing to do. I would wander up and down the Avenue Matignon looking in Maggy Rouff's and Jacques Heim's windows, and occasionally wonder in a vague way if I should ever find another subject to write a book about. This possibility seemed agreeably remote and life was most pleasant.

Then, out of the blue of South Kensington, Naomi's letter

arrived. Naomi and I had been together at St Catherine's at Richmond during what she calls 'the war' – it was the Spanish Civil War – and we had kept in desultory touch with each other ever since. We had been to each other's weddings, we remembered each other's birthdays, and about once a year had tea together at Gunther's to show off new hats.

Naomi, though a prefect, was artistic. At school, I remember, she played the viola one term, but changed to the cor anglais the next and afterwards took up the glockenspiel. She used to have Braque and Picasso prints on the walls of her room and books by Lorca and Rilke in their original languages. This used to impress her juniors immensely in spite of the fact that we suspected she couldn't read Spanish or German.

She was impulsive, generous and, she herself admitted, slightly scatter-brained; we were always surprised when she got her own way. She was warm-hearted and impractical; we were all relieved when she married Geoffrey Gordon-Smith, who was solid, rich and desirable. Dagobert, who met her once at a cocktail party last winter, said she was extremely decorative. At St Catherine's we had thought her rather 'quaint'.

Her letter began promisingly. 'Darling Jane,' she wrote in the gothic script which was the envy of St Catherine's, but unfortunately hard to decipher, 'I've just bought your book!'

I love letters which start like this, and I read on eagerly:

'Geoffrey, poor dear, who never reads anything but trash,' it continued, 'says it's not at all bad, though he spotted the villain immediately, which is apparently an undesirable thing. I wouldn't know. How do you ever think of such things? I think it's so clever of you – clues and bodies and Scotland Yard detectives in false moustaches! You must be making mints of money. I only wish I had time to write! My mink is beginning to look horribly shabby and London is desperately expensive. How intelligent of you to live in France! Do you run into Sartre and Anouilh often? I'm just rereading *Les Faux-Monnayeurs* for the dozenth time. Isn't it astonishing how little it dates?'

There were three or four pages of literary criticism which I didn't follow very closely, being unfamiliar with most of the names she mentioned. There was a postscript in which she said:

'I'm getting more scatter-brained every year. Senility, perhaps? Geoffrey – unkindly – reminds me I'm practically thirty! You were a form ahead of me at St Catherine's, weren't you? I can never remember. Oh, yes . . . Geoffrey's longing to try out his new Humber Super-Snipe in mountains, so we're spending a week in the Pyrenees. Of course, I immediately thought of you and Dagwood. Obviously we *must* forgather! Being almost next door, as it were. I can't wait to see you. We can bore our husbands to death by reminiscences of St C.'s. I only wish we could give you a lift in the car, but what with luggage and so forth. Anyway, I'm absolutely *relying* on you, Jane. Until the twenty-fourth, then, in the Pyrenees. Won't it be *fun*!'

'It might be at that,' Dagobert said.

I stared at him in astonishment. He explained:

'I mean I don't want you to feel you have to drop all your old school friends, Jane, because you married me. Which was Naomi? The one who was so good at hockey?'

'No,' I said, continuing to watch him. 'Naomi was the one at the Allisons' cocktail party in the flowered hat with the veil which kept getting in the way when you fussed around lighting cigarettes for her.'

He continued to look blank. I repeated thoughtfully: 'Dagwood . . .' and added: 'You *seem* to have made as little impression on Naomi as she *seems* to have made on you.'

'There's another P.S.,' he said, turning over the last page of Naomi's letter. It said:

'I nearly forgot! You'll never guess who's coming along with us. *Perdita !!!* Isn't it a small world! – N.'

I wrote back to ask who on earth Perdita was and weakly inquired whereabouts in the Pyrenees we were supposed to meet. I received a postcard by return.

'Sorry. Puig d'Aze. Everyone will be there. Kitson's playing and mustn't be missed. See last week's N.S. & N. But your own cousin, of course. She's adorable.'

'Who's Kitson?' I asked, handing Dagobert the postcard. 'And what's he play? Have I a cousin called Perdita?'

He stirred uncomfortably. 'No, but I think I have. Uncle Fortinbras married a woman who has three daughters. Two are named Titania and Portia. The other could easily be Perdita. We have some harpsichord records played by someone called Kitson.'

An announcement in last week's *New Statesman* cleared

up the Kitson mystery. As everyone knew, Kitson (apparently he had no first name) was, with the possible exception of Madame Landowska, the greatest living exponent of the harpsichord. In nineteen forty-five, after the death in tragic circumstances of his wife, Kitson had retired from the world to live the life of a hermit in the remote Pyrenean village of Puig d'Aze, refusing all offers to appear in London, New York and Paris. This June, for the first time in over six years, he had reluctantly consented to play once more in public. Admirers and disciples from all over the musical world had persuaded him to give a week's series of recitals. Thus the idea of the Puig d'Aze Musical Festival had been conceived – a unique occasion for the connoisseur to hear this remarkable artist probably for the last time. Tickets and information from the Hon. Sebastian Nevil, 6 Inner Temple Lane, London, or from the Syndicat d'Initiative, Puig d'Aze, Pyrénées Orientales.

A telegram a few days later also threw light of a sort on Perdita. It was from Cheltenham and was the first we'd heard from Uncle Fortinbras since the arrival of his wedding present to us, the mounted head of a stag, shot by himself. It read:

PERDITA DELIGHTED YOUR INVITATION. WILL HOLD YOU ENTIRELY RESPONSIBLE.

We thought of wiring back: 'What invitation and responsible for what?' but decided not to. There was clearly going to be enough confusion without our adding to it.

Chapter 2

THE bewildering thing about the shots which had sent us scurrying for shelter was that we had no more idea where they'd come from than what they'd been aimed at. Mist, churning up from the watercourse below, had so reduced visibility that we could scarcely make out the signpost at the cross-roads a few yards ahead. The reports, though I have taken some time to describe them, had followed each other in rapid succession. They were echoed and re-echoed by the walls of the gorge and died away in a mutter of angry reverberation down the valley. Whether we'd been shot at – or whether anyone had been shot at – from above, below or across the valley it was impossible to say.

I saw Dagobert peering intently over the edge of the road as though trying to pierce the rolling blanket of fog. I joined him hastily. Though it seemed an eternity since that gun had fired, only a few minutes had actually elapsed, and I was still in no mood to face things alone.

At that moment the mist parted beneath us. Our road hung over a precipice. I tugged at Dagobert's sleeve, but he refused to be moved. I followed his glance reluctantly, and as I did so a shaft of golden sunlight cut the gorge below. Above our heads the mist, suddenly light and fluffy, curled back, revealing the criss-cross ribbon which was the road to Andorra. But I hadn't noticed that yet.

I was staring down into the theatrically lit gorge. A thicket of larches, pale green in their new foliage, crept up the steep slopes as far as they could gain foothold. They looked like toy trees from this height. The man in a sheepskin jacket who moved at their edge looked like a toy figure too. He was carrying something that resembled a toy shepherd's crook. Or then again it could have been a toy rifle.

He glanced up in our direction and abruptly withdrew into the larches. Whether he withdrew as abruptly as I did is a debatable point.

I had no time to debate it; for at that instant the valley was shaken with an infernal roar which sent me scuttling across the road again. Dagobert hit the grassy inner verge of the road a split second after me. This time, I thought hysterically, they were after us with machine-guns, unless it was an earthquake. Again I was unable to locate the source of the noise, except that I realized it was approaching rapidly and was almost on top of us.

My heart thumped three or four times, as though measuring the moments before annihilation. Then feebly I began to laugh. High altitudes are said to have this distressing effect. My approaching annihilation was simply an approaching motor-car.

It had given us no warning. We decided afterwards that it must have been coasting and suddenly switched on its engine. It was a sports car, a Bugatti, and its muffler was cut out. It was also the first car we had encountered that day. Traffic had been largely ox-carts or an occasional flock of goats.

I realized a moment later that the Bugatti, though behind us, was not on our road. It was hurtling towards the cross-roads down a road above our heads – a road which doubled back towards the Andorran frontier. We heard the driver crash into a lower gear as he raced towards the fork, scattering loose gravel and raising dust. I caught a blur of bright crimson as the tyres tore round the signpost. The long, low body shuddered, skidded until its nose pointed nearly to us, but swerved again before it got clear round. I closed my eyes, waiting for the crash as it leapt the parapet and plunged into the gorge. There was no crash and I opened them again. The Bugatti miraculously, or so it seemed to me, was a disappearing flash of crimson down the road which led to Puig d'Aze. It left behind it a trail of dust and a disquieting sense of something out of control – or in a desperate hurry.

'Good driver,' Dagobert said admiringly.

'At least she's still alive,' I nodded.

He started slightly, frowned, and began to pick up the tandem.

'Yes . . .' he murmured, and to my surprise did not pursue the subject.

This, with Dagobert, is a rare phenomenon, and while he pushed the tandem towards the cross-roads I walked beside him with an air of expectancy. He drew my attention to the field of troilus which nodded their globes of waxen yellow in the sloping fields stretching down towards the spire of St-Justin-d'Aze. The Bugatti was no longer visible, having disappeared in the folding meadows of the fertile valley of the Aze. I hoped it was proceeding at a less suicidal pace.

I admired the globe flowers distractedly and continued – as I suspected Dagobert, too, was doing – to reflect upon the events of the last shattering (could it only be?) few minutes.

For some reason the apparition of the Bugatti had quite driven our friend with the shepherd's crook (or the rifle) out of my mind. The car had been an open so-called 'four'-seater. That is to say, it was the kind of car which has two comfortable leather bucket seats for the driver and the person beside the driver, and a cramped space behind where two passengers can crouch perilously and hold on to their hats. We have friends at home who sometimes offer us 'spins' in such vehicles. It's better than a tandem of course.... But my mind was wandering.

The back seat of the Bugatti which had just passed us was covered with canvas, of the sort which buttons down and forms a dust cover for luggage. I had caught the briefest glimpse of the two people in it. The driver was a young woman who looked rather tense as she gripped the steering wheel. A very striking crimson scarf – obviously dyed to match the car – trailed behind her in the wind.

I'd seen even less of her passenger: an impression of tousled dark hair, a sports jacket, an expression of grim amusement, as though he was enjoying it all.

'Though it may have been manly self-control,' I said out loud.

Dagobert glanced at me curiously and propped the tandem against the signpost. I noticed with misgiving that he had pointed it up the Andorra road. It was only Friday; our rendezvous with the Gordon-Smiths was for Saturday, when Kitson's recitals began. Dagobert felt that we just had time to 'work in' Andorra. I thought one peaceful day in Puig d'Aze would be agreeable, pressing the clothes we'd sent on by bus and disposing tactfully of the tandem.

'I also have to shorten that green tweed skirt.' I broke the silence again.

He didn't reply. He was walking back towards the spot

where we had taken cover during the gunfire. I caught up with him and said:

'I'll have to watch this habit I'm getting into of talking to myself all the time.'

He nodded absently. 'Yes, the new green skirt. Have I seen it?'

He was scrabbling up among the rocks and brambles above the road, ripping the sleeve of the corduroy jacket he'd bought in the Boulevard Sébastopol. The slope was nearly perpendicular. By it a particularly agile mountain goat might have reached the bend in the Andorra road somewhere above. I remembered the boulder which had come loose and rolled down across our road.

'It's the one I lengthened two years ago,' I explained without bitterness. 'What do you think you're doing?'

'Looking for the bullet.'

'What would you do if you found it?'

He lost his balance and came toppling down into the road again. For the first time in several minutes he smiled.

'I haven't the faintest idea,' he admitted. 'Only people always do look for the bullet in these cases.'

'What cases?'

He shrugged good humouredly. 'That's true. There isn't any case. I hadn't thought of it.'

We returned to the tandem arm in arm, feeling almost cheerful now that was settled. Our recent fog was hardly more than scattered wisps of cottonwool around the summit of the Pic des Quatre Vents and the late afternoon sun shone from a cloudless sky. Beneath it the tiled roofs of Puig d'Aze basked snugly. The shadows of the Pic, which would soon stride across the meadows to engulf the village, attained only the western slopes of the valley, deepening the green outlying fields of clover. The guide book was right: Puig d'Aze *did* nestle.

I turned away from this glimpse of the promised land with a sigh of resignation. Our road to Andorra zigzagged straight up the bare shoulder of the mountain, overhanging that horrifying gorge still associated in my mind with gunfire.

'If you're serious about the green skirt,' Dagobert said suddenly, 'we can go to Andorra some other time.'

I climbed on to the back saddle of the tandem with gratitude.

And then, because I'll never learn when a conversation is finished, I started all over again.

'If you think you really *ought* to find the bullet . . .' And added, even more fatuously: 'Though, of course, no one has been killed.'

'No,' he agreed briefly, and began to talk about harpsichords.

I tried to listen. Harpsichords, I learned, are not to be confused with clavichords, being diametrically opposed in principle – something technical about jacks and tangents. It was as well to clear up the point before meeting Naomi.

We rolled luxuriously down into the valley, stopping occasionally to examine wild flowers. The road had become wider and the bends less sharp. The Bugatti must have taken them in its stride; at least there was no sign of wreckage by the roadside. Coasting effortlessly, I could hear the clic-clic-clic of our wheels. It kept repeating my inane words to Dagobert: 'No one has been killed, no one has been killed.'

Now and again it invented a phrase of its own: 'No one that we know of.'

And once it added: '. . . yet.'

I think Dagobert, too, was worried by the thought which obsessed me. Those shots near the Col d'Aze could have been aimed not at us but at the occupants of the Bugatti.

Chapter 3

WE bounced into the narrow cobble-stoned street, and I suddenly had less morbid things on my mind: chiefly, the Hôtel des Voyageurs where, on Jean Delattre's recommendation, we had reserved a room. The Hôtel des Voyageurs was the Cycling Club's choice for Puig d'Aze and it gave special reductions for members. The Gordon-Smiths and Perdita were, of course, staying at the Grand Alexandra Palace.

We jolted into the cramped square in front of the church. The square was less decorative than it had seemed from the Col d'Aze, being full of motor coaches, souvenir shops and cafés advertising Coca-Cola. Dagobert was trying to distinguish the Saracen influence in the romanesque tympanum over the church door when we almost ran over a small, freckle-faced girl with pigtails who was licking an ice-cream cornet and gaping into a pastry shop. She addressed us in our native tongue:

'Look out where you're going, carncher? These bloomin' cyclists . . .'

As Naomi's postcard had said, 'everyone will be in Puig d'Aze.' I interrupted before the child could enlarge by asking her where the Hôtel des Voyageurs was.

'Never heard of it,' she shrugged. She thought this over and added: 'Yes, I have. It's down there somewhere,' and vanished into the pastry shop.

Dagobert wisely took the street which led in the opposite direction, and just behind the church we drew up abruptly beside an austere grey stone façade on which was painted in fading blue: 'Hôtel-Cafe. Confort Moderne.'

'Here we are,' Dagobert announced cheerfully.

I did not share his enthusiasm. It was going to be another of those 'picturesque' inns with large, draughty rooms, stone floors, a single feeble electric light bulb masked by an 'alabaster' bowl filled with dead flies, and a jug of cold water standing in a cracked basin.

Then, through the gate which led into the courtyard, I saw

the splash of crimson which had already caught Dagobert's eye. Our Bugatti was parked in one of the sheds under the inner eaves of the hotel.

We put the tandem in the shed beside the Bugatti. The luggage grid was empty and the canvas cover for the back seat had been removed. Presumably, the owners' things had been taken into the hotel. Perhaps they, too, travelled by the Cycling Club's recommendations.

I glanced over Dagobert's shoulder as he stooped to peer at the engraved plate screwed to the Bugatti's dashboard. It read: Squadron Leader John Corcoran, Craven Court, Knightsbridge SW1.' I thought for a second that the name meant something to Dagobert, but when I asked him he shook his head in a preoccupied sort of way.

The silences of Dagobert were beginning to get on my nerves, even though I suspected the effect was calculated. I jumped slightly when he struck a match.

'What are you doing?' I said. 'Stop it.'

But I knew exactly what he was looking for. If someone had shot at Squadron Leader Corcoran or at the woman driving a bullet might have hit the car.

If it had, Dagobert found no traces of it. He joined me a moment later at the door of the shed looking slightly foolish. I rubbed it in:

'Not riddled with bullets?'

When Dagobert is in the wrong he is always the second to admit it. He relaxed. 'It was an idea, anyway. And when you start writing up our adventures for the *Cyclist's Own* you'll need an idea.'

He saw me dubiously studying the courtyard. Chickens were scratching aimlessly among the cobble-stones, and a donkey, tethered in a shed opposite, watched us without interest. The first-floor bedrooms had a dilapidated wooden balcony joining them, leading (I suspected) to outside sanitation. He added quickly, improvising:

'But I've found a valuable clue.'

'I'm sure you have, dear,' I murmured, wondering why people with Bugattis – or even with tandems – stayed at the Hôtel des Voyageurs. 'If only we hadn't sent on our luggage...'

'The setting is excellent,' he continued. 'Quaint tiled roofs, romantic balcony, this ancient courtyard teeming with life.'

I thought of saying: 'Why wouldn't the Grand Alexandra Palace be a good setting?' but decided not to prolong the discussion. It was the same discussion which had been interrupted an hour ago on the Col d'Aze – about the book Dagobert felt it was time I began to write. Ever since the *Abersoch Advertiser* said: 'Though marred by excessive whimsy we quite enjoyed this yarn about Dagobert Brown and look forward to another'; ever since we cut out this review (omitting the bit about whimsy) Dagobert has striven to encourage my literary career.

This encouragement takes nightmare forms. Our neighbours become creatures with sinister pasts to investigate. Everyday events become fraught with mystery and menace. We find clues everywhere. In the midst of life we are in crime fiction.

This sometimes has unfortunate social repercussions (like the time in the Deux Magots when Dagobert didn't realize the two Existentialists at the next table were sober enough to understand English), but it enlivens domestic conversation and makes a change from my husband's other favourite topics like the Quantum Theory, Minoan Pottery, Fishing, and Medieval Metrical Romance.

'From what Jean Delattre told us,' I began, 'I got quite a different impression of . . .'

'Don't you want to hear about the clue I found?' Dagobert interrupted.

I apologized for my seeming lack of interest, and he opened his left hand. It contained the stub of a cigarette. As he obviously was waiting for my comment, I suggested:

'Corcoran smokes cigarettes? Or perhaps Mrs Corcoran smokes cigarettes?'

'No lipstick,' he said. 'Perhaps she doesn't use lipstick.'

'Perhaps she isn't Mrs Corcoran.'

'I like that,' he approved. 'That's the kind of doubt you want to start introducing. But doesn't something strike you about this cigarette butt?'

'No.'

'It's a Carmela. It says so on the paper. Carmelas are made in Andorra, where they cost threepence a packet. That's one reason I wanted to go to Andorra.'

He was leading me towards the door marked: 'Entrée de

l'Hôtel' while he spoke. I had an impression that he was talking in order to divert my attention, possibly from the extremely mangy dog on the threshold which was scratching itself half-heartedly. He's got me into worse places than the Hôtel des Voyageurs by this method. I stopped suddenly and said:

'And how does all this make it a clue?'

'A clue?' he muttered. 'A clue to what? Oh, yes, I'm glad you raised the question. This cigarette hints strongly that the Bugatti was coming from Andorra.'

'Yes, dear. So was the road. Remember?'

He saw my point and tossed the stub into the gutter. 'It wasn't a very good clue,' he admitted. 'But it shows I'm keeping my mind on your work.'

We had stepped down into a large, low-ceilinged room from which the chill had been partially removed by an iron stove which smoked in the far corner. A zinc counter with glasses and an array of bottles occupied one side of the room, lending it – Dagobert thought – a homey atmosphere. There were advertisements on the walls for Dubonnet and Cognac Camus, a large notice about 'Public Drunkenness', and, surprisingly, the programmes for Kitson's Harpsichord Recitals.

Two rustic types in the corner beside the stove were playing dominoes and drinking tumblers of red wine. They ignored us. A girl was sitting at a table by the window facing the street. Her long, glossy red hair came to the shoulders of the short ocelot jacket which she wore with blue jeans and high-heeled shoes. She was strikingly pretty in a kind of crude, sultry way.

As we entered she looked up from her book – Volume II of Schweitzer's *Life of Bach* – frowned, fidgeted, glanced out the window and finally returned with a pout to her book.

I joined Dagobert at the counter where he was studying the visitors' register. The most recent entry in bold, sweeping strokes was: 'John Corcoran, London. Room 2.'

Dagobert rang the bell on the counter. The only effect of the sound was to startle the dog who had come in with us. We gave it a packet of potato chips from the counter. It refused them, but wagged its tail amiably. It was a large, rangy mongrel with yellow shifty eyes and fur coming off in patches. I patted him without thinking. He gulped sentimentally, and I realized it was the beginning of one of those emotional entanglements which can prove so embarrassing.

Dagobert rang the bell again and called in his best French: '*Y a-t-il quelqu'un?*'

'If you are wanting a room,' the girl in the window said, 'there isn't one.'

Dagobert's French impresses me and I am always a little hurt that people invariably answer him in English.

'In that case,' I said hopefully.

'Why are you not going down to Aze-les-Bains?' she suggested. 'It's only ten miles from here and there you are finding tennis courts, a tiled swimming pool and a casino where you can be dancing in the evenings.'

I said that sounded very nice, but that we'd come for the music festival. She shrugged, conveying the impression that we were making a great mistake, and glanced out of the window again, biting her short unmanicured nails.

At that moment two things occurred and my attention became divided. The kitchen door opened and the landlady appeared. The street door opened and the child we had nearly run over in front of the church burst in. She saw us and said, 'Crikey!' in a disillusioned way, sank down beside the girl at the window, and yelled: 'Oh, no, you don't! That's mine.'

A tussle ensued for the possession of Schweitzer's *Life of Bach*, Volume II, interrupted by the child's suddenly saying in a stage whisper: 'I say, Vicki! *He's* hanging round again. I just seen him. Do you know what? I think he's got a crush on you!'

I didn't catch Vicki's reply (the landlady who'd clearly never heard of us was explaining to Dagobert that she had *plenty* of rooms, while I was muttering, 'what about the luggage we sent on?'), but I thought Vicki betrayed unexpected symptoms of humanity in blushing at the child's unlikely suggestion. I abandoned efforts to fathom the girl's doubtless sordid love life, and concentrated on essentials: namely, that Dagobert, ignoring wild nudges from me, had signed the hotel register. Shortly afterwards we found ourselves installed in that vast draughty room with stone floor, fly-filled electric-light bowl and jug of water in cracked basin that I had so accurately foreseen. The dog had already settled into the armchair.

Our room was Number 8. We had passed Number 2, John Corcoran's room, at the head of the stairs. I glanced at Dagobert curiously.

'It's an odd thing about our luggage.'

'It will be at the bus station,' he said. 'Probably. Is that six o'clock?'

It was. You could tell by counting the thunderclaps which at that moment shook the church spire next door and probably accounted for the cracked basin. The entire building trembled. The chimes of St-Justin-d'Aze are, the guide book states without exaggeration, famous for miles around. A large area of the Eastern Pyrenees can keep time by them.

'It will be fun trying to get to sleep in between times,' I said when the racket had died down sufficiently to make myself heard. 'What do you think of Vicki's suggestion about going on to Aze-les-Bains?'

'Does she look a little like Ava Gardner?' he mused. 'Or do I mean Pola Negri?' It was the first indication he had given that he had even been aware of her existence. He added before I could interrupt: 'By the way, the landlady says Corcoran arrived alone. I wonder what he did with the girl in the crimson scarf? I've got it! The Lady Vanishes. Or has that idea been used?'

We decided to pursue the subject elsewhere. By elsewhere, Dagobert meant in the café below. I explained to him as we descended the stairs that the first thing we were going to do was to go to the bus station to find our luggage.

'We'll take the tandem,' he said, 'and explore.'

The dog and I followed him out into the courtyard. I suggested that a walk would be restful. But we had already reached the shed. In our absence the doors had been shut. Through the cracks a glimmer of light escaped. It vanished as we paused. The doors were not locked and Dagobert jerked them open. A young man in a T-shirt and flannel trousers regarded us without visible embarrassment. He was about six-feet-three, very presentable, and must have been every day of twenty-one.

'I was just admiring the Bugatti,' he said with an attractive Texas drawl.

'You can see it better with the doors open,' Dagobert suggested. 'And that way you also save the battery of your torch.'

The young man grinned disarmingly and put the torch in his hip pocket. 'I guess you're right about that,' he agreed. 'Only I'm kind of unpopular around here already and I like to keep out of sight.'

I tried a shot in the dark. 'Are you the one that hangs around?'

This time he looked acutely embarrassed. 'Who said that?'

'Vicki.'

He flinched. 'Gosh! Do you know Vicki Stein? And that little horror?'

'With freckles and pigtails?'

'Yeah. Mitzi. Her sister. The infant prodigy.' He ran a huge hand through close-cropped fair hair, and added: 'She thinks I'm chasing her around.'

'Are you?'

He grinned again. 'Well, maybe I am at that.' He dropped the subject, returning enthusiastically to the Bugatti. 'She's a honey! Is she yours?'

'No,' said Dagobert. 'Our name is not Corcoran.'

'Mine's Tyler,' he said, extending a hand warmly. 'Tyler Sherman. I'm very pleased to make your acquaintance. Did you say Corcoran?'

We straightened it out eventually. We also learned, in about two minutes, that Tyler Sherman – Ty most people called him – was from Dallas, Texas, that he was a G.I. student specializing in something called 'Culture', that in search of this he had visited every art gallery in Europe, read Toynbee, Jung and Maritain, was taking in a few harpsichord recitals and was on his way to Rome, or maybe Madrid, before going back to the Sorbonne, or maybe Oxford, in the autumn. Ultimately he was going to get a job in the Dallas Mutual Life Insurance Company.

Dagobert felt we could go into all this more comfortably over a drink. Tyler Sherman said he knew a place down the street a way. He wanted to hear all about us, too.

'Brown?' he repeated as we reached the street and made for the church square. 'Funny about that name.'

'We're not sensitive,' I said. 'What's funny about it?'

'Not Dagobert and Jane Brown, by any chance?'

We tried not to look pleased; this must be a member of our public, perhaps even an admirer. I glanced at Tyler with new benevolence. He was scratching his head.

'Got it?' he exclaimed. 'It's on your baggage.'

'What baggage? Where?' I began.

'It's been stacked up in the hotel lobby for the last three days.'

'What hotel lobby?'

'At the place I'm staying – across the street and up a bit from the dump where the Steins are.'

'I know the dump you mean,' I nodded, eyeing Dagobert who was suddenly very occupied in trying to persuade the dog to go home again. 'We live in it. And *your* hotel is called . . .?'

'The Hôtel des Voyageurs.'

'Dagobert . . .' I called softly.

But he and the dog had already darted across the square; both were intently studying the *contreforts* which supported the apse of St-Justin-d'Aze.

Chapter 4

'DAGOBERT,' I repeated when he rejoined us a few yards farther down the street, 'do you know the name of the hotel you've got us into?'

He looked puzzled by the question. 'I can never remember the names of hotels. Isn't it the, er . . .'

'No. It's the Hôtel Commerce. The Hôtel des Voyageurs is across the street.'

'What an extraordinary thing! Imagine our making a mistake like that!'

'I'm trying to,' I said.

He shrugged. 'Still, does it matter?'

'Not in the least. We'll go back at once and explain.'

'You don't think,' he said, 'that we were led there by a kind of *destiny*?'

'Say!' Tyler Sherman broke in. 'If you stayed on at the Commerce you could ask me in to dinner tonight.'

'We're unpopular enough with Vicki without that,' I said unkindly. He looked so crestfallen that I at once relented. 'If we do, will you tell us what you were *really* doing with your torch in that shed?'

He coloured slightly and began to stammer. 'Well, er, there's a kind of ladder in that shed and I was kind of wondering where it led.'

'It leads,' Dagobert said, 'up to a box-room at the top of the stairs just next to Room 1. Room 1 is Vicki's room.'

'How do you know?' I demanded.

'I found out from the visitors' book.'

'So did I,' Tyler confessed.

I regarded both men (especially Dagobert) with distaste. Their common interest in the geography of the Hôtel Commerce seemed exaggerated.

'No wonder the poor girl bites her fingernails,' I said. 'How much farther down the road is this place you know?'

'The Grand Alexandra Palace?'

'No, the place where you said we could have a drink.'

'That's the place.'

I started to explain that I wasn't dressed for it, but both men received this so unsympathetically that I gave it up. Four days on a tandem had broken my spirit.

As we reached the hotel grounds Tyler Sherman exclaimed with that elaborate suddenness which indicates several minutes of careful preparation:

'Say, Jane! I wonder if you and Dagobert could be any relation of that cute little number who's just arrived at the Alexandra? Now I come to think of it, *her* name's Brown. The desk clerk told me. She's got some sort of screwy first name, too.'

'Not,' I said, 'as screwy as, for instance, Perdita?'

'Perdita! That's it! *The Winter's Tale*. Say, in that case . . .'

'In that case – nothing!' I said severely. 'Perdita Brown is our cousin and we're responsible for her.'

'Sure,' he placated me. 'Sure, I understand. I only thought you might introduce me, you know, as a friend of the family. Say, I've got it. We could make it a foursome and have dinner together tonight.'

'About two minutes ago,' I pointed out, 'you were having dinner tonight in the Commerce – in order to be near Vicki.'

'Gosh,' he sighed, 'that's right. I'd forgotten.'

'I think, Ty,' I said kindly as we turned into the gravel sweep in front of the Alexandra Palace, 'that your interests are almost too catholic. You must learn to specialize. One thing at a time. Besides,' I added disjointedly, 'Perdita's not supposed to be here until tomorrow.'

He wasn't listening. He had trailed behind us, suddenly overcome by an unfamiliar attack of timidity. He blushed, then went pale. He swallowed a couple of times, reminding me somewhat of the mongrel, who was still with us. It was fascinating to watch – in a slightly revolting sort of way.

'That's her,' he gulped.

We had nearly reached the broad veranda of the hotel. It was set with tables, where in the sunset a dozen reasonable-looking people were having cocktails and enjoying the view over the garden. Above clipped beech hedges the Pic des Quatre Vents was deep lavender against a pale robin's-egg-blue sky.

'Which is her?' I asked.

'The three in the corner,' he stammered.

But I had already recognized Naomi. She was wearing a fluffy white crêpe 'cocktail' dress with an uneasy neckline which slipped down her shoulders, and she had completely altered the style and colour of her hair. The older man beside her, solidly dressed in Harris tweed, was undoubtedly Geoffrey. But, like Tyler himself, I was mainly conscious of the third person at the table.

Perdita looked about nineteen. She was very fair, very slender and very beautiful. She looked like Botticelli's Venus rising from the sea, though she was wearing a simple well-cut navy cotton suit.

With it, however, she was wearing a chiffon scarf of a rather special shade of crimson. I was certain I had seen the same scarf about three hours ago, when the Bugatti had skidded so wildly down the road from Andorra.

Chapter 5

I'M afraid we totally forgot Tyler Sherman for the next half-hour. I was vaguely conscious of him once or twice, hovering in the background, luring the dog on with a salted almond and trying to catch our attention. Perdita herself once noticed him and said: 'Careful. There's that dreadful young American whom I had to snub this afternoon.' I said I thought he was very nice, and so did her 'Cousin Dagobert', but no one heard me. We were back to a mile-by-mile description of how splendidly the Humber Super-Snipe had behaved on every hill between Calais and Puig d'Aze, thus enabling them to arrive a day before schedule. I heard Geoffrey's pleasant voice saying mysterious things like 'gradient of one-in-six', and 'gearbox ratio', while Dagobert tried to work in a good word for tandems and catch the waiter's eye.

It was that slack period which comes about five minutes after you've met people you haven't seen for years, and you have so much to say to each other that you can't think of a word. We had exhausted such things as 'I love your dress' (me to Naomi hypocritically), and 'You're looking wonderfully fit' (Naomi to me, because that was the most that could be decently said of my appearance), and 'the time Geoffrey ordered *grenouilles* at the little *auberge* on the Loire and ate them before he realized they were frogs' legs'.

I wanted to find out more about Perdita; but she was reserved and shy. She remained a delight to look at, and on acquaintance would doubtless thaw out; but meanwhile she gave the impression of a young lady whose interest was only half engaged. She hadn't touched her cocktail. Her clear blue eyes were full probably of the long, long thoughts of youth. I was still capable of remembering what *those* were, and I recalled without enthusiasm Uncle Fortinbras's warning about holding us 'entirely' responsible.

Naomi, too, seemed to gaze out over the garden with more interest than she showed in Geoffrey's praise of the new Humber. To be sure, the sunset was heavenly and she may have heard her husband on the subject before. She stifled a yawn prettily with slim fingers (containing an immense emerald and a square ruby set in diamonds), and said to me:

'I hope they gave you one of the suites with its own balcony overlooking the mountains.'

I explained that we were not staying at the Alexandra. Dagobert (I said) had discovered an amusing little inn behind the church called the Hôtel Commerce.

The announcement caused a mild sensation. Naomi looked bewildered, and even Geoffrey arrested his account of today's triumphal lap between Toulouse and Puig. Perdita exclaimed:

'But that's where Johnny's staying!'

'Who's Johnny?' Dagobert asked, as though he didn't know.

'Johnny Corcoran,' Naomi said. 'Surely I wrote you that we'd persuaded him to come along and make up a fourth!'

'We!' Geoffrey laughed heartily. 'You mean, Perdita persuaded him!'

'Or *did* I mention it?' Naomi continued, ignoring her husband's remark. 'It's so like me to have forgotten! Yes, we thought it would be more amusing for Perdita.'

Something prevented me from saying: 'And has it been?' – a certain tautening of the girl's slim body, which I sensed rather than saw. She became aware of my glance and smiled much too quickly. Whatever 'it' had been for Perdita the adjective was not 'amusing'.

'You'll like him, Jane,' she said earnestly. 'Everyone does. He's grand.'

'If only I could persuade him to trade in that so-called racing car,' Geoffrey said, 'and get something reasonable like a Humber. These dashing supercharged jobs are all right for short spins, if you're willing to tinker around with them all the time. But take the run today from Toulouse. I arrive in good order in time to wash before luncheon.'

'How did you come?' Dagobert asked.

Geoffrey seemed surprised at the interruption. 'By Route Nationale No. 20, of course. There isn't any other way. But what happens to Corcoran and his fussy racing job? Supercharger gets bunged up. Carburettor trouble. Result? He arrives four hours afterwards, late for tea! If you're seriously thinking of a car, Brown . . .'

But Geoffrey wasn't holding his audience, except for me. I was interested to hear that Dagobert was thinking of a car, and even more interested to hear how the Bugatti had arrived in Puig d'Aze four hours after the Humber. If neither Perdita nor John Corcoran himself felt it necessary to explain to Geoffrey that a detour via Andorra would take at least four hours more, it was not up to me to point it out. Perhaps they didn't want to hurt his feelings. Perhaps I ought to mind my own business.

'Tell us about Johnny Corcoran,' I suggested, compromising.

Both Perdita and Naomi began at the same time: 'But surely you know!'

'No.'

'Don't you ever see the *Tatler* and the *Sketch*?'

'And the *News of the World*?' Naomi added with a touch of malice, which left me even more mystified.

Perdita looked uncomfortable and Geoffrey, whom I had not yet suspected of tact, said firmly:

'Squadron Leader Corcoran is one of the best test pilots in England. You remember that astonishing performance Boyce-Omega's Dark Star, fitted with the new Emerald Mark IV jet engine, put up between Hendon and Nice last month? Corcoran flew it. The Minister of Supply admits that nothing like it exists. The Mach numbers are sensational, though details are obviously secret. Even Corcoran says he doesn't understand them, though naturally he doesn't talk about it. . . .'

'Yes, dear,' Naomi interrupted sweetly, 'that's one of the most charming things about him. *He does not talk about it.* Are we all dining together? Jane, if you'd like to come upstairs?'

I said to her when we were alone in the lift: 'What was that crack about the *News of the World*?'

Naomi looked distressed. 'I could have bitten my tongue out! I mean saying that in front of the poor child. Johnny's married, you know.'

'No, I didn't know,' I said coldly.

'He's getting a divorce, naturally. A rather sticky one, it seems. Last Sunday's *News of the World* was full of it. His wife is a ghastly little tart. Johnny, I may hasten to add, is completely innocent.'

I remained unimpressed. 'In the circumstances,' I said, 'do

you think it was a very good idea to bring him along with you?'

'But why not? The trip has already done him a world of good.'

'Oddly enough, I wasn't worried about Johnny. I was thinking about Perdita.'

'But it was Perdita's idea! More or less,' she amended with a kind of smug smile which both puzzled and irritated me. 'Do I detect a faint note of disapproval, Jane?'

'You do.'

'I keep forgetting you're her aunt.'

'Cousin by marriage,' I corrected mechanically, but even the reminder of that less responsible kinship did not make me feel much happier. 'Is John Corcoran as much in love with Perdita as she is with him?'

The question took Naomi by surprise. We had reached the door of her room and she was fumbling with the key. She dropped it, recovered it and fussed for a moment with the lock before she replied:

'I suppose so. I must have taken Geoffrey's key. No. Well, anyway it fits. Johnny, yes, of course. He must be, mustn't he? Geoffrey and I expect they'll be married as soon as Johnny's free. I'm afraid I've left this room in a shambles! You must come home for the wedding, Jane. We can wax sentimental and shed a discreet tear as we remember our own hectic past.'

'Yes, that calls for a discreet tear,' I nodded absently, wondering why she seemed to contemplate this appalling prospect with such equanimity.

'If you're worried about Perdita and Johnny in the – er – meantime,' she laughed gaily, 'Geoffrey and I are most appropriate chaperons. We even arranged for Johnny to stay in different hotels. Hence the Commerce. I adore the view from this balcony! What a coincidence that you should be there, too!'

Naomi had a trick of talking breathlessly and seemingly at random as though she didn't really expect to be listened to. Then, disconcertingly, she would pause, fix large, motionless violet eyes upon you and wait for a response.

Since I was well aware that our being at the Commerce was not coincidence – though she couldn't possibly have known this – I found her sudden pause slightly embarrassing.

I said: 'Yes, isn't it?'

Her long dark lashes flickered into life again and she began examining herself critically in the three mirrors of her dressing-table. It was covered with an enviable array of Elizabeth Arden pots. There was a huge bottle of Lanvin's Scandale on the bathroom shelf and an equally large bottle labelled 'sodium ethyl iso' something or other – a sleeping draught, I imagine. Her white pigskin wardrobe trunk had been opened and partly unpacked. Matching hat-boxes, shoe containers, fitted week-end cases lay in a similar state all over the room, spilling out fascinating things with Dior and Fath labels. The score of *The Art of the Fugue* lay open on the bed and a handsomely bound edition of Marcus Aurelius 'without which I never move'.

'Geoffrey says that within five minutes I reduce every room I enter to a slum,' she apologized. 'His sanctum adjoins through the bathroom. It's full of motoring maps, fishing-rods and sporting rifles. Geoffrey's room, I mean. Not the bathroom. What, by the way, is the number of your room at the Commerce? I mean, if one wanted to telephone?'

I said I didn't remember, and that I doubted if the Commerce had such things as telephones. Apparently she'd already forgotten she'd asked the question. Graver thoughts occupied her.

'I wonder,' she mused, 'if Antoine was really wise about this streak of lavender. Who dyes your hair these days?'

She asked the question so ingenuously that I felt ashamed to admit that no one dyed my hair. Instead, I congratulated her on her own. It was a very interesting dark mahogany shade, swept back without a parting, straight except for short curls behind her ears. The streak of lavender was slightly startling, but on the whole successful. I couldn't have done it – that is, I couldn't have done it and continued to live with Dagobert – but it suited Naomi, elongating her triangular face with its broad, smooth forehead, immense eyes and small pointed chin. And, as she said, 'at *our* age one has to do *something*'.

She tried to lend me the score of *The Art of the Fugue*, which Kitson was playing on Monday, and looked surprised when I said I could not read music. She insisted that I borrow a dress (one she was thinking of selling) until my own luggage was unpacked, and said she felt sure she could 'sneak us in' to the private recital of Scarlatti sonatinas which Kitson was giving in his house tonight. 'I shall say you write books!' she exclaimed brightly. 'We shan't have to specify what *kind* of books!' When at last we went downstairs again she said wistfully, but without bitterness: 'No one will have noticed our absence. And Perdita, of course, will have cornered all the men.'

In brief, I rejoined the party in a simple black afternoon dress looking extremely satisfactory and feeling extremely depressed.

Chapter 6

NAOMI had been right in one respect: Perdita was surrounded with men. They had moved from the veranda to the bar and her radiant fair head was the centre of masculine attention. She seemed to be enjoying herself, which was fair enough. The far-away look in her eyes had vanished; she was flushed and a little silly. I heard her voice tinkling in adolescent badinage of some sort and wondered if she'd had too many cocktails.

Then I realized that her intoxication was of a different sort. Johnny Corcoran was present.

Naomi pointed him out. I did not tell her I had already caught a glimpse of Squadron Leader Corcoran this afternoon on the Col d'Aze. He was a little older than I'd realized – thirty, at least. He and Dagobert were draped against the bar counter talking and they looked more or less contemporaries. Dagobert was taller, but Corcoran was thicker set, more assured, more smoothly groomed. His features were more regular and his voice less diffident. He was, I suppose, good-looking; but I had started out on the wrong foot by comparing him with Dagobert, which meant that my judgement was biased and unreliable. I took an instant – if mild – dislike to him.

The fourth man (the third was, of course, Geoffrey) who had somehow managed to attach himself to Perdita's circle of admirers was Tyler Sherman. Perdita, who had ignored him until Johnny's arrival, was teasing him about his accent in, I thought, a rather forward way. Tyler, I must confess, was holding his own and teasing her about hers. They were both being very rude and sophisticated and unpleasant to each other – and obviously enjoying themselves immensely. It was not at first apparent that every word Perdita spoke was intended to impress not poor Tyler, but Johnny.

I joined Dagobert and was introduced to Johnny. He leaned over my hand gallantly and kissed it. Dagobert, more practical, got me a gin and french. Both little attentions had their points. Johnny looked at me with a slow, appraising smile which made me glad that the borrowed dress fitted.

'But Naomi gave me the impression...' He broke off, looked confused (which I don't think for a moment he was) and concluded: 'Er – *quite* a different impression.'

'That,' I explained, 'was Old School loyalty. Did she say I was good at games?'

'And... are you?' he challenged softly.

I recovered my hand, which he still retained, and said: 'I'm afraid this is all much too subtle for me. Tell me about your Bugatti. Does it frequently delay you for hours with carburettor trouble?'

He glanced at me with that intimate smile which I recognized as professional though effective. 'From time to time,' he murmured complacently. 'Why not come for a drive with me some day and see for yourself?'

'We'd love to,' Dagobert said, returning with my gin and french.

'I don't think that was altogether Squadron Leader Corcoran's idea,' I pointed out.

'Oh, wasn't it?' Dagobert said incuriously, and, to my horror, joined the others.

'At least he's been warned,' Johnny remarked smugly. 'There was some loose talk about dancing at the Casino at Aze-les-Bains tonight. Perdita's idea. I dance rather nicely, I'm told.'

'Isn't Perdita,' I said bluntly, 'a little too young for you?'

He fumbled with his gold cigarette-case. 'Much too young,' he sighed. 'But, as we say, *faute de mieux*. ... Besides,' he added as he extended his case to me, 'can I really help it?'

'No, I suppose you can't!'

My bitterness was wasted on him. He struck a match and held the flame to my cigarette. His fingernails were carefully manicured.

'What is the scent?' he murmured. 'Lanvin's Scandale?'

'Yes, it's Naomi's. That's why you recognize it.'

'But you wear it – with a difference...'

I went through the motions of stifling a yawn. 'I bet you say that to all the girls.'

Vulgarity, too, was wasted. He shrugged. 'Yes, it normally goes down rather well. Reverting to Perdita...'

'Reverting to Perdita,' I interrupted, getting rattled, 'why don't you pick on somebody your own size?'

He smiled slowly into my eyes. 'That, oddly enough, is just what I was going to suggest in the subtlest possible way to Perdita's charming cousin.'

'No,' I said, wondering if the cocktail was making my head spin or whether I merely needed the other half. 'No, Squadron Leader Corcoran, some sacrifices are too heroic. My cigarette's gone out. Do you mind if I ask Dagobert for a Gauloise?'

I caught Dagobert at that moment returning to the bar. This time I didn't let him go. He found a battered packet of Gauloises in his pocket, extracted one for me and tossed the remainder to Johnny.

'Try a Carmela, Corcoran,' he urged.

Corcoran regarded the dilapidated blue packet in his hand with distaste. 'Thanks, old boy. D'you mind if I stick to Gold Flakes? Never touch anything else.'

'Never?' Dagobert insisted with sinister casualness.

'No. Throat, you know.'

'Are you *sure*?'

'Of course I'm sure. What on earth makes you . . .?'

'Pity,' Dagobert broke in with a deep and mysterious scowl that left even me taken aback. He turned away thoughtfully to the bar.

Johnny remained frowning at the blue packet in his hand. 'I don't quite get the point of all that.'

'The Carmela routine?' I said innocently, delighted that something had at last shaken his self-assurance.

'In the first place, they're Gauloises,' he muttered. 'Not Cara – whatever he said.'

'I forgot to tell you,' I whispered confidentially, 'and probably I shouldn't mention it. My husband's a kind of detective, you know.'

'A . . . a . . . what?' he said rather carefully. 'I mean, what kind of a detective?'

'I'd rather not say,' I admitted honestly.

The charming smile came back again. 'You're joking, of course.'

'Of course.'

Perdita at that moment joined us. She had, I realized, exerted considerable will power in restraining herself so long. Tyler Sherman had disappeared and it was nearly eight.

'Johnny! If we're dining at the Casino in Aze-les-Bains . . .

Jane, what a shame you and Dagobert can't come with us!'

'Why, can't we?' I asked.

'Yes,' Naomi interrupted, 'it's all arranged! We four older people are dining quietly here at the hotel while the children dash off to the Casino. You'll bring her home at a reasonable hour, won't you, Johnny? We're going to Kitson's after dinner, but he's only playing for an hour, and we'll be home by eleven. No, Geoffrey,' she said to her husband who had taken my empty glass, 'we haven't time for another round. I'm sure Jane doesn't want it, anyway.'

I tried to convey the impression that another drink was the last thing in the world that had occurred to me. I felt vaguely as though I were still in the lower fourth at St Catherine's and Naomi still a prefect. Geoffrey began to arrange about a table, Johnny strolled off to fetch Perdita's coat and even Dagobert gulped down the drink he had just managed to order.

I contrived a word alone with Perdita while Johnny was bringing the Bugatti up to the front steps and Naomi was assuring Dagobert (who until that moment had been quite unconscious of what he was wearing) that no one cared how you looked in a place like Puig d'Aze.

'You *do* like him, don't you, Jane?' Perdita had whispered.

Instead of saying 'No,' which would, I felt, have broken off relations between us on the spot, I temporized:

'What does Uncle Fortinbras think?'

'They've never met. They will after . . . afterwards.'

'After the divorce,' I nodded. 'Why don't you . . .' I hesitated, conscious of her candid blue eyes on mine.

She was as aware as I was that Dagobert himself had been divorced before marrying me. There was no time to go into the fact that That Was Different. One's own past is very awkward during these moments of giving advice to the young.

'Why don't I what?' she challenged, knowing she had me.

I attempted to regain a position of authority by omniscience. 'Anyway, look out for the old gag about carburettor trouble,' I smiled. 'And tonight don't drive home again by way of Andorra.'

It was a bombshell, as I had intended it to be. She looked blank for an instant. 'But . . . how do you . . .'

'We happened to see you.'

'Where?'

'On the Andorra road about four-thirty this afternoon – as you well know.'

She turned away with a slight gasp. I saw the swift flush of pink which stained her bare neck. Johnny was already hooting at the bottom of the steps and she ran down to join him without even saying good night. I caught a further glimpse of her as the Bugatti moved forward. She had mechanically knotted the crimson scarf around her head and had slumped down beside Johnny as though someone had given her a punch in the stomach.

Chapter 7

I DON'T remember much about dinner that night. There was thin soup, chicken and probably vanilla ice cream. Naomi ordered a bottle of Graves *demi-sec*, but explained that there was no need to finish it, as, corked up again, it would do for tomorrow. We tried to be waggish about Miss Perk, the maths mistress at St Catherine's, while Geoffrey wondered if we could get out of Kitson's tonight. Dagobert proposed that we, too, might drive down to Aze-les-Bains, but Naomi said we were all much too tired.

We arrived at Kitson's on the stroke of nine. The Abbaye, Kitson's house, had once been a Cistercian monastery, fallen into ruin several centuries ago, but tactfully restored by Kitson himself. It was vast and rambling and only partially habitable. Kitson lived there alone, looked after by a series of 'housekeepers'. He was, Naomi told us, very rich, and had spent much more on music than he had ever made out of it.

Tonight's private recital was held in the refectory. Only a handful of people were there, among them the Honourable Sebastian Nevil, who was a 'particularly dear' friend of Naomi's and through whom she had got us invited. I think she was slightly disappointed when Sebastian turned out to be an old pal of Dagobert's from Cambridge days. The only other person present whom we knew was Mitzi Stein, who listened intently while Kitson played, twisted her pigtails viciously and forbore from applause. She bolted when the recital was finished, cutting us – and everyone else – dead.

Kitson himself was a fattish man in his fifties, with a huge, unkempt black beard. He wore rope-soled sandals and a checked flannel shirt. His fingernails were dirty and he was not quite sober. He spoke to no one and at half past ten exactly he shut the lid of his harpsichord and said: 'That will be all.'

There was enthusiastic applause and cries of 'bis' and 'encore'. Geoffrey woke from a sound slumber and said: 'Jolly good. What?' Kitson abruptly left the room, and we, when he didn't come back again, filed out, making polite chattering sounds.

Naomi said there was no one quite like Scarlatti, and Dagobert earned my gratitude by not pointing out (until afterwards) that the entire programme had been Couperin. We left the Gordon-Smiths, both stifling yawns, at the gates of the Alexandra Palace. Then we made as rapidly as possible for the nearest café.

'I think,' Dagobert said, 'I begin to understand the *New Statesman*'s rather sinister prophecy that Kitson is playing "probably for the last time".'

'Isn't he any good?'

'Weren't you listening?'

'No. I was thinking about Perdita.'

'Yes,' he said uncomfortably. 'One must have a long instructive talk with her some day. The older sister approach. When I'm not there,' he added, dismissing the subject. 'Beer would be fitting at this moment. Or do you think coffee and brandy, followed by beer?'

I objected that coffee might keep us awake, and we compromised on brandy. We had reached the beer – and a very interesting discussion about the tertiary geological epoch when the Pyrenees re-emerged from the Mediterranean – when I reverted to the subject of Perdita, pointing out that she was *his* cousin, not mine. It was also nearly midnight, and though the café window in which we were sitting commanded a view of the square and the street which led to the Hôtel Commerce, no Bugatti had yet been seen coming home. Dagobert asked rather sharply what I suggested: get out the tandem and cycle down to Aze-les-Bains? I knew from the tone of his voice that he had been, through Hercynian massives and geological epochs, as much on the qui vive for the Bugatti's return as I. I told him about Perdita's astounding reaction when she learned that I knew she'd come to Puig via Andorra.

'Of course, they'd lied to Geoffrey and Naomi about carburettor trouble and why they were four hours late,' I said, 'all of which seems elaborate and I should have thought quite unnecessary. Having lied, it's humiliating to be caught out. But you should have seen how Perdita took it!'

'Yes, I can imagine,' Dagobert said, ordering more beer in the face of a waiter who had arrived to say it was closing time. 'You missed some of the conversation when you were upstairs with Naomi. I'm afraid you put your foot in it.'

'What did I miss?'

He grinned faintly. 'The fact that this morning at Toulouse Johnny and Geoffrey traded passengers. Perdita arrived with Geoffrey at the Alexandra in time for luncheon. The woman with Perdita's scarf driving the Bugatti was Naomi.'

'Oh . . .' I murmured. 'That accounts for a lot of things. Including why Johnny and Naomi were in such a tearing hurry to get to Puig d'Aze. Poor Perdita!'

'Poor Perdita – rubbish!' Dagobert grunted unsympathetically. 'You mean poor Corcoran! When he tries to explain to Perdita why he concocted that story about engine trouble.'

'Yes,' I said with satisfaction, 'that may take a little doing.'

Midnight struck, rattling our beer glasses, and the waiter again began to hover. We ordered more beer, but our hearts weren't in it. The square was deserted except for a few late stragglers, among whom I recognized to my astonishment the stout figure of Kitson, weaving, I presume, homewards. When we finished our beer and left it was nearly twenty to one.

Tomorrow, we decided, we would get out the tandem again and proceed to Spain to inspect Baroque churches, having first sent Uncle Fortinbras a firm telegram saying, 'Refuse all further responsibility.'

It sounded practical at the time; as it turned out, the telegram was never sent. I had my first intimation that it would never be sent when we opened the unlocked door of our bedroom. The light was on and the dog, who had been waiting for us on the mat, preceded us into the room with hospitable wriggles. Then he stiffened and cautiously edged towards the bed.

On the bed a slight figure was stretched, face down. I recognized Perdita's blue cotton suit and fair hair. The crimson scarf lay in a limp ball on a corner of the carpet. Her body was motionless. Until her face suddenly jerked up from the bolster, mine was, too. Relief was only momentary. The white face was ghastly and streaming with tears. Hysteria twitched the corners of her mouth, and when she tried to speak no sound came. She buried her head again in the bolster and gripped hard at the counterpane as though trying to keep herself from being sick. I ran forward. The dog got there first and began to lick her cheeks. I heard the single word she articulated into the bolster. It was: 'Johnny.' And again: 'Johnny, Johnny.'

The repetition was an irritant and an explanation at the same time. So she had found out about Johnny and her heart was broken! She was nineteen and it would be broken dozens of times in the next few years. I felt like shaking her. Instead I put an arm around her.

She said: 'Jane . . . Dagobert . . . I thought you'd *never* come. It's . . . *Johnny*.' As she said the word yet again she tore herself violently away from me. She stifled a scream. 'Don't touch me! You don't understand!'

'Yes, I do,' I contradicted. 'You're a very young, very silly girl.'

My harshness seemed to sober her for a moment; she stared at me with a kind of defiance. Then her lower lip began to tremble and tears gushed from her eyes again, splattering down her nose.

'Johnny . . .' she quavered as though it were the only word she was sure of. 'Johnny . . . he's in Room 2.'

'Yes, I know. It's his room, and he can probably hear you blubbering.'

'No, he can't,' she said wonderingly, but dropping her voice nevertheless. 'No, he can't . . . because . . . he's dead.'

I swallowed hard, gripped her shoulders brutally and said: 'You're hysterical. You don't know what you're saying.'

I felt Dagobert standing tall and rigid behind me. Though it seemed likely that he was about to have two hysterical women on his hands, I was very glad he was there.

'But I do know what I'm saying,' Perdita said. 'Johnny's dead. He'd dead because . . . because I killed him.'

Chapter 8

PERDITA's appalling statement had the unexpected result of steadying her. I discovered afterwards that she had lain in agony for over an hour and a half on our bed waiting for our return, waiting for the moment when she could share the insupportable burden of her guilt with a fellow creature. Confession had lightened her. She was giddy, like a person who discards a heavy pack at the end of a long day's march. The relief was artificial but momentarily real.

She stopped crying and pushed her hair, almost silver in the feeble electric light, out of her eyes. What make-up she had worn had long since come off on our counterpane; she looked like a frightened child who has been caught cheating at school. The thought occurred to me that to her uncritical mind cheating at school and murder were equally reprehensible and about on a par. As she sat on the edge of the bed, her legs dangling, her fingers mechanically stroking the dog's ears, I dismissed this thought and fell back on my first instinctive reaction of utter disbelief. She had dreamt the whole thing!

Dagobert meanwhile had abruptly left us. We heard the door close softly behind him and the key turn in the lock.

'Does he think I'll run away?' Perdita asked uncertainly. 'Has he gone for the police?'

I thought I knew where Dagobert had gone, but I didn't go into the subject. 'We carry a flask of brandy in our saddlebags for emergencies,' I said. 'This, I think, is an emergency.'

She watched me fumbling with a tooth-mug at the washstand and said: 'If I could have just a glass of water, please, Jane . . .' She added in a whisper: 'What am I going to do, what am I going to *do*? Oh . . .'

I said quickly, trying to ward off the returning wave of hysteria: 'The brandy is for *me*. Here's a wet facecloth. Catch.'

The dog caught it instead and for a moment distracted us by tearing around the room, inviting us to chase him.

'His name's Fifi,' Perdita said. 'The landlady told me when . . . when . . .'

'Go ahead,' I prompted.

'When Johnny and I came in this evening. Isn't it absurd?'

We both laughed for about half a second, and then we both stopped. I began to bring her the tooth-mug full of water. She stood up and took it from me.

'Thanks. I don't know why I should be treated like an invalid. Jane, would you . . . shall I . . . talk about it?'

I didn't know, and busied myself recovering the facecloth from Fifi. Baulked, Fifi seized up the crimson scarf, but failed to gain our attention.

Perdita's voice became edgy. 'You can take it all down and use it in evidence against me. Isn't that the phrase?'

'I think the "against me" part is wrong. Shall we wait for Dagobert?'

'He's frightfully clever about – about these things, isn't he? Only . . . this time . . . there's nothing to be clever about, is there? I mean I . . . I shot him, and, well, there you are.'

'Why?'

I hadn't meant to ask any questions. In fact I had been trying hard not to. But having done so I realized that to let her talk was the only stimulant which could prevent her breaking down again.

'I shot him because . . . oh, it's so complicated! No, it isn't. Because I loathed him. Only,' she added, 'only I don't any more. Why is that? Oh, I wish I *hadn't* shot him.'

'That seems reasonable,' I murmured, 'if a little late.'

'All of us kill the thing we love,' she misquoted vaguely. 'Only I don't think I even love him . . . any more. That makes me vicious and cold-blooded, doesn't it?'

She stared at me with dilated blue eyes. Her hands were clenched and a convulsive shudder ran through her thin body. She looked anything but vicious and cold-blooded. I thought the water she had gulped down was going to make her sick.

'I'm glad you're not sorry for me, Jane,' she faltered, slumping down suddenly on the bed. 'I couldn't bear it if you were.'

I turned my back on her and rummaged busily on the table for matches and a cigarette. When I had regained sufficient courage to harden my features I glanced at her again. She had begun to cry softly, dabbing her eyes with the tassled edge of the counterpane. When she realized I was watching her she stopped.

'You don't seem to be getting on very quickly with what happened,' I said, keeping my voice level in an effort to maintain the pretence that I was not sorry for her.

She apologized. 'It's all rather mean and sordid and . . .' She broke off in sudden agitated distaste. 'I'll have to tell it all to the police, won't I?'

'Yes,' I said. And added immorally: 'It might be a good idea to have your story pat. He lured you back to his room . . . and . . .?'

She shook her head. She even attempted a faint smile, though the attempt was a failure.

'No. If there was any luring . . . I insisted on coming up to his room. He didn't particularly want me to.'

'We might omit that part from the official version,' I said hastily. 'But start at the beginning.'

'The beginning was when we drove away from the Alexandra to the Casino at Aze-les-Bains.'

'I was afraid of that,' I said. 'After I'd just let the cat out of the bag about Andorra.'

'Yes,' she nodded. 'You see. . . . How sentimental and horrid it sounds now! You see, he, Johnny, he'd promised to drive me over to Andorra. It was to be "ever so romantic", and we were going to "discover" it together and, ugh!'

'Be sick if you like.'

She apologized again and again began. 'I started right in on him, accusing him of driving Naomi there and lying to Geoffrey and me about carburettor trouble. He denied it at first, but finally said: "So what?" Then I remembered that Naomi and I have traded places two or three times previously during this trip. They were always late on those occasions, too.'

'So you jumped to conclusions.'

'Yes.'

'What did he say?'

'He denied everything. Then he laughed at me. Then he danced with me and, well, he told me I was adorable when jealous, and, well, he does that sort of thing rather skilfully. Only I kept on nagging him. I suppose I wanted him to keep reassuring me. He did . . . and I kept on and on. I ruined his evening all right!'

Recalling how the evening had ended, I swallowed slightly at this under-statement. 'Yes?'

'Finally, just after ten, he said he was going to take me home since I was being such a bore. We drove back, me still nattering. I said we *couldn't* say good night like this and invited myself up to his room for a final drink. . . . It wasn't eleven yet and he said I could stay five minutes. Of course I spent those five minutes nagging at him worse than ever. It seemed so *important* then that I should know the whole truth.' She had spoken quickly, almost unemotionally, until this point. Now her voice faltered and she avoided my eyes.

'I wish I had not learned the truth . . .'

I said nothing. The only sound I could hear was Fifi diligently scratching. It was broken by Perdita's muffled half-sob. She recovered herself instantly and said in a flat, impersonal tone:

'The truth, of course, was that Johnny had been Naomi's lover for months. He let me have it straight, I'll say that for him. No holds barred – as Tyler Sherman would say. He said: "Why do you think we brought you along on this trip in the first place? Did you honestly imagine that a child of nineteen – decorative though she be" – yes, he actually said that! – "that an infant like you could amuse an adult male for an entire fortnight? Grow up." Then he went on to explain, as though I hadn't grasped the idea already, that I had made a most convenient screen for him and Naomi, removing any possible suspicions that Geoffrey might entertain and – this was the most charming point he made – and "offering him occasional, not unamusing, *divertissement*". He was a bit tight, but he said it in the politest way. Yes, he was a nice chap, Johnny Corcoran, always the gentleman. . . .'

Her voice trailed away. She was, I saw, dry-eyed. I said: 'Do you mind if I use that tooth-mug for brandy?' and tried not to think very clearly what I should have done had I been Perdita.

'Then you shot him?' I said evenly. 'Why, why, Perdita, didn't you just walk out?'

Since she hadn't, it was a stupid question. She shook her head, swallowed and went on with an effort.

'No. Then I hit him – or tried to. He laughed and caught me in his arms. I bit him and he called me a "delicious little spitfire". It was the best-style melodrama. He said there was only "one way" to cure little girls who grew hysterically jealous and . . . Please may I not go into details?'

I nodded. I tried to sip the brandy, but couldn't swallow it. The key had turned again in the door behind us and Dagobert slipped in. Neither of us heard him.

'That was when I shot him,' Perdita concluded dully.

Fifi's joyous yap startled us both nearly out of our wits. Dagobert relieved me of the tooth-mug, looked suprised and grateful to find it still half full and sat down on the bed beside Perdita.

'What did you shoot him with?' he asked.

'He has a revolver. It was there in a holster on the table.'

'Didn't it make an awful noise?'

'Yes, I can still hear it.' She took her head in her hands. 'Ringing . . . ringing . . . in my ears.'

'Why didn't everyone in the hotel come rushing up to find out what was going on?'

'I . . . I don't really know.'

'Are you sure that ringing in your ears wasn't the church bell across the street? What time was it?'

'Yes,' she said thoughtfully. 'Yes! *That's* why! The sound's all mixed up in my mind. Eleven o'clock was just striking. It shook the whole room. I thought it was . . .'

'The explosion of the revolver,' Dagobert finished hopefully. 'There are striking similarities. I suggest you never fired it at all.'

Perdita smiled wanly. 'Only – unfortunately – that's not true. Because I did shoot him.'

'Did you see him actually fall?'

'Yes, he stumbled, threw out a hand, then I heard him collapse, I think. I didn't look. I couldn't. But . . . oh, it's no use! I killed him. I *killed* him, I tell you.'

'I wish you wouldn't keep saying that,' Dagobert snapped. He looked irritated rather than stricken. I felt a faint stirring of baseless hope. 'I suppose,' he sighed, 'we'd better have it in your own words. You shot him. How many times?'

'Once.'

'What happened next?'

'I – I don't remember exactly. I dropped the revolver.'

'Where?'

'I don't . . . Yes, by the door, while I was fumbling with the latch.'

'Did you turn off the light?'

'No.'

'Did you lock the door behind you?'

'No. I didn't think about that.'

'Fair enough. Have you seen many movies along this line?'

She looked bewildered. I began to feel much better as I recognized his tone of voice, though I thought he was being rather cruel.

'Sorry,' he said. 'You were too flustered to turn out the light and lock the door. You simply fled. Then what?'

'I thought I heard someone coming up the stairs, so I ran down the corridor. I remembered your room. Johnny had mentioned it earlier. He said even if you were there it was too far away for our voices to carry. Your room was unlocked, so I came in. I thought I'd leave as soon as the coast was clear. But I got more and more frightened and decided to wait for you.' She paused, waiting for Dagobert to say something. He said nothing and she concluded: 'That's all . . . I've been here ever since.'

'You didn't leave this room again?'

She shook her head.

'In all that hour and a half of waiting it didn't occur to you to go back to Room 2 and look around to make sure you'd left no signs of having been there?'

'No. What would have been the use?' she said miserably. 'The landlady saw us come in together and ... won't my fingerprints or something be on the revolver? Oh!' she broke off. 'My scarf! I may have left that!'

'You didn't,' I pointed out. 'Fifi is systematically demolishing it at this moment in the corner.'

Perdita glanced at the scarf, blanching as though at some memory once precious but now distasteful. 'I bought it at Marks and Spencers,' she murmured, 'because it exactly matched his car. . . .'

She began to snivel quietly, but at least she made no effort to retrieve the scarf. Dagobert intervened impatiently:

'You didn't leave this room?' he repeated. 'You didn't go down to Corcoran's room to switch off the light and lock the door?'

'No. Why do you keep asking me that?'

Dagobert grinned and I drew a deep breath. 'It's the kind of question that's essential in these "murder" cases,' he said. 'Make a note of them, Jane. You might use it all later.'

I recovered what was left of the brandy. 'I don't know what this is all about,' I reproached him, 'but aren't you being a little unkind?'

'I hope so.'

'Perdita has been through quite enough tonight. Even if she's deserved it.'

'So,' he reminded me grimly, 'have we.'

Perdita watched us, her bewilderment and distress deepening. I said:

'Tell us why you keep asking whether she locked the door and turned off the light.'

'Because,' he said, rising, 'the light in Room 2 is now off – and the door is now locked.'

'Then they've found his body!' Perdita gasped. 'What are we going to do?'

'We're not going to do anything,' Dagobert said roughly. 'Except bundle you back to the Alexandra so that we can get a little sleep. There isn't a body. I went in through the window and looked. He's not there and the Bugatti is not in the shed. He's obviously gone for a midnight drive to cool off, and I can't say I blame him.'

Chapter 9

WE took a dazed and chastened Perdita back to the Alexandra. She was still incapable of grasping the fact that she had not killed Johnny, and I thought two or three times as she clung to me on the way to her hotel that she was going to have hysterics. Dagobert was brusque and unsympathetic. I knew from his manner that he had been as shocked and frightened by the whole nightmare business as Perdita herself.

It was nearly two o'clock and the lobby of the hotel had only a dim light over the desk, behind which a night clerk dozed. Perdita had noticed from the garden that a single bedroom window on the top floor was still ablaze with light – Naomi's, or perhaps Geoffrey's next door; I wasn't quite sure.

'She's waiting up for me!' Perdita whispered, beginning to tremble. 'I *can't* see her, not tonight.'

I agreed that that might be awkward, and suggested we meet the situation tomorrow. Our immediate problem was solved when, at the sound of our footsteps on the gravel drive, the light went out.

On the way home I told Dagobert why Perdita felt reluctant to see Naomi. It was the first time he had heard the full story. He had only caught the end of it: when Perdita, defending her honour, had seized the revolver and fired. In view of the fact that she had come up to Corcoran's room in the middle of the night, he had been unimpressed. He listened uncomfortably while I gave him the unexpurgated version.

'In many ways,' he admitted, 'it seems a pity she missed him.'

I agreed. 'Yes. Now *you'll* have to do something.'

'Me? Why?'

'*In loco parentis*. You're responsible for her, remember?'

He sighed. 'And doubtless get punched in the jaw for interfering. . . . Hello!' he broke off hopefully as we entered the courtyard of the Hôtel Commerce. 'The Bugatti isn't back yet. Perhaps he's skipped town.'

'That would be the simplest solution certainly.'

I yawned while he struck a match and went through the open doors of the empty shed. He burned his fingers in sudden excitement and tried to strike another.

'Did you see it?' he said.

'No. What?'

'Neither did I!'

'Good,' I said. 'In that case we can go to bed.'

He struck another match and held it above his head. He glanced at me in wild surmise as though he had discovered at least a body hanging from the rafters. The shed, as far as I could see, was quite empty.

'You'll have to put it in words of one syllable,' I apologized. 'I've had rather a confusing day. What with hysterical girls and drunken harpsichordists, getting into wrong hotels and being ambushed on mountain passes, cycling across the Pyrenees and . . . oh!'

Our tandem wasn't there!

'This,' I suggested, 'is the work of a madman. Who else would steal a tandem?'

'At least,' Dagobert shrugged cheerfully, 'the plot thickens. 'If only,' he added with a tinge of regret, 'there was a plot.'

We had regained the courtyard door to the hotel when two o'clock thundered from the neighbouring belfry. Such is the power of habit that the landlady, who slept behind a screen on a cot at the back of the café, did not even stir at the sound.

'Quick,' Dagobert said, taking my arm. 'We have an hour to get to sleep before it happens again.'

I was asleep in roughly two minutes.

It couldn't have been the church bell which woke me – two minutes? – two hours? – later; though, like Perdita, I was still conscious of confused ringing in my ears. I was also conscious of an inert body lying across my feet. When I kicked gently it twitched, whimpered and finally began sleepily to scratch. Fifi, too, had been mixed up somewhere in the meaningless concatenation of Carmela cigarettes, rifle fire, crimson scarves and missing tandems that compounded the nightmare which made me fumble violently for Dagobert and then – not finding him – for the electric light switch.

It couldn't have been the church bell because my wrist-watch said twenty minutes past four. It may have been the brandy, but I prefer to think it was premonition. At any rate, I awoke with that false sense of alertness, of fatality and of my utter inability to cope that characterizes my nocturnal awakenings. Normally these are the moments when I know that I shall never write another line, when I realize with stark clarity that my overcoat cannot face another winter and that Dagobert is secretly in love with the blonde at the tennis club.

Tonight, however, I was consumed by other vaguer forebodings of the had-I-but-known-then-what-I-learned-later variety. When, next day, I did learn what-I-didn't-know-then, it was hard for me not to say: 'It happened at exactly four-twenty. I *felt* it!' This, parenthetically being untrue, might have considerably complicated Dagobert's investigations, which were complicated enough as it was.

In one respect my intuition was sound: I found Dagobert in Corcoran's room. He had got there the way I did, via our window and the creaking wooden balcony which linked the rooms facing the courtyard. The light in Room 2 was on and, through the half-drawn curtains, I got a momentary shock. My husband's body, in the cycling mackintosh he used as a dressing-gown, was stretched flat on the floor.

He came to life again before I actually screamed. I watched him backing as though in panic towards the door, his right hand clutching an imaginary revolver, which he let fall from nerveless fingers as he fumbled for the doorknob behind him. The pantomime was so realistic that it held me fascinated. I followed his glance as it searched the carpet in the region where the revolver ought to have fallen. There was no revolver there.

This seemed to bewilder him. Since the real revolver was lying as large as life just beneath the curtains of the window through which I was staring, I thought his bewilderment was overdone.

I cleared my throat and stepped through the window. He stared at me petrified. 'That's it!' he gasped.

'What is?'

'Stop where you are – in the window.'

Realizing he'd gone mad and might be dangerous, I obeyed.

'Now drop it,' he ordered curtly.

'D-drop what?'

'The revolver, naturally. Do you see?' he ended triumphantly, pointing at my feet.

I took my eyes off him reluctantly and glanced down. The revolver was, of course, just where I'd originally seen it beneath the curtain; that is to say, at my feet.

'What are you doing here?' he added before I had a chance to ask the same question. 'You're asleep.'

'Oh, is that what it is?' I asked hopefully.

'Can't I have any private life of my own?' he grumbled. 'But since you are here you might as well be useful. The essential point to determine is: who *are* you?'

I remembered conversations which began like this during the short but intense period when Dagobert had taken up metaphysics, but tonight I didn't like the glint in his eye. Even for me, who am not particularly sensitive, the events of today had been trying enough; it was possible they had unhinged him completely. I murmured something soothing and leaned down absentmindedly to pick up the revolver. He may have thought I contemplated defending myself with it, for he said tersely:

'Don't touch that!'

'I was only fidgeting,' I explained truthfully. 'Can't we, please, go back to bed now? It would be awkward if Corcoran suddenly came home. Besides,' I added, all at once awakened by this thought, 'didn't *you* put the revolver here?'

He shook his head. 'No, I haven't touched anything – except the bottle of Highland Fling whisky over there on the chest of drawers. Strictly speaking, all of this ought to be photographed from every angle. We should have kept your mother's Box Brownie. Then fingerprints ...'

'Dagobert,' I interrupted breathlessly, 'if this revolver was *here*, then Perdita couldn't have dropped it by the door.'

He relaxed. 'I knew you had it in you, Jane,' he said admiringly, pouring out four fingers of Highland Fling – a little finger in a glass for me, two and a thumb in a glass for himself. 'Go ahead. I like it.'

'Or else she could have flung it – or it could have rolled,' I added doubtfully.

He shook his head and waited for further suggestions.

'Someone else moved it afterwards?'

'Yes,' he said uncertainly. 'That has possibilities. Who? Someone who came in here after eleven o'clock? Me, for instance, while you and Perdita were in our room.'

'Did you?' I said, suddenly mistrustful.

He shook his head. 'I didn't see it. I should have, but I didn't. Not knowing at that time that a revolver was involved, I didn't look for one.'

'Finally,' I concluded, getting excited in spite of myself, 'someone could have fired it – from this window – *after* Perdita had gone!'

'No wonder your books sell like hot cakes!' he exclaimed, making himself comfortable on the bed. He brooded for a moment and added thoughtfully: 'Not that I've ever seen hot cakes selling. But we'll use your idea, anyway. I'm glad you thought of it.'

'You thought of it,' I said coldly, my brief excitement dampened as I saw this was turning into a story conference.

He helped himself to a Gold Flake from the packet beside the bed, lighted it and handed it to me. 'It has the advantage – indispensable in best sellers – of allowing us to suspect practically everyone who could have come into this room after Perdita thought she shot Corcoran at eleven. It gives us that diabolical cunning without which no murderer is really satisfactory. He realizes that Perdita thinks she did it. He knows she will break down and confess, leaving him scot-free to inherit the Corcoran fortune.'

'I'm going back to bed,' I said.

'I'm not riveting your attention?'

'No.'

'You're too bloodthirsty, Jane. Merely because there's not a real corpse stretched here in the middle of the mat you lose interest. You're disappointed. I sympathize, of course. Corcoran, from all accounts, would have made a most appropriate corpse; but we can't always have everything our own way.'

'I don't,' I said, moving back to the window, 'want to be here when Johnny Corcoran returns and finds you drinking his whisky?'

The thought also sobered Dagobert. He began to scramble to his feet, but at once regained his dignity. 'I think I can handle the situation,' he said. 'Besides, I'll be able to scram when I hear his car coming home.'

We both glanced at the leather travelling clock which stood beside the canvas revolver holster on the table. It said ten minutes to five, and for a moment both of us relapsed into silence. Neither of us expressed the disquieting thought which began to insinuate itself more and more into our minds. I mean the thought that Squadron Leader Corcoran, in spite of the fact that he had not taken his luggage, might not come home. Dagobert said quietly:

'Perdita actually did shoot at him, you know.'

'Yes, she swears she did. But how can we be sure?'

He pointed to a small neat hole in the wall about six feet above the bed. 'Not a very good shot,' he said, 'but have you ever tried firing a revolver?'

I nodded, having once aimed at a target on a cherry tree in the garden and hit the door of the wood-shed, not especially hard by.

'An expert,' Dagobert said, 'could probably tell us whether that shot had been fired from the door or the window. At least,' he added apologetically, 'he could have before I prised out the bullet with Corcoran's penknife.'

He removed the leaden pellet from the pocket of his mackintosh and regarded it without pride. He repocketed it with a shrug. 'Still, it doesn't matter. Perdita was making for the door. so she assumes she shot at him from there. She wouldn't remember where she was standing. Probably she was standing by the window since that's where the gun was dropped.'

I reminded him that all of this was of purely academic interest as there was no body. We had motive, we had opportunity, we had a weapon, but we had no body. He nodded absently and said if I felt like that I could work out the thing for myself. He was only trying to be helpful, and should we have just one more for the balcony? He poured out two more small whiskies, leaving a nightcap for Corcoran in the bottle. We lighted cigarettes, disguising our unwillingness to leave before we heard the sound of the returning Bugatti.

'After all,' I pointed out, 'we've already had more than two hours' sleep.'

He was prowling round the room, partly to keep himself awake. He eyed the still untouched revolver, began to pick it up, but remembered fingerprints.

'I wonder if this is really the best time of day for solving these knotty problems,' he said, borrowing my handkerchief. 'You remember your mysterious murderer who fired the revolver *after* Perdita had fled, thus committing the perfect crime? There's a flaw.'

'We'll put it right tomorrow.'

He had picked up the revolver cautiously in my handkerchief.

'The fingerprints,' I reminded him, 'will merely be Perdita's. What flaw?'

'Yes,' he nodded, examining the weapon gingerly. 'I suppose I should wipe them off. . . . The flaw would give the show away entirely. If somebody else used this thing after Perdita there would be two cartridges fired instead of only one.'

I grappled with this while he sniffed at the gun with distaste. I was about to suggest that our perfect criminal might replace the second expended cartridge with a fresh one he always carried around in his tobacco pouch for this purpose when I heard Dagobert gulp. He shook himself, as though to make sure he was awake. Then he said in a slightly strangled voice:

'Er – as a matter of fact, Jane . . . I don't like to mention it, but two cartridges *have* been fired.'

I sat down rather abruptly. There was doubtless a perfectly simple explanation of the two expended cartridges, but what it might be I couldn't imagine. Neither, to judge by the blank expression on his face, could Dagobert. Perdita could conceivably have forgotten what part of the room she had been standing in when she shot at Johnny, but she must remember whether she had fired once or twice; and she had told us she had fired once.

I had to remind myself that as no harm had been done the problem was still academic. I watched Dagobert carefully wrap the handle of the gun in my handkerchief. He replaced it in the holster and slipped the holster into his mackintosh pocket. I raised my glass before I observed it was empty, and noted that lack of sleep was making my hand shaky. Also it must have suddenly turned cold, for I was shivering. The first stroke of five o'clock caught me unprepared and I bit my tongue.

During the ensuing seconds of ringing pandemonium neither of us heard the key turning in the lock.

Chapter 10

WHEN I saw the door begin to open my first awful thought was that Johnny Corcoran had returned without our hearing the car. His key had not been hanging from the board in the café below, so presumably he had taken it with him.

Dagobert was standing by the window, gazing out over the courtyard. His back was to the door and he didn't see it open. I didn't have to warn him. The intruder's quick gasp did that for me. The intruder was Vicki Stein, who occupied Room 1 just across the corridor.

She had not seen me. I was sipping my empty glass in the corner beside the door. She was in dressing-gown and bedroom slippers and she wore no make-up. The vivid colour that came and went from her face was natural as, I am forced to confess, was the deep glinting red of her hair. Her eyes were immense – as well as they might be – before they blinked into two cautious slits. She looked like still another woman who had had no sleep that disturbing night, though being about Perdita's age she withstood the strain better than I.

'You!' she gasped softly as she stared at Dagobert's back.

It was one of those stifled, strangled 'you's' that suggest emotional relationship of some sort. I was beginning to wonder if I'd missed something when Dagobert spun round.

She looked blank and muttered: 'Oh . . .' I thought she seemed relieved. She swallowed, bit her lip and resisted an impulse to bolt. Her eyes flickered towards the key in her hand. A plastic tab dangled from it with the figure 2.

'Who did you think I was?' Dagobert asked.

The question filled her with confusion. 'But . . . but Squadron Leader C-C-Cochran, of course. I – er – well, you see . . .' She broke off with a deep blush.

'His name is Corcoran, actually,' Dagobert sighed, 'and I wish I knew his secret.'

She started at the word. 'His secret? I am not understanding . . .'

She saw me at that moment and her agitation increased.

'Shall we close the door?' I suggested tactfully, getting up. She beat me to it and the latch clicked behind us. 'Dagobert means,' I went on to explain, 'the secret of Corcoran's attraction – women creeping into his room in the middle of the night and so on. Is he a very old pal of yours?'

'I met him only today.'

'Then he must have a secret,' I nodded, recalling the speed with which Johnny Corcoran worked.

'I meet him tonight – he – he gives me this key. But where is he? What are you doing here?'

'When was this?' Dagobert asked.

'How am I to know? This is private between me and Squadron Leader Cork-What-You-Call-Him. I am, what you say, *Bohémienne* – what I want to do I do. When I want to come into a man's room I come!'

The defiance which had sustained her was suddenly exhausted. She sank down on the edge of a straight chair and looked rather ashamed of herself. She added in a more human tone of voice:

'Please . . . will you not tell anything of this to that American boy?'

'When did Corcoran give you his key?' Dagobert repeated gently.

'Does it matter?'

'No, but tell me, anyway.'

She began to bite her nails, stopped herself and pushed the hair out of her face. Her expression was thoughtful and guileless.

'It would be just five or six minutes after midnight,' she said rather carefully. 'We are meeting in the corridor, talking and laughing and . . . as you say, he has this secret. With some men it is like this. You . . . you know,' she finished lamely.

I murmured a girlish: 'Quite,' and Dagobert restored her poise by giving her a Gold Flake. She gazed thoughtfully into his eyes while he held his own lighted cigarette to hers. She touched his hand lightly with her fingers as though to steady it. Probably the gesture was necessary, but I thought it was slowing up her confession unconscionably. Finally she whispered:

'So I say . . .' She paused again, her eyes still raised tragically to Dagobert's so that it was uncertain whether she was addressing him directly or merely recounting what she'd said to Corcoran. 'I say . . . *yes* . . . I take his key and promise to come. It is foolish of me, but with *some* men one is foolish. I think,' she added, at last averting her eyes and colouring prettily, 'I think you, too, are having this secret.'

'What secret was that?' murmured Dagobert, who had lost track. He caught my eye and added hastily: 'Oh, yes. But we seem to be straying from the point.'

'That,' I remarked, 'could be the idea.'

She protested passionately. 'You are so *hard* towards me!' She obviously meant me, but she spoke to Dagobert. 'You think everyone else is strong – like you. You condemn me because I am weak, *human*.'

She began to dab her eyes with a small lace handkerchief. They were quite dry, but the gesture was effective in a ham sort of way. She remembered – a moment or so too late – to clutch her dressing-gown modestly to her bosom. The entire performance was so bogus I almost forgave her. It even embarrassed Dagobert. Or something did.

'What were we talking about?' he rumbled.

'Vicki,' I said, restoring a little order into the narrative, 'has just blushingly accepted the key to Corcoran's room. Why she couldn't rap shyly at his door and be let in in the normal way remains obscure.'

'He was going for a drive,' she said. 'He likes to drive by himself, through the night. But he comes back soon to find me waiting for him. That is why he gives me his key.'

'And you wait until five o'clock the next morning before using it.'

'I fell asleep,' she explained simply.

'While Corcoran doesn't bother to turn up at all,' I nodded. 'This is one of the most passionate stories of love at first sight I've ever heard! I'm going to bed to dream on it. Are you coming, Dagobert?'

'I'll wait up with Vicki for a few minutes, if you don't mind.'

Vicki herself looked so acutely uncomfortable at this proposal that I made one of my split five-minute decisions, smiled back at him with nonchalance and said: 'No, of *course* not, my dear,' and graciously retired.

If I'd been physically able to stay awake I might have tossed restlessly on the lonely bed I shared with Fifi. In any case, Dagobert rejoined me about five minutes later – that is, he said it was five minutes later. Conversation was a little one-sided since I took no part in it. Something patently absurd about there being a man in Vicki's room already and (I think) something about our tandem having turned up again – both obvious dream fragments of a fevered imagination.

They were, oddly enough, the first two things I thought of when I woke up next morning. It was slightly after midday and Dagobert slumbered beside me, grunting gently when nudged, but showing no further signs of life.

'Not that it's really any of my business,' I said, 'but if there was already a man in Vicki's room, why was she prowling around in search of Corcoran? Love of variety? This restless modern pursuit of novelty?'

There was no answer. I rang for breakfast and there was no answer to that either. I got out of bed, chattering brightly, flung back the curtains and made as much noise as possible with the cracked jug and basin. Dagobert slept beatifically through it all, though I did get some reaction out of Fifi, who watched me with reproachful yellow eyes from the arm-chair.

'Then there was the bad news about the tandem being returned,' I went on, falling over Dagobert in order to reach the bell again. He sighed profoundly, but did not stir. 'I hope these investigations are not going to prove too exhausting for you, Dagobert,' I said. 'What time *did* you come to bed?'

I gave it up and sallied forth in search of breakfast. I couldn't find anyone except the domino players in the café. I wandered out into the courtyard, wondering suddenly if the Bugatti had at last come home.

The shed was still empty. No Bugatti and, I noticed with wonder, no tandem. So I had dreamed the bit about the tandem's turning up again and about the man in Vicki's room and, presumably, about Dagobert's coming to bed a few minutes after I'd so nonchalantly left him!

I went back into the hotel, deciding to get straight on these points at once. This time I found the landlady emerging from the kitchen. She was garrulous, but disinclined to talk about breakfast. When I grasped in rough outline what she was talking about, I forgot about breakfast, too. I reclimbed the stairs two at a time and burst into our room.

Dagobert was sitting up in bed with a breakfast tray across his knees – shaved and brushed – while Fifi was toying with a croissant. He poured out a cup of coffee for me and congratulated me on my smiling morning face. Then he looked at my face and continued to pour coffee, mainly on the counterpane. I told him what I had just learned from the landlady.

The wreckage of the Bugatti with Squadron Leader Corcoran's body in it had been found in the gorge below the crossroads on the Col d'Aze.

Chapter 11

HAD Dagobert been constitutionally capable of letting nature take its course the rest of our stay in Puig d'Aze could have been very pleasant. The weather was perfect, the woods and meadows were full of wild flowers, there were delightful walks to a dozen fascinating shrines and ruined monasteries in the neighbourhood and even Kitson, after his shaky start, played well. Geoffrey and Naomi, Vicki and even Perdita gradually grew accustomed to the idea that Johnny Corcoran was dead, while I, somewhat cold-bloodedly, felt that his demise was exactly what Puig d'Aze had needed.

Dagobert felt so, too, but in his own peculiar way. 'This,' he said, finishing the jam with his spoon, 'is going to take my mind off romanesque architecture.'

I suggested that we ought to know what 'this' was before getting too worked up and that – if I could rely upon my interpretation of the landlady's French – Corcoran had died, according to the authorized version, in a motor accident.

'We'll revise it at once,' he said, leaping dynamically out of bed.

'Where are you going? You're not dressed.'

'We must strike while the iron is hot.'

I tried to explain as I followed him out into the corridor that the iron wasn't hot. Corcoran's body had been found at dawn this morning, identified, and the cause of the accident already determined. And didn't he want to hear the facts?

'We'll get them afterwards,' he said, making for Vicki Stein's room.

'That reminds me,' I said. 'Did I dream that about men in Vicki's room?'

'Not men – *signs* of masculine occupation. I'll explain later.'

He paused, turned and tried the handle of Room 2, opposite. To his astonishment the door was unlocked. He opened it. The room had been cleaned and the linen changed. Corcoran's luggage had been removed, and a complete stranger glanced up from unpacking. He glanced up with an unfriendly expression.

He was a man of about thirty with short sandy hair and very little chin. He wore suède monk's shoes, beige flannel trousers, a bright checked jacket and an open-necked sports shirt with a zip fastener, all brand new and obviously bought for the occasion. A British passport lay on the table – it looked brand new, too.

He regarded us with yellowish eyes which reminded me of Fifi's, though they were less loving. He cracked the joints of his fingers in a rather menacing way, though he may have been merely nervous, having been warned before he left home what to expect in foreign hotels.

'Yes, old boy?' he snapped.

Dagobert tore his admiring gaze from the suède monk's shoes.

'*Je vous demande mille pardons,*' he said suavely.

'A froggy, huh?' he muttered. He took the cigarette from his lips and raised his voice, knowing this to be the way to make yourself understood on the Continent. 'I said what the devil do you want? *Compris?* This is my room. You've made a mistake. Now buzz off. *Allez!* Scram!'

'*Vous venez d'arriver, Monsieur?*' Dagobert inquired politely.

He caught at the word hopefully. '*Arriver*. Yes, that's right – I just *arriver*. Okay? By the ten o'clock bus from Perpignan. This is my room. You make bigga mistake. *Compris?* Whatever you sell I not want any. *Compris?* Now get the hell out!' He saw me at that instant and modulated his voice. 'Sorry, madam; no offence intended. . . . You – *parler anglais* – hein?'

'I speek a leetle,' I admitted, feeling that if we were going to stay we ought to have a language in common.

'Then explain to this bloke that this is my room and I want to unpack.'

Dagobert looked perplexed. '*Dites-lui que la chambre appartenait à mon ami Corcoran.*'

'He say,' I translated, 'that thees room was belonging to his fren' Corcoran.'

He lighted another cigarette from the stub in his mouth.

'The squadron leader chappie? The one who had the accident?'

Dagobert shook his head excitedly. '*Non, celui qui était assassiné.*'

The man looked from Dagobert to me with a blank expression. He cracked the joints of his forefinger and of his middle finger in thoughtful succession. 'What's he on about now?' he asked.

'He say he mean ze chappie is murdaired,' I explained.

Dagobert glanced at me in such astonishment that I thought for a moment I had mistranslated the word *assassiné*. He said:

'I can't imagine why you keep talking like that, Jane. Between ourselves, old boy,' he explained confidentially to our friend who had sat down slowly on the edge of the table, 'she speaks English as well as I.'

'Come again!' he muttered feebly. He turned from habit to me for explanation. 'Look here!' He reddened. 'What the blazes is all this?'

'I haven't the faintest idea,' I said. 'But it's nice not having to talk broken English, isn't it?'

'Who *are* you, anyway?'

'Our name is Brown,' I said. 'We live down the corridor. We often pay little visits like this to our neighbours.'

'I'm Fred Evans,' he murmured absently, eyeing Dagobert. 'Pleased to meet you.'

'Haven't we met before?' Dagobert asked.

'I very much doubt it. I've just got here.'

'That could be,' Dagobert conceded generously. 'I wish you'd let me have the name of your bootmaker some time.'

Fred Evans continued to eye Dagobert nervously, taking in the bare feet, the orange silk pyjama legs and, over all, the cycling mackintosh. He took still another cigarette from the box of a hundred Players on the table and lighted it from the butt. The ash-tray was already full of them. He glanced at me for enlightenment.

'Barmy?' he suggested with sudden hope.

'You can't always tell,' I said fairly. 'Sometimes there's method in it, but usually there isn't.'

'Did you move the calendar, Fred?' Dagobert asked, 'or was that done by the management?'

We both followed his glance towards the wall over the bed. A calendar, which last night had hung on the opposite wall, now covered the small bullet-hole Perdita had made when she fired at John Corcoran. While we were looking at it – each with his own private brand of bewilderment – Dagobert carelessly flicked through Fred Evans's passport.

'Oi!' Fred shouted. 'Oh, no, you don't. That's a valuable document. I was warned about letting that out of my possession before I left London.' He crooked a forefinger. 'Come on, give it back.'

Dagobert returned the passport with a grin. 'Good likeness, Fred,' he said. 'What kind of a journalist?'

'Free-lance. Any objections?'

'None at all. Where do your things appear mostly?'

'They don't – very much,' Fred admitted with a sudden modesty which quite won me over. 'I'm – I am,' he repeated with a return of his normal aggressiveness, 'a special correspondent of *Workers' Playtime*, and if you don't believe me you can see my credentials. I'm covering the Puig d'Aze Musical Festival, and they paid for my railway ticket. Well, for half of it,' he amended. 'I say! Maybe you could give me the dope. Just *entray noo* I never heard of this chappie Kitson before I sold them on the idea of sending me, and I'm not too sure what a harpsichord is.'

'Could I see these credentials?' Dagobert asked.

Fred's momentary amiability vanished. 'What for?'

'You said I could if I didn't believe you.'

'Look here, laddie,' he growled, caressing the knuckles of his left hand with the affection of a boxer who is itching to use them, 'I don't think you and I are going to hit it off very well. How about getting the hell out of here before I lose my temper?'

He reached into his jacket pocket none the less and handed Dagobert the typed letter with the heading: WORKERS' PLAYTIME, 22 Euston Crescent, NW 1, the information that one Fred S. Evans was their Roving Correspondent on the continent of Europe, and that all assistance rendered him would be appreciated. His photograph was also attached.

While Dagobert studied this impressive document Fred studied Dagobert; both seemed unhappy about it.

'I don't get the hang of you,' Fred grumbled, more or less taking the words out of my mouth. 'Come to that, what are *you* doing around here?'

Dagobert glanced up casually. 'I'm trying to find out who murdered Corcoran. Didn't I mention it?'

Fred glanced at me questioningly. I smiled nervously and nodded, as though to suggest that the safest thing was to humour him. Fred murmured quickly:

'That's okay, chum. You go right ahead. Glad to help you if I can. Got any clues?'

'One or two.'

Fred again sought my eyes and lit his fourth cigarette. 'Is that on the level?' he began dubiously. 'Because if it is . . . well, *W.P.*'s roving correspondent might be interested. Only, as I get it, the thing's already sewn up. Famous test pilot smashes himself up. Okay. That's worth a paragraph, but . . .'

'I can't understand,' Dagobert interrupted with a puzzled frown, 'how you manage to smoke so many cigarettes without staining your fingers. Have you noticed it, Jane?'

I hadn't; nor did I see the point of suddenly changing the subject – except, of course, for the sheer pleasure of irritating Fred. In point of fact, Fred's fingers were quite free of that yellow stain between forefinger and middle finger that generally betrays the chain smoker.

'Look, fellow,' Fred said with remarkable restraint, 'we were talking about this squadron leader type who bumped himself off . . . I say!' – he broke off suddenly, swept by enthusiasm – 'how about this for a lead? "Puig d'Aze, June the whatever it is. Your roving correspondent is typing this from the very room that Squadron Leader Corcoran occupied on the night of his tragic death. Does an aura of mystery linger in this strange room? Are *all* the relevant facts surrounding this sinister event yet known? Will further dramatic revelations come to light? Your own roving correspondent is here to find out the truth!"' He paused expectantly... 'What do you think?'

'How can you be typing it?' Dagobert said. 'You haven't a typewriter.'

'Oh, for chrissakes!' Fred exploded.

'A minor point,' Dagobert agreed hastily. 'In a pinch, Jane could lend you hers. How do you like the idea that Corcoran was killed in this room?'

Fred choked violently over the cigarette which hung between his lips and almost swallowed it. Dagobert thumped him helpfully on the back. 'I don't,' he managed to splutter. 'And stop whacking me.'

'I thought it would help to account for that lingering aura of mystery,' Dagobert explained. 'But skip it.'

'How,' Fred asked, 'could he have been killed in this room? He was found at the wheel of his car at the bottom of a cliff miles from here.'

'Ever hear of moving a body after death? He could have been killed in this room and driven to the Col d'Aze afterwards.'

Fred Evans considered this, the roving correspondent in him tempted by it. I, too, stirred uncomfortably. It was not, of course, the first time that this possibility had crossed my mind. It had been crossing it at regular intervals: every time I remembered that Corcoran's revolver had been fired *twice*. Finally, Evans shook his head.

'It won't do, old boy. Ever try to move a dead body?'

'No,' Dagobert said. 'Hard work, is it?'

'How would I know?'

'I supposed,' Dagobert said mildly, 'you'd found out in the usual way. By trying it.'

'Okay, laddie, keep your shirt on,' Fred said. Realizing that it was he and not Dagobert who was in danger of losing his shirt, he smiled. When he smiled his upper teeth protruded rather fetchingly. 'So your murderer drags the body downstairs through the café, hoists him into the car and nobody notices.... See what I mean?'

'You can reach the shed where Corcoran kept his car via the boxroom just next door at the head of the stairs. There's a ladder. You could get him into his car that way without being seen. I point out all these little possibilities in case you want something to work on.'

'Thanks, old boy.' Fred nodded absent-mindedly. 'Makes you think, doesn't it?'

He cracked in slow succession each individual finger of his left hand. The thumb didn't respond at the first jerk and he tried it again. The sound set my teeth on edge. He glowered at Dagobert and then looked at me for sympathy.

'Damn this chappie,' he said querulously, 'he gets you so worked up you begin to go barmy yourself. He's got me clean forgetting that someone apparently saw this laddie Corcoran driving off.'

'*Apparently*,' Dagobert, to whom this was news, repeated significantly. 'Who?'

'See what I mean?' Fred complained again, appealing to me. 'I don't know who. And then the way I heard it he was drunk.'

He paused and crossed to the mantelpiece. On it rested the bottle of Highland Fling we had nearly finished last night. The maid had forgotten to remove it.

'See this?' Fred said, shaking it. 'Dirty great bottle of whisky he practically knocked off last night.'

'No. Jane and I practically knocked that off.'

Fred sank down again on the edge of the table.

'Jeeze!' he said feebly.

'That part's true,' I assured him.

Fred stared at me reproachfully as though I'd let him down. 'Okay, okay,' he murmured in a tone of conciliation, 'he wasn't drunk, and no one saw him. And everyone's crazy around here, including the cops. And,' he added, cheering up suddenly at the thought, '*and* that luscious cookie across the hall.'

Dagobert recognized this description before I did. 'Vicki Stein?'

'The toothsome little morsel in Room 1? Is that her name?'

'In what particular way is Vicki crazy?' I inquired.

'She's *apparently* told everybody she saw Corcoran *apparently* alive and kicking about five past twelve – in other words, a moment or two before someone *apparently* saw him drive off,' Fred explained with heavy sarcasm.

Dagobert looked discouraged. 'It's going to be difficult, isn't it?'

'Yes,' Fred agreed briefly. 'Maybe I'd better stick to the harpsichord angle . . .' He began his fifth cigarette and fixed his pale amber eyes on me through the veil of smoke. 'Why,' he said slowly, 'would anybody *want* to bump off Corcoran?'

When I didn't answer, he laughed bitterly. 'There I go again! Forget it. Next you'll have me lying awake at night worrying about it.' He rose and paced the room, pausing to thump Dagobert heartily on the back. 'Speaking of that little red-head, Gertrude Stein, or whatever you called her, how about introducing me? Huh? For background material, you know. Personalities at the Puig d'Aze Festival. I'll mention you in my articles, too, if you like. How about it, old boy?'

'Put that way, I don't see how we can refuse,' I said.

Dagobert, too, approved of the idea. In fact, it seemed to

appeal to him especially, just why I couldn't for the moment make out. He thumped Fred with equal enthusiasm between the shoulder blades and said:

'Well played, old boy.'

They grinned in a silly masculine way at each other and then simultaneously stopped grinning. I thought, as Dagobert led the way across the corridor and knocked at Vicki's door, that Fred seemed a little thoughtful. He brightened as Vicki immediately opened the door. She must have been waiting just behind it.

Vicki herself did not look quite so bright this morning. Her face was as white as a sheet and her eyes were haggard with sleeplessness. They flickered uncertainly from Dagobert to Fred and me in the background. I had the fanciful impression that she was about to scream, but her voice, though hoarse, was steady.

'What is it, please?'

'A friend of mine wants to meet you,' Dagobert smiled.

'Fred Evans is the name,' Fred said, taking over with that suave mastery which betrayed the man of the world. He glanced over his shoulder at us, winked and clicked his teeth. 'This is where I get a little background material,' he explained. Then he turned the full charm of his protuberant teeth on Vicki. 'Where have you been all my life?' he murmured confidentially.

'That,' Dagobert said, when we had withdrawn to let them work out the answer for themselves, 'is quite an interesting question. . . . You know those signs of masculine occupation I mentioned a while ago . . .'

'In Vicki's room,' I nodded, brooding. 'So you went into Vicki's room.'

'Don't wander, Jane. The signs I had in mind were a pair of suède monk's shoes under her bed. They're not there this morning. I think Fred has them on.'

Chapter 12

WE found Perdita in our room, picking at the scraps which were left on the breakfast-tray. Perdita was looking pale and tentative, but, I was thankful to see, well under control. She had that fresh, clean look of persons who stay in hotels with private baths, and her crisp blue-patterned frock made our wallpaper seem dingy. She smiled at us shyly.

'Sorry to keep barging into your room when you're not here,' she said. 'I'd have waited downstairs but Tyler Sherman was hovering about, being most tactful and rather sweet, I suppose. I'm afraid I wasn't very gracious. I, er, I seem to have gone off men, if you know what I mean.' She turned away and concentrated on stroking Fifi. Her voice was reasonably casual as she added: 'You've heard, of course. I mean about what happened. To Johnny.'

We said we hadn't heard the details, having just got up.

'You're lucky,' she said wryly. 'The Brigadier des Gendarmes called on us at about half past eight this morning. Geoffrey had to go and identify the . . . body, isn't that the phrase?' She gave her attention to Fifi again. 'The car caught fire when it crashed. He – it – was rather dreadfully burned.'

'So badly as to make identification difficult?'

'No, I don't think so. That is, Geoffrey didn't say . . .'

'But badly enough,' Dagobert suggested, 'to make it impossible to say, for instance, whether he was dead before the crash?'

'I don't quite understand.'

'If he'd been shot, say, before the accident.'

She stared at Dagobert and blinked. 'But I thought . . .' She took a deep breath. 'Then I *could* have killed him, after all!'

'He means,' I interrupted bluntly, glaring at Dagobert, 'that *someone* – not you – could have killed him.'

She didn't hear me. She shivered, as though someone had walked over her grave. The dark shapes of last night's horror took form again, like a nightmare remembered on waking. She was still staring at Dagobert.

'*You* found him dead,' she whispered, 'and, and disposed of the body to save me. And told me he'd gone, so I think I'd misfired.'

'It's an idea,' Dagobert said. 'Though I doubt if I'd have had the time. Before we get too tense, I didn't.'

He wandered around the room, collecting socks and boots. 'We've covered this ground before,' he said, 'when it wasn't very important. Now it is important, Perdita, and I want you – as we say – to give the matter due consideration. Where were you standing when you shot at Corcoran? If you can't remember for sure, say so.'

'But I can,' she said promptly. 'I was standing between the table and the door. The revolver was on the table. I took it and backed towards the door, fired, and dropped it while I was fumbling for the door-knob.'

Dagobert nodded, but made no comment. I wanted – out of Christian charity – to say that we had found the revolver under the curtains at least fifteen feet away from the door, but decided to let Dagobert do this in his own way.

'And you fired – how many times?'

'Once,' she said, her bewilderment increasing.

Dagobert put on one sock and looked round vaguely for the other. I recovered it from Fifi and gave it to him.

'Why not tell her why that question is important?' I suggested.

'Oh!' Dagobert glanced up at his cousin with a grin. 'It means you didn't shoot him, Perdita. Go on with what happened this morning. If I'm going to solve the mystery it's high time I found out what it's all about. Geoffrey identified the body and the police have come round to grill you.'

'Yes,' Perdita said. 'You see, the Brigadier knew I'd gone up to Johnny's room. He knew when we'd left the Casino at Aze-les-Bains, and even that Johnny had been a bit tight. The Casino doorman reported it. He was very polite, the Brigadier, I mean. He has a huge moustache and looks like an old-fashioned gendarme in the films. He was very paternal and said he only had to ask me a few questions for the record. His chief concern seemed to be that the accident might ruin my holiday.'

'What did you tell him?'

She hung her head. 'Well, not very much. That's what I

want to ask you about. Should I go back to the police station and explain exactly what happened?'

'Good heavens, no!' Dagobert exclaimed in alarm.

She looked relieved, then remembered something 'But they'll have found the revolver! And if they take the fingerprints . . .'

'They won't,' Dagobert said with a smile. 'But I may . . . which reminds me. May I start my collection with yours?'

Perdita breathed again when he smeared her fingers with ink from my fountain pen. 'You have the revolver?'

'Yes.'

'Oh, good!' she said with a frankness I found refreshing.

Dagobert took prints of her fingers on the back of our Cycling Club membership card. He examined them with admiration. 'What precisely *did* you tell the Brigadier?'

'I told him we had a quarrel,' Perdita replied, wiping off her fingers on Fifi. 'That was true, anyway – and that I marched out of the room just after eleven. I told him how I'd gone to your room and waited for you and how we'd all walked back to the Alexandra. He knew that, anyway.'

'By the way, whose light was on when we took you home? Geoffrey's or Naomi's?'

'I don't know. I went straight to bed and didn't see either of them – thank heavens!'

'The Brigadier didn't ask you what you and Corcoran quarrelled about?'

'No, luckily,' Perdita said, flushing at the thought. 'Geoffrey was present at the interview, and, well, for obvious reasons I couldn't have gone into details. It would have meant mentioning *her*.'

'How is Naomi?' I inquired curiously.

'In a bit of a state.' She added, with almost a note of compassion: 'Poor Naomi! She can't let Geoffrey or even me see how she *really* feels. She has to pretend to be sorry for me. The trouble is I no longer feel very sorry for myself. Does that shock you? Because, well, whether I shot him or not, I am morally responsible for Johnny's death.'

'How is that?'

'If I hadn't nagged him all evening he wouldn't have drunk so much. If it hadn't been for that ghastly row and my attempting to kill him he wouldn't have taken that crazy midnight drive. So, in a way, it *was* my fault.'

'Does that hurt much?' I asked unsympathetically.

'Not much. It ought to. I suppose.'

'I'm working on a scheme to assuage your conscience,' Dagobert grinned. 'That is, if you have one. The police are satisfied with the accident theory?'

'Aren't you?' she asked shrewdly.

'If the police are, he isn't,' I explained. 'If they aren't, then he is.'

Perdita smiled faintly. 'He must be fun to live with . . . Geoffrey will give you the details. Geoffrey's been grand, incidentally, through all this – a pillar of strength. He says he's been half expecting Johnny to break his neck in that Bugatti all along, can't think why it hasn't happened before. Naomi says that Johnny used occasionally to go for midnight drives after parties in England. Funny how much better she knew him than I. I can't get used to it.'

'Was coming to Puig,' Dagobert shot off at a tangent, 'originally Naomi's idea?'

'Now that you mention it,' Perdita said reflecting, 'no. It was Johnny's. Rather ironic, in view of everything.'

'At any rate, rather confusing,' Dagobert nodded. 'Go on about Geoffrey.'

'You should get it from him,' she said. 'It seems Johnny was seen a few minutes after midnight by a girl who lives in this hotel, and he told her he was going for a drive. I gather the landlady didn't actually see him come downstairs, but she says he could have reached the car by a ladder into the shed. Anyway, he was seen driving out of the courtyard – by Kitson, oddly enough.'

I remembered that we ourselves had seen Kitson just after midnight last night, weaving past our corner café. We had not seen the Bugatti because it had taken a back street to avoid the church square.

'That was the last anybody saw of him,' she continued steadily, '. . . until this morning at dawn, when a shepherd discovered the burnt-out wreckage. Geoffrey says that from the state of the ashes the Brigadier is sure the accident took place not long after midnight. There's apparently a very bad turning just above the gorge and the car smashed through the parapet. And that,' she added in a small voice, 'is that.'

I saw that she was not quite so unaffected by her narrative as she pretended to be. She had closed her clear blue eyes and her lashes were wet. More than a crimson Bugatti containing the body of an egotistical bounder (alive or dead) had plunged over that parapet to oblivion. Something of Perdita herself had gone with it. In its twisted wreckage her first love had perished.

Dagobert, waving a pair of dilapidated corduroy trousers, roused me from these high-falutin' reflections.

'Strictly speaking,' he sighed, 'we ought to pedal the tandem up to have a look at that parapet this afternoon.'

'You can't,' I said. 'I forgot to tell you. The tandem's disappeared again.'

'Good. Then I'll borrow Geoffrey's car. *What?* Are you sure?'

'I'd recognize that tandem anywhere. And it's not there.'

He began to crawl into his trousers in a distracted way. Perdita, recovering herself, said: 'I'll wait downstairs while you dress, shall I? I ought to go back to the hotel, I suppose, only . . .'

'You can have luncheon with us,' I said. 'You've missed it at the Alexandra, anyway.'

'Oh, may I, Jane?' she said eagerly. 'I, er, I'd much rather. Unless you and Dagobert object to my tagging around with you.'

She was pathetically grateful when we assured her that we'd be delighted. Her reluctance to return to Naomi was not hard to understand.

'Besides,' Dagobert said, 'Jane will be glad of your companionship. I have some rather subtle investigations to make this afternoon, such as . . .' he paused, trying to think of something to investigate.

'Such as who murdered Corcoran?' I suggested mildly.

'No, I want to find out where our tandem is.'

Chapter 13

PERDITA and I spent a pleasant and useful afternoon together after getting rid of Dagobert, or perhaps it would be fairer to say after Dagobert got rid of us. He said good-bye abruptly in the church square, strode briskly up the main street and disappeared into the post office.

We had already shaken off Tyler Sherman. Tyler had been lingering in the Café de Commerce when we came downstairs, looking awkward and sympathetic and obviously longing to join us. Perdita's polite but chilling smile discouraged him; we left him in the café, probably hoping to be consoled by Vicki's eventual appearance.

'Isn't it a pleasant sensation not having any men around?' Perdita sighed when we finally stood deserted in the church square.

'Yes,' I said. 'But it doesn't last.'

'I suppose one gets over these things – in time,' she mused. 'Oh, I say! There's an English tea-shop just across the way that advertises poached eggs on toast! I'm starving.'

The tea-shop – which really was called Ann's Pantry – might have been transplanted from Perdita's native Cheltenham. Doubtless, long before the First World War, it had been. Puig d'Aze then had been one of those English 'discoveries' which are dotted around so many of the most attractive and least expensive corners of Europe. King Edward the Seventh had once spent a month here and a Royal Duke had built the startlingly pinnacled château, now the lunatic asylum, overlooking the new town. Other signs of former occupation are still discernible to the observant: an English library, an English chemist, a stone basin on the edge of the square with the half-effaced legend: FOR OUR DUMB FRIENDS. In the church there is a guide book in English with a life of Saint Justin written by the Reverend Thadeus Pepper, The Vicarage, Nether Stoke, Hants, 1903.

But Puig d'Aze has moved with the times. The Travel Agency in the Avenue Prince de Galles, which used to offer old ladies escorted donkey rides to the Pic des Quatre Vents, now advertises day excursions in special sight-seeing buses to Carcassonne, Perpignan and Lourdes. The English library has become the Anglo-American Library. There are placards in the windows of neonlighted cocktail bars saying: ENGLISH SPOKEN. Though, to be fair, there is also SPEEK ENGLISCH, and once, in the Auberge des Gourmets (Son Restaurant, Sa Cave, Ses Spécialités), the happy translation: 'His Restaurant, Her Cellar, Their Specialities.'

Puig had adapted itself to the new visitors – the Steins, Fred Evans and, of course, the Browns.

Ann's Pantry, however, has not radically changed. There are copies of the *Tatler* and the *Sketch* – not dated 1903, though nearly – Wedgwood china and photographs of the Royal Family. To be sure, the original Ann has gone; otherwise we probably would not, at three o'clock in the afternoon, have been served with fresh poached eggs on crisp buttered toast, vast quantities of ham, a huge salad, several kinds of cheese, a pot of China tea with an adequate jug of boiling water and (for Perdita) an immense dish of ice cream with fresh strawberries and whipped cream on top of it.

The sight of the latter was too much for Mitzi Stein, who for the last ten minutes had been peering in at us, flattening her nose against the plate-glass window and making funny faces. She opened the door, letting in Fifi, who had been ejected by the management, and wandered around with a grave air of preoccupation, pretending she hadn't seen us. She stopped suddenly on one foot, twisting a copper pigtail thoughtfully.

'What's that?' she said.

'It's called *coupe maison*,' Perdita replied.

'Ummm . . .' Mitzi sniffed dubiously. 'I might try one some time. If I feel like it.'

She was turning slowly away when I suggested rashly: 'Why not try one now?'

She leapt into the extra chair at the table with astonishing rapidity. 'I don't mind if I do,' she said, signalling urgently for the waitress.

I introduced her to Perdita.

'I know who *she* is,' she said. 'She's the one who sneaked up to the bloke what killed himself's room.'

Perdita tried to smile. 'My reputation seems to have got around.'

'Everybody knows everything in this place,' Mitzi pointed out equitably. 'It's worse than the Malden Road.'

'The Malden Road?'

'Don't pull that stuff!' Mitzi sneered. 'You know where the Malden Road, Camden Town, is as well as I do, and I was brought up there. Vicki,' she added with an unexpected note of pride, 'was chosen Usherette Beauty Queen at the Gaumont Palace this spring.' She shot a disdainful glance at Perdita. 'Some blonde came second. You probably saw Vicki's pitcher in the *Daily Mirror*.'

I said I was sure I had, and ordered a double *coupe maison*. While waiting for it Mitzi became fascinated by the inkstains on Perdita's fingers.

'I've got it!' she exclaimed disconcertingly. 'Dagobert took your fingerprints. That's what he was doing.'

Perdita was quicker to grasp this than I was. 'I'm afraid, Mitzi, you peep through keyholes,' she said.

'Anyway,' Mitzi evaded the accusation, 'it's just the silly sort of thing Dagobert would do.'

'You speak about my husband with great authority,' I said, slightly dazed.

'Ye-ah,' she admitted grudgingly, 'I know him. I was in hospital last winter with mumps.'

Dagobert had not, to my knowledge, ever been in hospital, so I waited for the mystery to clear. Mitzi added:

'They brought me one of those books about him – Gosh!'

'What do you mean, "Gosh"?' I asked stiffly. 'I hope in a way your mumps were extremely painful.'

'I mean – well, work it out for yourself!'

'I have,' I said, turning to look for the waitress. 'Cancel that order for the *coupe maison*.'

'Maybe,' Mitzi said quickly, 'I wasn't really old enough to appreciate it. I'll bet it was jolly good, really. The nurse said it was. She said she'd read every one of them. She wouldn't miss one for anything. She can hardly wait for the next. They're the best things she's ever read in her whole life. And when I grow up I'm going to read them all, too. I'll love them, I bet. I'll . . .'

'Never mind,' I interrupted with a kindly smile. 'The waitress didn't hear me cancel the order, and perhaps the *coupe maison* will make you very, very sick.'

It didn't.

Neither did an equally copious second helping. We tactfully avoided the subject of literature and talked about music. Mitzi was almost as unimpressed by Kitson as a musician as she was by me as an author, though he had, she admitted, given her a few useful tips during the half a dozen private lessons she had taken from him. This made the trip to Puig worth it, in spite of the awful people who had come to the Festival.

'Coming to the Festival was, of course, your idea,' I said.

'It was not,' she contradicted belligerently. 'It was Vicki's, though she says it was for my sake. She thinks she's crazy about music. But if you ask me she's only crazy about men. Tyler Sherman! He's not so bad. But, then, talking to that man in the corridor after midnight – euh!'

'Did you actually hear her talking to him?'

'No. I was asleep. I got an attic room on the top floor, but everybody knows about it. Then there's a new bloke, Fred Somebody, what's just arrived. You introduced her to him!' she accused with disgust. She added more tolerantly: 'Vicki's all right, 'smatterafact. It's only her age. She'll grow out of it.'

'Do your mother and father live in London?' Perdita asked.

'Nope.'

She concentrated on polishing her second plate of ice cream, sighing regretfully. I suggested a third helping, which she refused with an even deeper sigh. I asked for the bill.

'Father,' Mitzi said suddenly, 'was Solomon Stein. You know who Solomon Stein was.'

I didn't, but I nodded. She saw through me instantly.

'He was only just about the greatest flautist that ever has been!' she said scornfully. 'The Nazis got him – in forty-four, when I was a baby.'

'Oh,' I said, swallowing. 'It's a wonderful afternoon. Shall we all explore the town?'

'My mother,' Mitzi said impersonally, 'died a year later – in a Soviet concentration camp. Vicki was there, too. And Anna. . . .'

'Who is Anna?'

'Our sister. She's in Warsaw – we think.'

'Oh.'

'Rudolph,' she went on, 'Rudolph – that's our older brother – he'd got away in nineteen-forty and joined the R.A.F. He somehow got Vicki and me away from the Commies and brought us to London. He couldn't get Anna away because she was older and very beautiful and . . . Vicki knows about it. She was almost thirteen years old, but I was only about three.'

'Your brother Rudolph must be grand,' I said inadequately.

'We've never seen him,' she said indifferently. 'He went off somewhere. I guess he died. Vicki brought me up. That's why I kinda feel responsible for her. There she goes now! Think I'd better run along and bust it up?'

I came out of my reverie, wondering what she wanted to bust up. Vicki had just passed the tea-shop, looking flushed and bright-eyed. She was teetering along as fast as she could on her high-heeled shoes. Tyler Sherman was walking lazily beside her. He was obviously teasing her and she was obviously not disliking it as much as she pretended. He took her arm as they crossed the church square. She make only a token protest. Mitzi watched with disgust.

'Mind you,' she admitted, 'Vicki can't help being so beautiful. But she never was like this before, silly and – ugh! – you know. . . . Maybe it's only a phase. In London she always said boys were silly. You know what she done with the money she got in that Beauty Contest? She bought me a new Dolmetsch harpsichord – a real beauty.'

Her small, grubby fingers did scales on the checked tablecloth. She stopped and said with a sudden solemnity:

'I think maybe I could eat another *coupe maison.*'

Chapter 14

WE settled the bill and left Mitzi in the middle of her third *coupe maison*. She urged us not to wait as she might take a little time finishing it, and afterwards she had to see Kitson about something called 'short octave fingering'. I said to Perdita when we regained the street:

'Some day I'm going to learn about not judging people on first impressions.'

Perdita grimly echoed the sentiment: 'Me, too!'

She, of course, was thinking of that noble hero, Johnny, while I was thinking about the Beauty Queen of the Camden Town Usherettes who used her prize money to buy musical instruments for her small sister. Characters, I find, are always stepping out of line like this. One, I remembered with a slight shiver, could have stepped out far enough to commit murder.

We had neither of us mentioned the Gordon-Smiths, but both of us were conscious that we couldn't very well go on avoiding them. Perdita, in a sense, was their guest – although she was paying her own hotel bills and a third of the petrol – while Dagobert and I were supposed to have come to Puig d'Aze expressly to join them.

We turned unwilling footsteps towards the Alexandra. It was only two or three hundred yards up the Avenue Prince de Galles, and to the right after you crossed the broad Place de la République. You could also reach the Alexandra more discreetly by two or three narrow streets overhung by ancient jutting eaves, much featured in the picture postcard shops – streets which radiated from the church square. Naomi, I reflected uncharitably, would doubtless have found these more devious routes to the Hôtel Commerce had Johnny's week in Puig d'Aze not come to such an abrupt end.

We kept to the Avenue Prince de Galles, looking enviously at the British export tweeds and into shoeshops. Neither of us was in a hurry to rejoin our dear friends. We stopped in the Place de la République to examine the begonias planted by the municipality and to admire the stucco chalet which was the

Gendarmerie Nationale. Dagobert came down the front steps just as we passed.

'Oh, good; I wanted to see you,' he said. 'Enjoying the shoe shops? Was our tandem a Speedster, a Roadster, or a Sportster? It has to go on a form, and since the form is in quintuplicate it's essential to get it right.'

'Dagobert,' I said, 'I think we may have been wrong about Vicki.'

'Yes, I know,' he said. 'That's why I rejoined you last night within about thirty seconds.'

'You said five minutes!'

'Is this the kind of vulgar squabble to have in front of Perdita?' he reproved me.

I asked gently: 'Did you during those thirty seconds find out by chance that coming to Puig was Vicki's idea, not Mitzi's?'

'Puig seems suddenly to have attracted the oddest people.'

'All,' I nodded, 'making straight for the Hôtel Commerce.'

Perdita had followed this as well as she could. 'You mean Johnny?' she said.

'He means Johnny *and* Vicki.'

'I see,' she said shortly. 'Another of his – er – "*divertissements*".'

'But she didn't even know his name,' I remembered. 'Only that he was Squadron Leader somebody – Cochran, she called him.'

'Engrossing, isn't it?' Dagobert said. 'I wish I had time to talk it over with you. Of course, she may *not* have known him. Or she may have been acting. Or – she may have known him under a different name. . . . I wish I could give you a lift. Shall we meet at the milk bar around opening time?'

He glanced at his wrist-watch, smiled apologetically, and got into the Humber Super-Snipe which was parked at the corner. He drove away with a horrible grinding of gears which Geoffrey was luckily not present to hear.

We walked on towards the Alexandra unhurriedly. I broke the lengthening silence.

'Thinking about Johnny?'

Perdita flushed. 'Yes. But not the way you think I'm thinking about him. I feel quite . . . cold inside. Curious – like you and Dagobert – wondering, asking myself questions, but impersonal questions. If I found out he'd had a hundred affairs, which he probably had, I couldn't be less interested.'

'I can see that.'

'Not,' she smiled quickly, 'that my girlish emotional reactions are very absorbing!'

'I'll keep them down to a minimum if this turns out to be one of Dagobert's "cases". What kind of impersonal questions?'

'Like the one you and Dagobert were asking: why he chose, of all places, the Hôtel Commerce.'

'Naomi told me he always stayed in a different hotel – for the sake of propriety.'

'Yes, but generally he stayed in an equally expensive hotel, or, if he could find one, more expensive. Economy was not one of Johnny's hobbies.'

I recalled the Bugatti, the gold cigarette-case, his clothes and luggage. 'No. I don't know what a test pilot earns, but he probably had private money. A rich family?'

'I don't think he has any family, except,' she remembered, 'that wife who's divorcing him. He pays her something fairly substantial. I gather from what Geoffrey and Naomi say that he was rich and poor by fits and starts. Perhaps Naomi "lent" him money!'

Personally, I didn't think even passion would drive Naomi to that extreme, and I pointed out that Johnny's source of income did not help us to solve the mystery of why he picked out the Hôtel Commerce.

'Last night,' Perdita said, blanching in spite of her new-found coldness, 'while he was telling me the facts of life he said the Commerce would be handy for Naomi because of back streets and that ladder in the shed.'

'He makes it sound delightfully romantic.'

She made a face. 'Yes. Poor Naomi – in a way! . . . Speaking of the Hôtel Commerce, why did you go there?'

'It's a long and involved story. Being married to your cousin Dagobert frequently gets me into long and involved stories. It's like the tandem.'

'You two *are* lucky,' she sighed.

'I don't see how that follows, but without waxing too sentimental about it, I have no complaints. . . . Yes, I have!' I added suddenly. 'Our luggage – it's still at the Hôtel des Voyageurs.

But here' – I gave her hand an encouraging squeeze as we mounted the Alexandra veranda – 'we are!'

Good news awaited us at the reception desk. Geoffrey had gone out with Sebastian Nevil to play golf. Naomi had left a note for me saying she was in her room 'resting'. (So essential, as she explained later, for women of 'our' age.)

There was, however, a darker side to the picture. We were *all* expected for dinner that evening. Eight o'clock promptly, as Kitson's first public recital began at nine. Evening clothes, of course. Black tie, if Dagobert preferred. There was no hurry about the return of the afternoon dress. Be *especially* nice to Perdita.

'How,' I said, putting this into immediate effect, 'would you like to move into our hotel?'

'Could I?'

'Life may be a little austere after the Alexandra,' I warned. 'But I dare say you can learn to rough it.'

We packed Perdita's things, paid her bill, and found a taxi. The next hour or so was hectic. Perdita tried on all my clothes; I tried on all of Perdita's clothes; and by the time we again issued forth to see what was going on in the village we had nearly forgotten that drama surrounded us.

It was brought home to me abruptly when Dagobert suddenly materialized from the narthex of St-Justin-d'Aze, where he had been taking a quick rubbing of a troubadour's tombstone. Excitement was depicted in every line of his face. He is rarely given to such displays of emotion and my heart stopped beating. Clearly he had found out who had murdered Corcoran.

He drew me aside recovering his normal poise. He said:

'You remember, Jane, that idea we discarded of mysterious attempts against us personally? The shots on the Col d'Aze and so on.'

'I remember the shots, but not the "and so on" part. No one's . . .' I went slightly pale, 'I mean, shot at you again or . . .'

'No one's exactly shot at me,' he admitted, aware of the anticlimax, 'but our unknown enemy has struck again. Our room – Room 8 – has been rifled! And not merely rifled – *everything's gone*.'

I let out my breath very slowly. 'This may hurt you more than it does me,' I said. 'They ought to have told you.'

'What?'

'*I* rifled our room. I mean, it isn't our room any more. I've moved our things over to the Hôtel des Voyageurs, where we have a most comfortable room with bedside lamps and a bathroom attached.'

He looked so downcast that I added kindly: 'But perhaps you've made other thrilling discoveries this afternoon, my dear. I know! You've found the tandem.'

He shook his head, but cheered up slightly.

'No,' he said. 'But I've bought a new one.'

Chapter 15

SUCH is the power of suggestion that I said to Dagobert that evening while I was plucking my eyebrows, preparatory to dinner at the Alexandra:

'*Re* our room at the Commerce being searched, I'm not dead sure that it wasn't.'

'Don't!' He flinched painfully.

'I know I shouldn't say so without being certain.'

'I mean don't do that to your eyebrows!'

'You needn't watch.'

'It has a dreadful fascination. I can't tear my eyes away. Couldn't you possibly make it Vicki?'

'No,' I said, 'I can't honestly make it anybody. But ever since you suggested the possibility little things keep coming back to me. I'm sure, for instance, we hadn't closed the saddlebags; they were neatly buckled when I began to repack.'

'The maid?'

'She hadn't done the room. Then the new tube of toothpaste we bought yesterday. It was still in its packet but the seal on the box I now see has been neatly cut. The letter I'd forgotten to post to mother was still in the guide book, but in the section "Toulouse", while I'm pretty certain I last used it to mark the Val d'Aze twenty or thirty pages on.'

He concentrated on his shirt studs, but he was paying attention.

Dagobert, to my relief, had put up no resistance to tonight's arrangements. Even dressing for dinner did not discourage him. 'We'll be the only people there who are dressed,' he pointed out, 'but it will please Fred – a detail for his report to *Workers' Playtime*. We'll go on the new tandem.' I had decided to face that problem when the time came and had gone up to Perdita's room on the floor above to borrow her electric iron.

'Why,' I now asked, 'do you want it to be Vicki?'

'For the sake of tidiness,' he explained. 'Vicki was about to search Corcoran's room last night – she may have even done so after I weakly came back to bed. If she searched our room today there'd be a pattern in it: it's a hobby of hers to search hotel rooms.'

'But why?'

'I must get her to tell me some time.'

'You mean,' I said, extracting the wrong eyebrow in my excitement, 'that Vicki was looking in our room for something she had failed to find in Johnny's!'

'I was working along that line,' he confessed. 'At present I am working along entirely too many lines. If some of them don't meet soon I'm going to give it all up.'

'Would it confuse me too much to hear about some of the other lines you're working on?'

'Probably,' he nodded. 'It confuses me. For instance, this isn't the first time Corcoran has visited Puig d'Aze. He was here two years ago and the year before that.'

'How do you know?'

'The Brigadier reluctantly volunteered the information. Hotels turn their registration slips over to the Gendarmerie, you know. Corcoran on both occasions stayed at the Alexandra and only remained one day.'

'Then,' I pointed out, 'it wasn't so strange, after all, that it should have been he who proposed coming to Puig d'Aze. If he already knew the place. . . .'

'No. . . . Though he never told Geoffrey or Naomi he'd been here before. I asked them when I took the Humber back. I warned you it was confusing.'

'You didn't discover,' I said, 'that Vicki, too, has been here before?'

'No. It's not that confusing. But I found out that the light which was on in the Alexandra last night was Naomi's.'

'How?'

'I asked the doorman at the Alexandra to point out Naomi's room and Geoffrey's room from the drive where we were standing. It's fantastically simple, detecting, when you go about it in the right way. It's half past seven. You don't seem to be awfully dressed yet, Jane.'

'How can I, when you keep interrupting?'

'There's no hurry,' he said inaccurately, trying the telephone. 'We'll have our drinks up here.' The telephone worked and he ordered dry Martinis. He returned to my side, softened by the prospect of their imminence. 'I love you in that creamy satin gown,' he murmured.

'It's my petticoat,' I said, 'and go away. If you haven't anything better to do you might find my stockings.'

'But I have.'

The arrival of the Martinis restored order. 'It's the southern night and the spring,' I sighed, '*and* a decent hotel.'

'We could telephone the Alexandra and say I have malaria.'

The idea was appealing. 'If I hadn't spent an hour ironing this dress,' I began. 'Besides, there's Perdita.'

'She's almost old enough to walk around to the Alexandra by herself.'

I changed the subject. 'Is spotting Naomi's room and finding that Johnny's been here before the sum total of your day's work?'

'Now you've broken the magic,' he complained, sipping his cocktail. 'Still, we'll be seeing a great deal of each other. No, I met a man in Aze-les-Bains who is very enthusiastic about my book on Bertran de Born. Of course, he can't read English.'

'I'm glad you're meeting such nice people,' I said, taking off a stocking which I had put on wrong side out.

'His name's Perrault and he's the *médecin-légiste* for Aze-les-Bains.'

I put on the stocking wrong side out again. 'The police doctor?'

'Yes. He doesn't think much of his Puig d'Aze colleague, whom he calls a "*couillon*", a word which is not in my pocket dictionary. He is convinced that if Dr Couillon – I mean, our local man – thinks Corcoran died in an accident, then Corcoran must have been murdered. And vice versa. Now, Dr Couillon has, in fact, signed the death certificate without question and without even a proper autopsy.'

'In other words – according to Dr Perrault – it logically follows that Corcoran was murdered.'

'Yes. A purist might object to this reasoning, but . . . Shall I ring down for something to drink?'

'We haven't time for another.'

'*You* haven't time,' he corrected sympathetically. 'Both Dr Perrault and I think it odd – and most convenient – that the body was so burned that no one can tell whether Corcoran was dead before the crash or not. Fred Evans thinks so, too. Fred and I had a glass of beer together. He doesn't think much of French beer, but he was fascinated by the fact that Corcoran's body was so efficiently burned. It's shaken him into half believing in the "screwy" theory of dirty work. If it were not for the libel laws he says he'd write something pretty snappy about it for *Workers' Playtime*. At any rate, that makes three of us who now believe Corcoran was murdered.'

'Three and a half,' I said uncomfortably. 'I'm the half.... Perhaps we have just time for a quick one – tell them less gin this time.'

When he returned from the telephone I said, though without conviction: 'We must be wrong! If there was a second fatal shot, why didn't anyone hear it?'

'Why didn't anyone hear it when Perdita fired?'

'Because eleven o'clock was striking. No one would have had time to ... oh!' I broke off, wishing the drinks would come. 'Oh! I see. The second shot could have been fired at *twelve* o'clock.'

He grinned. 'Thirsty work, isn't it? We'll be able to relax during the recital – if we ever get there. Remind me to pay Naomi for our tickets.'

'She'll remind you.... But if he was killed at midnight, how could Vicki have seen him at five minutes past midnight?'

'He was dead – but she could still see him.'

'She said she talked to him.'

'Yes. She said that to us, to the landlady, to Fred, to the police, to everybody she's talked to. She seems to consider the point important. If she'd just seen Corcoran dead and didn't want anybody to know she'd just seen him dead, it *would* be important. Especially if she'd killed him herself....'

'But why?'

'I suggest a perfectly good murderer to you, and you want to know why. You always rush things, Jane. Except,' he added, answering the door and collecting our drinks, 'things like dressing. Anyway, if you see me during the next week or two in a huddle with our Vicki you'll know what I'm doing.'

'I shall guess.'

He glossed over the point. 'So long as there's no misunderstanding. But we must not keep darting from subject to subject. We were talking about ... what were we talking about?'

'Murder,' I reminded him grimly.

Dagobert, in spite of the reminder, seemed to be in increasingly good spirits – possibly the result of the dry Martinis. He was pleased with himself and he was pleased with me. Since I had made only minor progress with dressing, I sought the explanation of this elsewhere. Clearly, there had been suppression of vital information.

'All right,' I said, 'what is it?'

'I meant to keep it until you were dressed,' he shrugged. 'It's about Dr Perrault. He's also a dab at fingerprints.'

'You left the revolver with him.'

'Yes.'

My mind flew off at a tangent. 'Could Vicki – or whoever it was – have been searching our room for the revolver?'

'In the toothpaste and between the pages of the guide book?'

'I see what you mean. Go on.'

There was a knock at the door. Perdita, letting her side down badly, was dressed and ready before me. Before Dagobert let her in he finished off his cocktail. He murmured:

'Don't let this go any further, but Dr Perrault got a smudged but legible set of prints off the handle of that revolver. *The fingerprints were not Perdita's.*'

Chapter 16

SOMEONE else, then, had fired Corcoran's revolver after Perdita! Someone's fingerprints had obliterated hers. This paramount fact over-rode everything else that I had thought about up to this moment. In spite of Dagobert's warning not to jump to conclusions, I jumped to the one which seemed obvious: find out whose fingerprints were on the revolver, and you knew who had fired the second shot and killed Corcoran.

There were, as Dagobert suggested, certain loose ends: such as the murderer's subsequent disposal of the body. Carrying Corcoran down the ladder and getting him into the Bugatti would be – as Fred had pointed out – no mean task for an able-bodied man, and a task which practically eliminated the women from my then sketchy list of suspects. There was also the question of why our murderer – though carefully removing the body – had left the weapon for us to find. Had he remembered it only later, and come back for it? But Vicki was the sole person (we knew of) who had attempted to visit (or revisit?) Corcoran's room. And since she was a woman I'd already eliminated her. Again, there was the remote possibility that someone (a third person) had handled but not shot the revolver between the time Corcoran had been shot (while midnight was striking) and the time (4.30 a.m.) when we had found the revolver.

This way madness lay. If it confuses the reader, you can imagine what it did to me. I clung, therefore, to my simple faith in the formula: find the owner of the fingerprints and you've found the murderer. This kept me sane, though I did develop an odd tic of stealing surreptitious glances at people's fingertips.

We weren't very late for dinner and Naomi was charming about it. 'It's quite all right,' she smiled. 'We'll merely miss the pudding. It was only *crêpes suzette*, which actually they do rather well here. You've had cocktails, I imagine.'

Perdita hadn't, but I was glad to hear her murmur: 'Yes.'

Naomi's rest that afternoon had done wonders. I don't

know exactly what I'd expected; something in the tragic line, I suppose, with a brave, patient expression and sorrow-laden eyes. Instead, she was almost aggressively cheerful and plainly determined to ignore Johnny Corcoran's death entirely. Perhaps, in her 'scatter-brained' way it had simply slipped her mind!

She made only one oblique reference to it as we preceded the others into the dining-room.

'It was so thoughtful of you, Jane,' she whispered. 'I mean to have poor Perdita with you. We *must* do all we can for her, mustn't we? I was wondering about that nice young American, Tyler Sherman. . . . Ah, here we are!' She broke off in the kind of voice which makes others immediately realize you've been talking about them. 'Dagobert on my right and, yes, Perdita *here* on my left! No, that means Jane will have to sit next to her husband. I could never work out these problems, could I, Jane? – even at St Catherine's. *How* to seat three women when there are only two . . . oh . . .'

'I'll see if I can't find another man,' Perdita remarked dryly, but fortunately in an aside to me. Naomi had already recovered herself.

'Geoffrey, you attend to the wine. I'm *sure* we'll need to start another bottle. The soup *may* be a teeny bit cold. Foolishly, I told the waiter to serve it at eight. Isn't it exciting hearing Kitson again after all these years!'

I said yes, though I had the impression that we'd heard him last night, and Naomi said he was going to play 'nothing but pure Bach – the forty-eight Preludes and Variations,' she believed.

I saw Dagobert jump, but it may have been the soup. Naomi added:

'I have your three tickets, you know. But, well . . . we can settle that later, can't we? Tomorrow I thought we'd all take out a picnic luncheon in the car. Our hotels will give us each *petits paquets*. We might persuade Tyler Sherman to join us, Jane. He lives in your new hotel, doesn't he? Now, where shall we go? Font Romeu? Vernet-les-Bains? You choose.'

'How about Andorra?' Dagobert said.

She hesitated, as though to weigh the suggestion. She bit her lip. 'Why not? Talk it over with Geoffrey. He *may* consider the roads a little rough for the new car.'

Geoffrey looked up from his soup plate, about to protest against this aspersion on his Humber. Naomi smiled at him firmly, and said before he could open his mouth:

'Finish your soup, my dear. The *garçon* is waiting. Shall we all have the chicken?'

I had seen the flicker of a smile in Perdita's eye when Dagobert mentioned Andorra. The flicker was malicious but at least it meant the wounds were healing.

Naomi's wounds, too – for I presume Johnny's death must have meant *something* to her – seemed to be doing nicely. Apart from a slightly heightened tendency to manage everybody, there was no indication that last night's tragedy had left any mark at all on her. The fanciful thought crossed my mind that Johnny's death was a relief to one and all. Geoffrey alone looked occasionally distressed when the conversation skirted subjects which recalled Squadron Leader Corcoran.

We got through dinner in record time, omitting the *crêpes suzette*, which flamed merrily on neighbouring tables. Geoffrey already had the car at the door, though it was only ten minutes' walk to The Abbaye.

After the briefest exchange of 'No, *you* must sit in the front seat,' Dagobert, Perdita and I climbed into the back. Geoffrey said we were going to be early after all and why not stop on the way for coffee? Naomi said the car clock was fifteen minutes slow and that coffee kept one (her) awake all night. Geoffrey said that in view of tonight's ordeal that might be a jolly sound scheme.

Perdita laughed at this mild sally and Naomi said: 'Not amusing, Geoffrey dear. Besides, you know perfectly well what I mean. Last night after coffee – and, of course, after the excitement of hearing Kitson – I had to take *two* of those new capsules Dr Hervey prescribed, and one is supposed to be the absolute limit.'

'I wish you'd stop taking those things,' Geoffrey growled. 'Hervey's an idiot to let you have them.'

'Dr Hervey's a pet,' Naomi said dreamily.

Dagobert nudged me. I said:

'But last night even two of his capsules failed to work.'

'They certainly did not!' she contradicted me shortly. 'They put me out like a light.'

'When was that?'

'When we came back from Kitson's, of course. When would that be – a bit before eleven? Anyway, I blacked out in a rather frightening way without even creaming my face! The next thing I knew it was eight o'clock and the maid was bringing in my breakfast.'

'That's funny . . .' Perdita said. She thought again and relapsed into silence.

Naomi herself prompted: 'What's funny? Forgetting to cream my face? Jane will tell you that a thing like that is far from funny – at our age.'

'No,' Perdita said, 'I mean I thought your light was still on when I came home about a quarter to two. It must have been Geoffrey's next door.'

'As a matter of fact . . .' Geoffrey began. He broke off and concentrated on a sharp bend in the street before concluding: 'Yes, I sat up in bed into the small hours, reading.'

I remembered the bedside reading lamps at the Alexandra. They were modest pink-shaded affairs and would certainly not have lit up the third-floor window that we had seen at a quarter to two last night. And then, unless Dagobert and the hotel doorman were mistaken, the light *had* been Naomi's.

Again Naomi herself kept the subject alive. 'You might easily have seen my light on,' she said cheerfully. 'I probably forgot to switch it off. It's just the kind of thing I would do.'

'But . . .' Perdita stopped.

'But,' Dagobert continued for her, 'the light was switched off just as we walked up the drive. You probably did it in your sleep.'

'Probably,' Naomi agreed. 'Why do we keep on discussing it? Careful, Geoffrey, it's the next turning on the right. And do hurry!'

Geoffrey said, after he had negotiated the turning:

'As a matter of fact Naomi did forget to turn off her light last night. That's why I dislike those dam' capsules so much. She was sleeping like a log – much too soundly for a healthy person. I went into her room and switched off her light. It would have been about a quarter to two, as a matter of fact.'

'Then that explains everything, doesn't it?' Naomi said sweetly. 'I'm sure Dagobert and Jane must be utterly fascinated, darling, by our nocturnal habits! Oh! . . . we're here. I'd better let you have your tickets.' She opened her gold brocade handbag. 'They were twelve hundred francs each, rather dear, I thought, but then one doesn't hear a Kitson every day.'

Naomi had been right about the clock on the dashboard being slow. She had also been right about skipping the *crêpes suzette*. We arrived, as planned, at nine sharp.

It was not really Naomi's fault that Kitson himself had not appeared and that it was at least three-quarters of an hour later before the lights went down, programmes ceased to rustle and the recital began.

The big harpsichord had been placed on a platform built over the well in the abbey cloister and chairs set on the grass surrounding it. Cheaper seats were provided by benches further back under the cloister arches. They were filled with hikers in shorts, locals and the sort of people who came on tandems. Half of them brought music scores.

We sat among the *élite* – the municipal dignitaries and the priest, a handful of people from the Alexandra, half a dozen music critics. Sebastian Nevil fluttered among us, pointing out the charm of the abbey cloisters, assuring us that the moon would rise above the cloisters at any moment, that the Maître was in superb form and would play divinely.

Mitzi, who had strayed among the twelve-hundred-franc ticket-holders from the benches behind, told me in a whisper that the 'Maître' was being sobered up by his 'housekeeper' and that we'd probably have to wait all night.

We caught a glimpse of Vicki Stein beneath the arches, leaning against a broken edge of the cloister wall beyond which the Val d'Aze, already blanched by the moonlight Sebastian had promised us, shimmered beneath the lavender shape of the Pic des Quatre Vents. She looked very decorative in a patterned dress. Tyler Sherman leaned beside her.

'I bet,' Mitzi commented nastily, 'they're saying, "Isn't it *ever* so romantic!"'

'It is,' I pointed out.

Naomi had also been studying the couple. 'Who,' she asked, 'is the glamour girl poor Tyler Sherman seems to have got himself involved with?'

'My sister,' Mitzi replied fiercely. 'And what's it to you?' She turned away with dignity, muttering: 'These tarted-up hags!'

'Charming friends you have, Jane,' Naomi smiled.

'Yes,' I said, wondering how she would take to Fred Evans, who, with his complimentary critic's ticket, was bearing down on us.

Fred had changed for the occasion into plastic sandals, linen slacks and one of those sports-jacket-shirt arrangements worn nonchalantly outside the trousers which I always have to hurry Dagobert past when we look in Shaftesbury Avenue shop windows. He gripped my hand warmly.

'This is a bit of all right, isn't it?' he said enthusiastically showing protruding teeth in a cordial smile. 'Is that the harpsichord? Looks,' he lowered his voice in a disillusioned aside, 'just like a dirty great piano to me.' He rustled his programme importantly. 'Bach, I see. No one in the world like him. Give me Bach every time. Which reminds me. They sell beer in the refec . . . refrec . . . in that big room in there. That's called Bach, too, you know, in frog talk. You ask for a *demi.* For some reason a *demi* is twice as big as an ordinary one. Doesn't make sense, but then nothing does around here.'

I introduced him to Naomi. He squeezed her hand until she winced. 'Pleased to meet you,' he said. 'You're the one whose old man identified the late lamented, aren't you? I'd like an interview with you two some time.'

I rapidly explained that Mr Evans represented *Workers' Playtime.* Naomi said, really, how interesting, and turned to drag Dagobert from Sebastian Nevil. Fred, unconscious of the snub, watched her approvingly, cracking his finger-joints with the air of a connoisseur.

'Real style there,' he confided. 'I go for it every time.' He brought her suavely back into the conversation. 'I say, Naomi, if hubby hasn't anything better to do in the evenings than wander around by himself, how about you and me stepping out, *hein*, as we say locally?'

Naomi smiled and let out her breath cautiously as though to prevent an explosion.

'I'm afraid, Mr – is it Evans? – that I haven't the remotest idea what you're talking about. . . .'

'Crickey! Have I put my big foot into it?' Fred flushed.

'He was talking about Geoffrey', Dagobert explained helpfully as Geoffrey himself walked off with Sebastian in search of more programmes.

'That's right,' Fred nodded. 'How are you, Dagobert?

Doing all right, I see. You want to watch out for that, Jane.'

He eyed Naomi, who, conscious of his admiration, went white, pink and white again. She said to Dagobert in a small voice:

'*What* about Geoffrey?'

Dagobert looked blank, but Fred volunteered: 'They tell me that hubby was wandering around all by himself late last night.'

'Who told you that?' Naomi said quickly.

'They,' Fred shrugged. 'You know, "*they*". The famous Evans Spy Service. Village gossip. You can't rely on it, but as I always say, "where there's smoke . . ."'

He glanced around. It was nearly a quarter to ten and the local inhabitants, wiser in these matters than the visitors, were arriving for the recital. Fred suddenly spotted Vicki and Tyler, who had not moved from their position overlooking the valley.

'Uh-huh!' he exclaimed. 'That Yank's making a pass at my red-head popsy! Something must be done about this. See you later, chaps. Don't find any more dead bodies!'

And he disappeared with a gay display of upper teeth towards the cloister arches. The mayor of Puig d'Aze stepped on to the platform at that moment, and I could not observe whether Fred's infectious smile was reflected in Naomi's eyes.

Chapter 17

I ENJOYED the mayor's speech and understood nearly a quarter of it. It was full of fine resounding phrases like '*ce grand Maître*' who has made of our remote but proud village a place of musical pilgrimage, renowned throughout '*le monde entier*'. He drew our attention to '*la beauté féerique*' of the setting, the ancient abbey cloisters, the moon '*pure et éternelle*', the night '*douce et solennelle*'. It was his intention – if re-elected next year – to make the Puig d'Aze Musical Festival a joyous annual event. He touched lightly upon the commercial advantages which hotels and tradesmen would reap from this, but ended up – some twenty minutes later – by reminding us that tonight was consecrated to Art alone. We had not come to listen to an account of his modest efforts to save Puig d'Aze from the deplorable state into which it had fallen under the former administration, but to hear the magic of the Maître . . . '*que la musique parle* . . .'

He paused and mopped his brow. Everybody clapped and looked expectantly round. No Maître.

The mayor caught Sebastian's eye and began again, sketching out a plan he had in mind for a Casino. He was working us up to a pitch of excitement over the tiled swimming pool which would make the one at Aze-les-Bains look silly when Sebastian, who had crept inconspicuously out, returned with Kitson.

Kitson looked surprised and slightly annoyed to find us all there. He blinked his eyes, giving the impression that tonight's recital had slipped his mind. The mayor shook hands with him warmly and assisted him on to the platform.

Kitson was wearing a dark plum-coloured velvet dinner jacket. His black beard had been neatly trimmed and brushed. His face looked very clean. It ought to have been, Sebastian explained later; he and Paulette (the housekeeper) had thrown a bucket of water into it.

He sat down without fuss and began to play. A seraphic expression settled over Naomi's face which I tried in vain to imitate. I was handicapped by Dagobert's tendency to keep time with his left foot and by the fact that – although the programme announced Preludes and Fugues – he was playing the Chromatic Fantasia of which we have Kitson's own recording at home. I was dying for it to come to the end so I could tell Naomi.

I had no opportunity. When he finished he began without pause to play the Fifth French Suite (the programme said Goldberg Variations), and when that was finished he immediately began again. He continued for two hours on end without playing a single piece announced on the programme. Dagobert, more cunning than the rest of us, spotted each item. I was impressed until he showed me page six of the programme. Kitson was simply playing next Thursday's concert.

For the first hour I listened intently, especially enjoying the passages I was familiar with.

There was supposed to be an intermission at the end of an hour. Kitson ignored it. My mind began to wander as, regrettably, it always does after one hour of musical concentration. I thought about wardrobe accessories for a while, and about an article I'd recently read in the Continental *Daily Mail* entitled 'Ten Amusing Things to Do with Diamonds'. As there was clearly no message in this for me, I looked cautiously around and caught Fred's eye. He made an eloquent gesture towards the bar, began to whisper, 'How about . . .' but was promptly shushed by Naomi.

Perdita, on the other side of Dagobert, was listening in a private world of her own. I saw that her eyes were wet. Geoffrey, beside me, had gone quietly to sleep. His pleasant, undistinguished face looked gentle and relaxed. His chin, dropping forward, bulged slightly over his stiff collar, and once, when Kitson struck a series of jangling chords, his face twitched.

Geoffrey had had the most exhausting day of any of us: the police at breakfast, identifying Corcoran's body; golf with Sebastian this afternoon while Naomi rested. And, according to his own statement, he had read into the small hours, turning off Naomi's light at a quarter to two. According to the Evans 'Spy Service', he had also been seen strolling around the village late last night.

I glanced at Naomi on the other side of him. She had gone off into her trance again; it looked to me uncommonly like a short nap. She was ten or fifteen years younger than Geoffrey, and she looked it. She was also, I suspected, ten or fifteen times as intelligent. Was she intelligent enough to carry on a love affair with Johnny Corcoran under her husband's very eyes without being suspected? Given Geoffrey, the answer was probably yes.

I remembered something else about Naomi suddenly. Yesterday, on the way to her room, when I had asked if Johnny was in love with Perdita, Naomi had reacted most oddly. The question had disturbed her, and she had answered me only after dropping the key of her door. It could have been the first time the thought had occurred to Naomi – her lover *might* be attracted to Perdita after all. My innocent question could have sown the seeds of jealousy in Naomi's heart, and jealousy is the most devastating of all emotions. If, for instance, Naomi had witnessed that scene in Room 2 when Johnny had taken Perdita in his arms. . . .

But Naomi had at that moment been in a deep, drugged slumber. And, I reminded myself, we had just paid twelve hundred francs each for a concert I wasn't listening to.

I concentrated on Kitson, if not entirely on what he was playing. By this time he was considerably wider awake than most of his audience. He had, of course, more to do than the rest of us. I followed him through the *courante* of the Partita in B flat (identified by Dagobert's finger on page six of the programme) and through the first bars of the *sarabande* before I drifted off again, this time brooding about Kitson himself.

In Paris one of the first things Dagobert had done when we decided to come to Puig was to find out what the *New Statesman* meant by that reference to the 'death in tragic circumstances' of Kitson's wife.

Kitson, he had learned, was married in May 1945 during the German collapse and the event had passed almost unnoticed. The woman he'd married had fallen out of the fifth-storey window of a London hotel on their wedding night. There had been a small party in their hotel suite before the accident, during which much drink had been consumed; the coroner's verdict had been death by misadventure. But everyone who had known the couple was convinced that Sheila Kitson had thrown herself out of the window.

We had been reluctant to probe any deeper into a half-forgotten personal tragedy which seemed to have no bearing on the present. Sebastian Nevil had been at the wedding party, but he could (Dagobert reported) add little to the bare outline above. Whether Sheila Kitson had fallen by accident, or had committed suicide, no one could blame Kitson for his precipitous retirement to Puig d'Aze.

In my romantic way I decided I detected new depths of pathos in Kitson's interpretation of Bach – in spite of the fact that at the moment this thought occurred to me he was just finishing the programme with a particularly gay and sparkling *gigue*.

Kitson interrupted our applause with an impatient gesture, announced that tomorrow night's concert would be given at nine o'clock on Monday morning instead, and disappeared into the house. When he didn't reappear in response to the continued ovation the mayor got on to the platform to express our gratitude in a few well-chosen words. While he was choosing them everyone filed out. In the confusion I somehow found myself being propelled by Fred Evans towards the bar which had been set up in the refectory. It was after midnight, and the awful thought had crossed Fred's mind that this might only be the intermission.

The sole person in the bar was Kitson himself. He put down the tumbler of red wine he'd just drained, wiped his beard with the sleeve of his velvet jacket, glared at us and grunted:

'Who are you? Did you pay for your seats? Or did Nevil let you in free?'

'Mr Evans,' I said, 'is the distinguished critic. I paid twelve hundred francs for my ticket, which I think is excessive.'

Kitson glanced round and lowered his voice. 'Get them directly from me after this,' he said quickly. 'I'll let you have ten per cent off. And what,' he stared at Fred, raising his voice again, 'does the good Mr Evans know about music, pray tell?'

'Sweet eff ay,' Fred admitted gracefully. 'Just *entray noo*, I'm more in the line of crime reporter. How do you get a beer around here?'

Kitson nodded impatiently towards the long refectory table, which was lined with bottles and glasses. 'You are not, I presume, physically incapable of helping yourself. The prices are clearly marked and I'll give you change if you need it. A crime reporter is precisely what is wanted in the realms of musical criticism. The connexion between the genius and the criminal, though obvious, has never . . . Get out!' he thundered at two people who had floated uncertainly into the room.

They fled. Kitson hitched his velvet trousers above his expansive belly and refilled his glass. Fred poured out two glasses of lukewarm beer and extended a five-hundred-franc note. 'The artist,' Kitson said, pocketing the five hundred francs, 'needs privacy.'

'I should think you go the right way about getting it,' I said.

He ignored the interruption. 'So does the criminal. This conversation begins to bore me,' he added, clearing a space on the long refectory table.

He stretched himself out at full length in the space he had cleared and closed his eyes. He was apparently sound asleep.

Fred tapped his forehead and murmured: 'And I thought I'd met some!'

I asked curiously: 'Is it lots of fun, Mr Kitson, pretending to be an eccentric genius?'

He opened one bleary eye and studied me. 'Yes,' he said. He closed the eye again and added: 'Though, strictly speaking, to do the thing properly one ought actually to be a genius. I'm not. But so long as only we three know it doesn't matter. There is, by coincidence, a genius in Puig d'Aze at the moment. Her name is Mitzi Stein. Why don't you go away now?'

'Oh, no you don't, chum,' Fred said. 'Not till I've had my five hundred francs' worth.'

'Suit yourself,' Kitson said haughtily, and began to breathe like a man in deep slumber.

Naomi, followed by Geoffrey, came into the room at that moment. She saw Fred, but not Kitson.

'Oh,' she said, avoiding Fred's eager smile of welcome, 'there you are, Jane. We couldn't imagine what had happened to you. Dagobert's been looking everywhere for you. I'm taking Geoffrey home. He's had such a day, poor dear. Dagobert said you and he would walk. I rather envy you. Hasn't it been sheer heaven! One has never heard the Chromatic Fantasia played quite like that! And, oh yes, I rescued Tyler from the red-haired siren and he's coming with us tomorrow for our picnic to Font Romeu. He's walking back to the hotel with Perdita now. So something may be starting *there*, if you know what I mean! We must rush. Isn't it an amusing idea to have the next concert at nine o'clock in the morning! One's morning self is so much more receptive. At home I always have ten minutes of Mozart before breakfast. It makes –'

'Cannot somebody,' Kitson's voice boomed sepulchrally from the inert mass on the table, 'stop that silly bitch from chattering?'

Naomi gasped, but recovered her poise at once.

Fred cracked the joints of his left thumb. 'Come now, none of that,' he purred gently, 'or I'll break your blinking neck, genius or no genius.'

The arrival of Dagobert and Sebastian eased the momentary tension. Naomi, smiling gaily, said good night and led a flustered Geoffrey away. Sebastian said, with a sigh:

'I suppose Kitson's being insufferable again. Paulette and I can do absolutely nothing about it!'

Fred greeted Dagobert with satisfaction. I don't know what gave me the impression that there was some kind of conspiracy between them. Possibly the impulsive jocularity with which Fred exclaimed:

'I've got it, old boy! Why couldn't we pin Corcoran's murder on this laddie Kitson?'

'It's an idea,' Dagobert said doubtfully, studying the recumbent figure on the refectory table.

Kitson, I observed, did not stir. His eyes remained closed and he might, indeed, have been sound asleep. Sebastian said solicitously:

'Please don't do anything to upset him before the Festival's over. Kitson, dear boy, you played very nicely tonight. Mitzi Stein said so. And the Decca people have definitely decided to do those recordings of the French suites.'

'Just before you came in,' Fred went on portentously, 'he was talking in a very queer way; about how geniuses are always criminals. He's a big, strong fellow. He could have done it, too!'

'Done what?' Sebastian asked distractedly. 'Kitson! Do sit up. We have visitors.'

'Lugged him down that ladder,' Fred said.

'Yes, yes, of course,' Sebastian muttered absently. 'Do help yourselves to anything you want, everybody.'

'What's more,' Fred concluded triumphantly, 'he was the last to see him alive. Did you see *him*, Kitson, or did you just see the Bugatti?'

Kitson continued to sleep in peace. Sebastian, wringing his hands, murmured:

'Do answer when you're spoken to, dear boy. . . . Oh, where is Paulette? She's the only one that can do anything with him.' He slid with a movement of helplessness towards the door leading into the hall. 'Who,' he whispered in my ear as he left, 'is that dreadful man, and what on earth is he talking about?'

There was a moment's silence after Sebastian left the room. The cloisters beyond the french windows were dark and finally deserted. The last motor-car had driven away. Across the valley the bell of St Justin's struck one. Even from this distance the sound was a sudden jab which made my pulse quicken uncomfortably.

Fred glanced at Dagobert. Dagobert was nibbling a sandwich in a corner, pretending – and probably wishing – he wasn't there. I wondered if the absurd, fat, bearded figure on the table was not equally uneasy. He gave no sign of it.

'Ask him if he *recognized* Corcoran,' Dagobert said.

'The chances are he wouldn't exactly recognize him,' Fred frowned. 'He'd probably never seen him before. He'd only spot the car, with a driver of some sort.'

'True,' Dagobert said as though he could think of nothing more constructive to suggest. He added, a moment later: 'I wonder if he can ride a bicycle?'

'That's a damn silly question!' Fred grunted. 'Can you, laddie? He can,' he added when there was no response. 'I saw him on a bike this afternoon. The point is, what was he doing, hanging around the Hôtel Commerce at midnight last night!'

'Yes,' Dagobert agreed. 'And ask him if he's ever tried riding a tandem-bicycle alone . . .'

Fred spluttered slightly over his beer. 'Look, old boy,' he said, 'I give up. You carry on.'

'All right,' Dagobert said. 'Why, Mr Kitson, did you go to the Hôtel Commerce last night?'

There was no answer, and Dagobert himself supplied it. He talked quickly now, as though to get it over and done with. He said:

'Because I wanted to have a word with Corcoran. . . . What about? Probably I wanted to settle his hotel bill. . . . Why on earth would you want to do that? Because it is my custom to settle Corcoran's hotel bills when he comes to Puig d'Aze.

I did it two years ago when he stayed at the Alexandra and again the year before that . . .'

'No! Really?' Fred interrupted. 'Now we're getting somewhere!'

'Why,' Dagobert continued, 'was it Mr Kitson's custom to settle Corcoran's hotel bills?'

'I say,' Fred cut in, in a whisper, 'I think the chappie really is asleep.'

'No,' Kitson said without opening his eyes. 'I'm waiting for a dramatic moment to intervene. I paid – what's-his-name – Corcoran's bills because I do not like my fellow countrymen to leave unpaid bills in Puig d'Aze. As the leading resident Englishman in the community I felt this to be my duty. Does this bore you, or shall I go on?'

'Please do.'

He continued unhurriedly and without stirring from his position on the table. 'You may find this explanation a little difficult to believe. Nevertheless, I advise you earnestly to believe it. Let me digress for a moment. About my position in this community. I am a lovable, eccentric and extremely rich foreign resident who has contributed much to the amenities of Puig d'Aze. I am a close friend of the mayor, the *médecin-légiste*, the *gendarmes* and other leading citizens. I am also, as you know, a public asset. The Puig Musical Festival, which I intend to hold annually, will bring hundreds of tourists to the place. I have innumerable friends locally, many of them rough Catalan peasants, who would go to any length to spare me pain. . . . I wonder if, in my pompous though rather sinister way, I make myself clear?'

'I'm afraid you do,' Dagobert confessed.

'Threatening us, huh?' Fred began aggressively.

'Yes,' Kitson said. 'Would you be good enough to pour out a glass of red wine for me?'

He sat up, opened his eyes and stroked his black beard, while Fred refilled the tumbler with red wine.

'Thank you,' he said. 'Five or ten minutes' total relaxation is wonderfully refreshing. Let me recommend it to you, Mr Evans. It will cure you of those jitters you try to conceal by chain-smoking. Now where were we? Yes, of course, you had just decided not to go on attempting to discover who murdered Squadron Leader Corcoran.'

'You did say . . . murdered?'

'I thought that was your word. Please don't interrupt. The sad part of it – I say sad because you have given up your investigations – is that Corcoran probably *was* murdered. I told my friend Brigadier Petitjean that I recognized Corcoran driving away from the Hôtel Commerce. Now the truth is, I was in a deplorable state of intoxication at the time and it is more than likely – in fact, I'm certain – that it was somebody else at the wheel of the Bugatti.'

'Who?' Fred snapped.

'It really doesn't interest me who,' Kitson sighed gently.

'He didn't have a big black beard?' Dagobert suggested.

'No, he didn't have a big black beard,' Kitson said. 'Corcoran himself, we must presume, was unconscious or dead, in the back seat. There was a canvas cover stretched over it.'

'You noticed that,' Fred put in shrewdly, 'but you didn't spot who was driving?'

Kitson ignored this and accepted Dagobert's smooth silver cigarette-case. He took a cigarette carefully wiped his fingerprints off the case with his dirty silk handkerchief and handed it back.

Dagobert pocketed it with a grin. 'D'you mind,' he asked, 'if we hang around Puig d'Aze until your recitals are finished?'

'Do, dear boy,' Kitson urged. 'I was telling your good wife that I can let you have tickets at reduced rates. Ah, here's Sebastian with Paulette, who is, between ourselves, beginning to be a teeny bit of a bore. Shall we change the subject?'

We stayed for nearly two hours longer. Paulette was charming. She was pretty, though almost as fat as Kitson himself, and she insisted on making *soupe à l'oignon* to go with the contents of the bar which Kitson had decided would not keep until the next concert. Kitson, to Sebastian's horror, told us that he himself had had that notice inserted in the *New Statesman* about the Puig d'Aze Festival, even to the bit about the 'death in tragic circumstances' of his wife, which, he added, was one of the luckiest escapes of his life. He was, he told us, a technically competent but uninspired harpsichordist whose reputation was based almost exclusively on his revolting manners. Dagobert argued that he exaggerated and Sebastian fluttered around filling glasses and looking distressed. Fred got very drunk and disappeared early. Paulette and I retired to the kitchen to make Welsh rabbits. Just before we left I seem to remember Dagobert's playing the harpsichord, while Kitson sang 'Her Father was the Keeper of the Eddystone Light'.

It was pleasant walking home through the deserted village under the light of the full moon. For some reason Fifi frisked beside us. The apparition of the dog seemed to revive unpleasant memories, and Dagobert said:

'I hate to spoil a good evening, but, I'm afraid, Jane, we've just been hobnobbing with a murderer.'

'Kitson.'

He nodded, and we walked across the silent church square. I became conscious for the first time of how painful high heels were on cobblestones.

'You got his fingerprints after all, didn't you?'

He nodded again and said: 'What do you think of his suggestion that we drop the whole business?'

'I like it, but of course we won't.'

'No, I suppose not.' He tossed a stick for Fifi. 'It's a pity.'

'You believe,' I said carefully as we approached the hotel, 'that Kitson murdered Corcoran . . .'

He frowned and shook his head. 'Not Johnny Corcoran . . .' he said. '*Sheila* Corcoran. Kitson's wife was named Corcoran. And she didn't fall from that window. *Or* jump. Kitson pushed her.'

Chapter 18

No drama awaited us in our new hotel. Our room had not been rifled, there were no hysterical girls in it. The bed had been turned down and our night clothes put out invitingly. Three o'clock had just struck (less overwhelmingly than at the Hôtel Commerce) and we had an hour of heavenly silence before us. It was sensual pleasure to get out of my shoes.

'I wish,' I said, 'you wouldn't choose those rare occasions when I'm about to go to bed to tell me things like that!'

'We'll discuss it in the morning,' he said.

I borrowed the cigarette he had just lighted. 'We'll discuss it now. I'm used to doing without sleep, and tomorrow I'll take one of Naomi's capsules. How do you know her name was Sheila Corcoran?'

'Sebastian told me.'

'Did Sebastian also tell you that Kitson pushed her from the window?'

'No. I worked that part out all by myself. Only Kitson and ourselves know it. And, of course,' he added, 'Johnny Corcoran.'

I shivered slightly. 'Yes, and look where that got him.'

Dagobert locked the door, bolted it, and began to undress. 'Johnny Corcoran was at the famous party in the hotel suite. Johnny gave the bride away, or whatever you do with brides at Caxton Hall.'

'What was he? Her brother?'

'That's the part that remains, to quote Sebastian, a little *louche*. She was supposed to be a kind of cousin, freshly imported from Galway. She was very simple and sweet and spoke with a captivating brogue – at least she did until half-way through the party, when, under the influence of R.A.F. gin brought back from Germany, things began to warm up. Sebastian feels that Sheila may indeed have come from Ireland, but via the Mile End Road and Shaftesbury Avenue, whose dialects she had also mastered. Sebastian, disliking scenes, went home at this point to mind his own business.'

'One could do worse than imitate Sebastian,' I mused. 'What scenes?'

'A rather odd one, in a way. Johnny, at that time a Flight Lieutenant covered with medals and very compelling in his R.A.F. uniform and moustache, was making his usual pass at a blonde in the service pantry when Sheila found him. She nearly scratched his eyes out. Sebastian is vague about details; but putting two and two together he realized that Sheila's relationship to Johnny had been more intimate than was supposed. She was, as everybody later discovered, a girl Johnny had picked up somewhere, lived with, and literally "given away" to Kitson. Kitson, with the extraordinary blindness which sometimes strikes hard-boiled men around the age of forty-five, had fallen head-over-heels for her. Kitson was very wealthy, and Johnny and Sheila seemed to be on to a good thing. Johnny provided her with his name and vaguely respectable relationship; then unselfishly stepped out of the picture. She would be more useful to him as the wife of a rich man. It was a pity that he had to spoil it by being caught philandering in the pantry. And yet – financially – it wasn't a pity after all. As it turned out, Johnny did pretty well. At least he did until last night.'

'Yes,' I nodded, 'getting his hotel bills at the Alexandra paid, running a Bugatti ...'

'Obviously there's even more in blackmail than in being the lover of a rich man's wife,' Dagobert agreed thoughtfully. 'The only thing is ... well, something Kitson himself volunteered tonight while you and Sebastian and Paulette were making Welsh rabbits. But you're already in bed!'

'I can listen lying down.'

'I'll keep it back until you're dropping off to sleep,' he promised. 'Meanwhile, to go back in our narrative six or seven years – and I mean to the moment when Sheila went for Johnny in the pantry. Kitson, too, witnessed this scene, and not being completely a fool, realized its implications. When Sebastian left, Kitson was having a few disillusioned words with his newly married bride. No one heard those words except Johnny, who was present, and they were not mentioned at the inquest. Other guests said, however, that Sheila seemed alternately moody and drunkenly hysterical from then on. That was why they thought she probably committed suicide. She fell from the window a moment after the last guest had departed. The last guest to depart was Corcoran. Corcoran *said* at the inquest that Kitson had at this instant been in the hall saying good night to him. In other words – *if* what Corcoran said was true – Kitson had not been near Sheila when she fell, and she fell either accidentally as the Coroner found (having leaned out of the window, it was presumed, for a breath of air or to wave good-bye to her guests), or else she jumped, as the other guests at the party suspected, but at the inquest did not say.'

'In other words, Kitson's alibi depended entirely upon Johnny Corcoran's word.'

'Yes. And Corcoran has been blackmailing Kitson ever since. You know Kitson. Would he have allowed himself to be blackmailed unless he had in fact killed his wife?'

I tried to think of another answer, but there wasn't one. It was as obvious that Kitson had pushed Sheila as it was impossible to prove. The only person who could prove it had been found dead in the gorge below the Col d'Aze.

'I suppose,' I said, 'we'll discover that the fingerprints on the revolver are Kitson's.'

'We might . . . they ought to be.' He got into bed beside me and turned out the light. We pretended to relax. He let out his breath cautiously, as though fearing to disturb me. I said: 'Yes?'

'Why do I feel so certain Kitson did not kill Corcoran?' he complained. 'I wish I'd get these hunches in the morning, instead of just when I'm trying to go to sleep.'

'You said a moment ago that Kitson had volunteered something tonight which puzzled you.'

'It may have been intended to puzzle me – I don't know. It certainly sends the mind reeling off in other directions. Incidentally, Jane, if we – I mean you – ever write this business up, could you depict me as being rather less at sea: you know, one of those keen, one-track types who keep strictly to the point, who shrug off the inessential with a quizzical smile and put their finger immediately upon the crux of the matter. How, I wonder, do you go about shrugging off the inessential before the thing's solved? Is what Kitson told me tonight inessential? Or is it the nub of the business?'

'My advice would be more valuable if I knew what he told you.'

'You could have me sum up the affair,' he went on, 'by saying something like, "It first became obvious to me that Geoffrey didn't do it when I found that the fingerprints on the revolver were his." Or, "The single blunder Vicki made was stealing our tandem." Or even, "What completely gave the show away was the lack of nicotine stain on Fred Evans's fingers. The rest was merely a matter of verifying who Tyler Sherman really *was*."'

'What did Kitson tell you?'

'Oh,' he came down to earth. 'Kitson said, apropos of nothing, that he'd "lent" Corcoran "*small* sums" on three or four occasions in the past, but that they probably totalled less than five hundred pounds altogether. I said, "Really, how interesting." He looked at me blearily and began muttering something about not giving a damn how the swine got killed, so long as he did get killed – but that he, Kitson, though something of a swine himself, was not a damn traitor, and if by any chance I was working for "those people" he didn't want to be obstructive. He repeated seriously that he did not know who was driving the Bugatti just after midnight; but it was *not* Corcoran. Maybe it was one of "those people".'

'It just needed "those people",' I said. '*What* people?'

'The same question flitted through my mind,' Dagobert said. 'I said, "yes *and* no" rather quickly. He said "quite" and we changed the subject. We were both being terribly subtle; we'd finished the brandy and were going back to the red wine again and the finer shades of meaning doubtless escaped us both. We exchanged two or three significant glances and he added: "Not that I'm telling you anything, dear boy, but one doesn't run a Bugatti and God knows how many women on a Squadron Leader's pay, plus the five hundred he's had out of me." I said "quite", and he said "quite", and then you and Paulette came in."

'The implication is that Corcoran had a third source of income,' I said.

'You see what I mean about the mind reeling.'

I suggested doubtfully: 'Women? Perdita and I wondered if Naomi could have contributed. You might as well turn on the light. We can go to sleep after four o'clock strikes.'

'Still,' Dagobert said, more cheerful now that we had given up trying to go to sleep, 'all of this takes our mind off the sordid domestic angle, jealousy and sex. In fact I like it, unless Kitson was merely trying to drag a red herring across the track which leads straight to him. Who had Corcoran come to meet in Puig d'Aze? The obvious answer is Kitson, whom he sometimes touched for sums of money. But Kitson intimated that these were small sums, scarcely worth the journey. So what is the real answer?'

'That Corcoran came to meet someone else, from whom he could obtain a worthwhile sum of money?'

'Yes. Now what else had Corcoran to sell which was worth money, besides his knowledge or suspicion that Kitson pushed Sheila out of the window?'

'Yes,' I said, going pale at the thought. 'It would be silly to have a drink at this hour, wouldn't it?'

'I don't know how much a test pilot actually knows about the mechanical aspects of the plane he flies, but the Emerald Mark IV jet engine which Corcoran recently tried out is obviously high on the War Office's Secret List.'

He stopped pacing the room and sat down on the bed again. He ran his fingers through his hair and scowled. He murmured:

'I hope Corcoran was murdered *before* he saw the enemy agent he'd come to meet . . .'

Chapter 19

I WENT downstairs for breakfast next morning. It was nearly ten, and the maid wanted to do the room. Dagobert, I learned, had gone off two hours earlier, having ordered sandwiches for today's picnic, an ordeal I was still not strong enough to think about.

There was a small enclosed garden at the back of the Hôtel des Voyageurs, shady and cool, with iron tables covered with bright checked cloths. I asked for my coffee to be served there. It came while I was admiring the pink and blue convolvulus which the maid called *belles-de-jour* and Tyler Sherman, still more appropriately, called Morning Glory. With coffee came *brioches*, fresh butter and honey, and I decided to write at once to the Cycling Club and congratulate them on their recommendation of hotels. While I was wondering how to phrase this in French, Tyler Sherman drifted out into the garden. He asked if he might join me.

He and Perdita, it seemed, had been trying out our new tandem, while Dagobert had borrowed the small Renault which Tyler had hired for his summer holidays. Perdita was now upstairs changing for the picnic. We were supposed to start about eleven, which would allow us to have luncheon in Andorra. I raised an eyebrow at this.

'Does Naomi know it's to be Andorra?' I inquired.

'Not yet. Last night Mrs Gordon-Smith suggested Font Romeu, but we all think Andorra would be more fun.'

'Will you,' I said, 'take a small bet that we go to Font Romeu?'

Tyler sprawled out in the wicker chair opposite me and smiled. His smile was good-humoured, but his chin was stubborn. 'Any size bet you like,' he drawled. 'Five hundred francs?'

I agreed and poured out the remainder of my coffee. He watched this with distaste.

'Can you drink this French coffee? I've at last broken them into giving me milk – in a glass, and not boiled. It nearly broke their hearts.'

I asked him how he liked the concert. He said he like it fine and added sheepishly: 'Especially before it began and after it finished.'

'Yes, I noticed you came with Vicki and left with Perdita. I warned you against that sort of thing the other evening.'

He sighed heavily. 'I wonder if you were right.'

'In troubled waters already?'

'Not exactly. That is,' he frowned, 'am I acting like a drip to talk like this?'

'Probably. I don't know what a drip is, but go on. No one's listening.'

'Neither of them has ever mentioned the other, if you mean that kind of trouble. No subtle cracks or anything – except maybe at me. Only . . .' The scowl deepened. 'Only, well, it's *me* I'm worried about, Jane.'

'You seem to be bearing up reasonably well.'

He shook his head. He looked so worried I almost felt sorry for him. 'No,' he muttered, 'I'm not bearing up at all well. Gosh darn it all, I've fallen in love with *both* of them!'

I laughed outright. He continued to look so miserable that I ended up by feeling exasperated.

'You don't know what being in love is!'

'Okay. You tell me what it is!'

'Well,' I began, 'it's . . . this is ridiculous. Ask them to bring me some more coffee and two aspirins.'

'Is it feeling very tender and kind of protective towards someone?'

'Yes, among other things.'

'Then I feel that way about Vicki and Perdita both. . . . Is it also wanting to grab them in your arms and kiss the hell out of them?'

'Have you been doing much of that sort of thing?'

'No, but I'd like to. To both of them.'

'There's probably a medical term for that.'

'Yeah, satyriasis,' he grinned. 'You needn't worry. It's not as bad as that. I guess it will all work out. Maybe, in fairness to everyone concerned, I ought to explain that neither of them is exactly crazy about me.'

'That will doubtless come in time. Did you say you were going to fetch me some more coffee?'

He returned with the coffee-pot, looking ashamed of himself, as well he might. He talked for a while about things which were profoundly indifferent to us both. Since he was very young and very tall and very good-looking, I relented.

'Go ahead and talk about your sex-life, if you want to.'

The word embarrassed him and he blushed. 'I ought to change for the picnic, I guess. . . . Maybe I'll go like this. Was Perdita pretty far gone on that guy Corcoran?'

I hedged. 'Has she said so?'

'Never mentioned him. Only the other night at the Alexandra I kind of got the impression . . .'

'I doubt it,' I lied. 'He was a friend and naturally his death has been a blow. He was years too old for her.'

'I thought so, too,' he said eagerly. 'And, to tell the truth, I hated his guts on sight. He was too damn English to be true, if you know what I mean.'

'He was Irish, presumably.'

'Why do you say . . . presumably?'

'Because of his name,' I explained, puzzled by the way he'd asked the question.

'You know him better than I,' he continued thoughtfully. 'Could he, do you think, have been . . . No, skip it! It doesn't make sense. He's been well known in the R.A.F. for years.'

'What were you going to ask?'

'If he could have been putting on an act? You know, pretending to be frightfully British, doncherknow? Not that it's any business of mine. I don't know why I brought up the subject. Anyway, he's dead, and I'm darned if I'm going to pretend my heart's broken.'

'Since we're asking each other all these penetrating questions,' I said, 'where, actually, were you the night Corcoran died?'

To my surprise he smiled broadly. 'Everyone keeps asking me that,' he said. 'I'm getting my answer pat. I was sound asleep upstairs from ten o'clock onwards. Alibi and everything.'

'Who is "everybody" that keeps asking you that?'

'Well,' he confessed, 'well, I guess I mean Perdita and Vicki. Perdita . . . well, maybe it's natural in a way. I mean with her going up to, you know, his room and perhaps not realizing that everybody in Puig already knows it, anyway . . . but wondering if I . . . I'm getting awfully bawled up,' he broke off in confusion.

'Keep trying,' I said.

'Okay,' he exclaimed, getting angry. 'She goes up to this guy's room. Being an ordinary decent young woman, she hopes I don't know about it. The point is, I don't give a damn. Of course, I'd enjoy breaking the guy's goddam neck for him if he hadn't obliged by doing it himself. But I don't for a moment believe that anything took place in that room that Perdita ... oh, hell! – that Perdita wouldn't want her mother to know about! Only I can't tell her so without sounding like a sanctimonious heel.'

'She spent most of that evening,' I said soothingly, 'in our room with us.'

'I don't care where she spent it,' he insisted. 'She's free, white and – no, I guess she's not twenty-one. Gosh!' he added naïvely, 'she looked cute on the tandem this morning!'

I changed the subject firmly. 'Why do you suppose Vicki was so anxious to know where you were on Friday night?'

'Huh? What's that?' He came out of his brood about Perdita. 'Vicki?'

'You know – the other fair charmer.'

His sheepish grin gave way to a look of solicitude. 'Poor Vicki,' he murmured. 'I – I wish I could explain. She's so different from Perdita, kind of shy and scared like a kid who's been knocked around a lot by life. Sorry to talk in clichés, but I don't know any other way to put it. The funny thing is that Perdita, who looks like a child that's led a sheltered life, is twice as grown-up and self-assured and able to look after herself. Vicki, who looks like a sophisticated Hollywood star, is a babe in arms by comparison. She bites her nails and fidgets, doesn't know whether you're serious or kidding her. Half the time she's scared as hell of me; doesn't know whether I'm a wolf or ... or what. Maybe *we* wouldn't be such smart alecks if we'd been brought up in a concentration camp.'

I nodded. 'You found that out?'

'Yeah ...'

He had picked a dandelion which grew between the garden paving-stones and was tearing off its petals one by one. I wondered if he were playing 'she loves me, she loves me not', and if so, whether 'she' was Perdita or Vicki. He gave up halfway through.

'She's got an older sister who's still in Poland,' he said.

'Works in Warsaw for a Government official. Anna Stein.'

'Yes, Mitzi told me. And a brother named Rudolph, who may or may not be alive.'

'That's right.' He sighed deeply and put the stem of the dandelion between his teeth. 'The funny thing is – no, funny's hardly the word! – but as it happens a buddy of mine knows something about this Anna Stein which . . . Sorry if I keep breaking off in the middle of sentences. I shouldn't shoot my mouth off so much, I guess.'

'You were talking about this mysterious friend of yours.'

'Yes, he's from Dallas, like me, and has a job in Germany in one of the semi-civilian branches of the army. He's been in Warsaw recently. We had some drinks together last week in Paris, and Anna Stein's name cropped up. Would you believe it?' he exclaimed, struck by the monstrosity of the coincidence.

'No,' I said, 'not for a moment. What about Anna Stein?'

He bit the dandelion stem in two. 'There was a purge in the department where she worked. They shot Anna as she was trying to get away.'

'I see.'

He rose and kicked a pebble smartly across the garden. I noticed that he was wearing suède monk's shoes, not unlike Fred Evans's. 'If I had any sense,' he said savagely, 'I'd high-tail it out of this dump today! I've persuaded Vicki to have dinner with me tonight. What a little ray of sunshine I'm going to be as I hold her hand and announce that her sister's just been bumped off by those so-and-so's!'

He sat down again and added: 'Not that she'll believe me, even if I have the guts to tell her. She'd think it was a trap. She doesn't trust anyone. She's practically convinced I'm one of them myself! She calls me a spy!'

My stomach moved queasily at the word. It had been haunting me ever since last night. Corcoran, we half believed, had come to Puig to meet a secret agent. My smile felt tight around my cheekbones, like a mask which didn't quite fit. I said lightly:

'And are you?'

Tyler's mind was elsewhere. 'Am I what?'

'Secret Service.'

He grinned suddenly and scrambled to his feet. 'Oh, yes,' he murmured. 'Sure . . . *Hi*, there!'

The disarming grin was not, I realized, intended for me. I glanced over my shoulder to see Perdita, freshly changed and more attractive than ever. Early-morning tandem rides clearly agreed with her. She kissed me affectionately and looked disappointed when I said I must rush upstairs to get things.

Tyler's reluctance to see me go was less marked. The problem of Vicki was, I felt, temporarily shelved.

Chapter 20

NOT really having anything to rush upstairs to get, I wandered out into the street, trying to recapture those first fine careworn raptures of budding love. For I – like Tyler – had once been torn between an earnest young man with horn-rimmed spectacles who worked in the Ministry of Information and took me to the ballet and Lyon's Corner House afterwards, and a Commando captain who had a booming laugh and used to trample on my feet at the Coconut Grove. I was desperately in love, shortly before the time I was side-tracked by Dagobert, with them both.

So it could be done. I sighed sentimentally, and felt very grateful that such stresses and strains were now comfortably remote.

Then I saw Tyler's Renault parked a few hundred feet down the street outside the Hôtel Commerce. Dagobert had warned me that he might have to go into a huddle or two with Vicki. Remembering Vicki's technique – corny, but efficient – I decided to chaperone the *tête-à-tête.*

Through the window I caught a glimpse of Dagobert in the far corner of the Commerce Café, *tête-à-tête* to be sure, but not with Vicki. He was deep in a game of chess with Mitzi. Both were too absorbed to notice my approach. Dagobert looked worried. He touched a knight nervously and Mitzi gave him a look of low cunning. He withdrew his hand hastily and murmured:

'Yes, I see. If I do that you take my rook.'.

'Don't be silly,' Mitzi said. 'I advance my queen's bishop's pawn and it's mate in three.'

'Oh, is it? So it is. Er – in that case . . .'

'You might as well castle,' Mitzi advised, 'at least it'll make the game last longer. Anyway, here's your wife.'

Dagobert looked glad to see me. 'We'll finish it off some other time,' he said, relieved.

'Don't let me interrupt.'

'We've had two or three games already.'

'I won them all,' Mitzi said.

Dagobert smiled at me. 'Just working my way into the innocent child's confidence,' he explained.

Mitzi corrected him. 'He's trying to pump me about Vicki and Tyler Sherman. Tyler is a spy – we think.' She added: 'They've got the best liquorice cupies you ever tasted, locked in that case over behind the counter!'

'Why didn't you explain that before?' Dagobert asked, getting in touch at once with the landlady who kept the key.

He returned with a large paper bag of assorted liquorice objects, chewed one and smacked his lips. 'You're right,' he said, slipping the bag absentmindedly into his pocket.

Mitzi said: 'Spies are *always* hanging around us, even in London.'

'What for?'

She tore her gaze away from his pocket long enough to articulate: 'I dunno.'

'You don't know,' Dagobert repeated thoughtfully. He produced a second liquorice and offered it to me. I shook my head.

'Yes, I do,' Mitzi corrected herself quickly. 'It's because we're mysterious foreigners – like in Rip Kirby.' She extended a small capable hand and added in a strange whisper: '*We've got the secret papers.*'

Dagobert popped the sweet into his mouth. Mitzi watched him sadly.

'Honestly, I dunno . . .' she confessed.

This was so patently true that Dagobert nearly relented. Instead he hardened his heart and restudied the situation on the chess-board. 'My move, isn't it?'

Mitzi wound the tip of her pigtail around her forefinger and put it in her mouth. 'Tyler had a pitcher of Vicki – the one where she was Beauty Queen, cut out of the *Daily Mirror*. He saw us get off the bus last Wednesday when we came, and he was studying the pitcher. So's he'd recognize her. That's why I warned her he was probably a spy. . . . I bet,' she smiled timidly, altering her technique, 'I bet those cupies are pretty good.'

'They really are,' Dagobert nodded. 'I'm glad you recommended them. And what did Vicki say to that?'

'Are you going to eat another one?'

Dagobert reached without eagerness into his pocket. 'Er – oh, yes.'

Mitzi watched him slowly put the neck of the tiny black cupie doll between his teeth; her mouth was drooling slightly. 'Vicki was sort of scared, especially when he trailed after us and said could he carry our suitcases? She said, "What do you take me for?" But he only sort of laughed and said, "What hotel were we staying at?" I told him. Vicki was furious. But he'd have found out, anyway.'

'You fixed up the hotel you were going to stay in before leaving London?'

'It's not,' Mitzi said with sudden dignity, 'very nice to cross-question a little girl like I.'

Dagobert nibbled off the liquorice head reluctantly. 'If I moved my bishop . . .' he began.

'Yes, we did,' Mitzi said. 'I don't know why, so don't ask me.'

'Perhaps you were to meet someone here,' he suggested.

'I don't know, I'm sure,' she said demurely. 'Grown-ups don't confide in children who are only ten. Maybe you don't want to finish that . . .'

Dagobert stopped nibbling and swallowed the thing. His hand returned with a conscious effort to his pocket. His face was beginning to look slightly green. Mitzi, misinterpreting the gesture, said eagerly:

'Do you know what I think? I think Tyler came here to spy on Vicki and then fell in love with her instead. You know, like the films. He's torn between his duty and his love. He's got a gun, too. Yanks always carry guns. How many cupies have you got left now?'

'Lots,' Dagobert winced, forcing the legs of a fourth between his lips. 'You're making up the bit about the gun.'

'Yes,' she said, 'but not about them becoming beloved enemies. Vicki was crying last night when she came home after the recital, on account that her heart was so torn with conflicting emotions.'

'Were you anywhere around when Vicki first met Squadron Leader Corcoran?' Dagobert asked.

'No,' she said shortly.

Dagobert didn't press the point. It would not have done any good if he had. Mitzi knew, of course, about her sister's midnight encounter with Corcoran, even though she had not witnessed it. I remembered her disgust as she spoke of it yesterday in Ann's Pantry. Dagobert toyed with the chessmen and mechanically removed the paper bag from his pocket; for a moment even Mitzi's interest was unaroused. He rustled the bag feebly; then with a shudder handed it to Mitzi.

'This,' he said, 'is doubtless a tactical error.'

Mitzi's thoughtfulness had vanished like magic. She plunged an avid hand into the bag. She hesitated and then with a supreme effort offered the bag politely to me.

'If there's anything else you want to know,' she said, 'go right ahead. I can get you Vicki's fingerprints if you want.'

Even Dagobert looked a little ashamed of himself.

'No thanks,' he grinned. 'Shall we finish off this game very quickly?'

'Righto.'

For about half a second she studied the board, then Dagobert.

'Oh, no, you don't!' she sneered. 'You've moved twice while we were talking!'

By a nice bit of timing Dagobert was saved from utter humiliation by the sudden toot of the Humber Snipe outside the window.

'Naomi's picnic!' I cried, leaping as though I were still in the lower third and late for hockey practice.

Dagobert, resigning the game to Mitzi, hastily joined me in the door. The liquorice had stained his lips a cadaverous black.

'I think,' he said, swallowing hard, 'I am going to be sick.'

Chapter 21

NAOMI had the seating in the cars already arranged – me beside Geoffrey, she and Dagobert in the back, the two 'young folk' in the Renault – so I had little opportunity to tell Dagobert how accurate Mitzi's guess about Vicki and Tyler probably was. It seemed clear, at least, that Tyler had come to Puig d'Aze to meet Vicki, even if Vicki had come to meet someone else. (Corcoran?) It was also clear that Tyler had fallen for her – at any rate before Perdita came. It was reasonable to assume that Tyler had been sent to meet Vicki – and given her photograph – by his mysterious 'semi-civilian' friend who had recently been in Poland and knew of Anna Stein's death.

But that Tyler had been sent to Puig merely to bear these sad tidings seemed a little extravagant. Had that only been part of Tyler's job? I remembered our first encounter with him – in the shed where our tandem and Corcoran's Bugatti were kept. Tyler *said* he'd been exploring, wondering what the ladder led to. It led, he had agreed, to the box-room next to Vicki's room. The box-room was also just opposite Room 2, where Corcoran had last been seen alive.

But as I saw the Renault drive off with Tyler at the wheel I could not even begin to convince myself that we were perhaps entrusting Perdita to a killer. Any more than I could imagine that I might be sitting next to a murderer myself. Or that Dagobert's companion in the back seat could have shot her lover . . .

Just before we started, an incident occurred which resulted in my losing five hundred francs. It had been decided that the smaller car should lead the way and Naomi was showing Tyler on the motoring map the best route to Font Romeu. Tyler said he thought we were going to Andorra. Perdita chimed in with: 'Oh, let's do!' She'd always longed to see Andorra. Even I (who had a financial interest in going to Font Romeu) said that if we didn't drive to Andorra Dagobert would make me cycle to the place.

'We've heard the road is so appalling,' Naomi objected.

'Geoffrey's not very keen on ripping our new tyres to pieces, are you, dear? If it rains we'll have to put on chains. Besides,' she added, 'how stupid of me to forget! I've already telephoned the hotel at Font Romeu to expect us!'

'I thought,' Tyler said, 'it was going to be a picnic.'

'I told them we'd come in for coffee afterwards.'

'I'll telephone them again,' Dagobert said helpfully, 'if you can remember the name of the hotel.'

If Naomi scented rebellion in the air she showed no sign of it. Her smile remained frank and charming. 'I know!' she exclaimed, as though she had just thought of a nice surprise for us all; 'we'll arrange Andorra for tomorrow! Shall we?'

I was just planning how to spend Tyler's five hundred francs when a blow was struck from an unexpected quarter. Geoffrey said, very quietly:

'We'll go to Andorra today, Naomi. Everyone obviously wants to, so that's what we'll do.'

To my utter astonishment, Naomi gave way without a murmur.

'Of course, if everyone wants to go to Andorra,' she said submissively, 'that's quite different. Personally, I don't care one way or the other. I only thought . . .'

'Carry on, Sherman,' Geoffrey said. 'We'll follow.'

This brief contest of will-powers left no tension in the atmosphere that I was aware of. Naomi took defeat as graciously as she normally accepted victory. Perhaps it was because Geoffrey so rarely expressed a definite opinion that she deferred to it when he did. Perhaps, even, a subtle change had taken place in her attitude towards her husband since the death of Johnny Corcoran. Several times that Sunday I thought I noticed, not exactly a new sympathy, but a new respect in Naomi's treatment of Geoffrey. She contradicted him less flatly than usual. She looked less noticeably bored when he talked, and once or twice even brought him into the conversation. All of this was so vague that I may have imagined it.

She was completely mistress of herself by the time Geoffrey had backed the car around to follow the Renault.

'I was against Andorra,' she confided with a frankness which nearly deceived me, 'because of Perdita. The road passes that awful Col – doesn't it, Geoffrey? – where the accident took place. But perhaps Perdita won't realize.'

In the Humber it took us such a surprisingly short time to reach the cross-roads on the Col d'Aze that we'd passed the fatal spot almost before I knew it. A glimpse of the parapet, already repaired, and a dizzy vision of the gorge and the larches below where the Bugatti had crashed. That was all. The burnt-out wreckage was still there, but I didn't see it. We did not stop to admire the view.

Geoffrey took the left-hand fork which zigzagged up the side of the Pic des Quatre Vents, keeping just far enough behind the Renault to avoid its dust. Naomi, as usual, had been right about the road surface – it was shocking. But then, I recalled with an effort, Naomi was the only one of us who had been over it before. I say I recalled this with an effort, because it was she who kept exclaiming at the savage grandeur of the scene, saying that she had never seen anything quite like it, and gradually working herself up into imagining that it was she who had insisted on today's Andorran excursion. She, too, it seemed, had 'always longed to go to Andorra'.

Well before noon we had reached the frontier. Formalities were casual. The French officials glanced at passports and car papers, but stamped nothing. If they recognized Naomi from three days before they gave no indication of it. I thought she drew a breath of relief when they courteously waved us on. The Andorran officials didn't even stop us.

We found a picnic spot about an hour later and waited until Tyler, who had been giving a driving lesson to Perdita, caught up with us. It was a green valley thick with wild narcissus, a few miles before the village of Andorre-la-Vieille, the capital of the republic. (It isn't really quite a republic, but since 1278 a fief owing feudal allegiance to two co-princes who are the Spanish Bishop of Urgel and the French Assemblée Nationale. It is very complicated and doubtless fascinating, but details of 'viguiers and bayles' as Dagobert explained them to us during the picnic fortunately slip my – and his – memory.)

We lay stretched out on the grass after luncheon and listened to the mountain stream. It was the only hurried note in the landscape. Overhead, an invisible skylark was singing its heart out and cattle grazed lazily on the high slopes which stretched up to the dark lines of mountains, still patched with snow. In late June the narrow strip of upland valley was enjoying its brief, fragile spring. To us, too, perhaps to all six of us, it was a brief, fragile moment of deep, living peace; for no one showed any inclination to push on.

Geoffrey, after regretting that he hadn't brought along his fishing kit, had closed his eyes and dropped off to sleep. Perdita had tried wading in the icy brook and had finally wandered off with Tyler to pick gentians. Naomi chatted desultorily about her two children, aged five and six, who were staying with Geoffrey's parents in Kent. She called them the brats and was careful to explain that they were ill-behaved savages, trying to disguise from us – and herself – the fact that she was missing them. It was the first time she had mentioned her children, and I found her more likeable as she spoke of them.

During that too-brief half-hour which followed our picnic we were far from Johnny Corcoran and the grim images which his name evoked.

And yet the very word Andorra must have brought him near to most of us. Dagobert had engineered today's outing largely because of Corcoran. Naomi had first visited these scenes with him. And Perdita had romantically planned 'to discover' Andorra with Johnny.

Personally, I felt sure she had lost nothing in waiting to discover it with Tyler instead, and as far as I could make out Perdita would probably have agreed with me. Naomi may have been thinking – with reference to herself rather than to Perdita – along parallel lines, for she suddenly breathed, apropos of nothing:

'This is the way it *ought* to be . . .'

I opened an eye and glanced at her. She was watching Geoffrey, curled up asleep on his mackintosh in the shade of a clump of vivid yellow broom by the side of the stream. She became aware of my glance and flushed.

'I mean it's pleasant, isn't it?' she said. 'Peaceful, uncomplicated. We ought to take out picnics every day. Must we drive on into that wretched village?'

'Is it wretched?' Dagobert inquired.

'Probably. Most of the local villages are.'

Dagobert said: 'I'm being awfully unfair, Naomi. Jane and I saw you driving the Bugatti on Friday afternoon.'

'Oh!'

It was a small, quickly stifled gasp. Naomi's half-hour of peace had come to an end. I noticed that her first reaction was to glance again towards Geoffrey. He was sound asleep, and even if he had not been he was out of earshot. The colour came gradually back into her face. She smiled brightly. 'And does that matter? Everyone knows that I came in the Bugatti.'

'But not from Andorra.'

'Er – we – we lost the way. It didn't seem worthwhile going into countless explanations.'

'I'm afraid I'm going to ask you to do so now,' Dagobert smiled.

'I'd really rather not, if you don't mind,' she said pleasantly, but firmly.

Dagobert didn't insist. He rose, stretched himself and wandered a hundred yards downstream. Naomi watched him, looked at Geoffrey, and turned to me. She began to say something, but instead rose and followed Dagobert. I went with her. Geoffrey slept peacefully on. She said:

'Not that it really matters, but have you told anyone else? Geoffrey?'

'No, of course not.'

She tried not to show her relief. 'Please don't,' she begged. 'I mean, not having mentioned it before, it would seem so odd if . . . well, you know.'

'Jane, unfortunately, mentioned it to Perdita. That was before Corcoran died, and we thought the woman in the car with him was Perdita. You were wearing her scarf.'

'Yes. . . . Oh dear,' she smiled faintly, 'what a twisted web we weave when first we something or other to deceive. . . . Not that I meant to deceive anyone! Could you ask Perdita, *please*, not to breathe a word about it?'

'I already have,' Dagobert said.

'Oh, good. Then we needn't think any more about it, need we?'

'Where did you have luncheon that day?'

'In a café in the village. I don't remember the name of it. Of what possible interest could it be?'

'I thought we might have coffee there.'

She laughed. 'I do remember that we had the worst coffee I've ever tasted. Following a greasy and thoroughly unsatisfactory luncheon.'

'The Guide Michelin speaks nicely of several restaurants in Andorre-la-Vieille.'

'Not of the one *we* went to! Johnny thought it looked "picturesque". Frankly, it wasn't even that. Poor boy, I suppose the truth is he thought it looked cheap.'

'Like the Hôtel Commerce in Puig d'Aze,' Dagobert nodded.

'Yes. He was nearly broke, I gather. The trip had been more expensive than he'd reckoned for, but he told me he was expecting money shortly.'

'He didn't say where from?'

'No. I imagine he'd sent to England for it. I, incidentally, lent him five pounds that day to tide him over until it came.'

'He didn't pay it back by any chance?'

She shook her head with annoyance. 'No, he borrowed it that evening in order to take Perdita to the Casino at Aze-les-Bains.'

This, unaccountably, seemed to please Dagobert. Upon reflection, I understood why. It suggested at least that Corcoran had not been paid for any information that afternoon in Andorra, and narrowed down his opportunity for having sold information to the hour between eleven o'clock when Perdita had left him and midnight when we were convinced he had been shot. For he must have been shot at midnight while the bells of St Justin were ringing. Otherwise someone would have heard the revolver.

That he had been shot after midnight seemed equally unlikely: Kitson had told us that the unidentified person driving away in the Bugatti at a quarter past twelve was *not* Corcoran. Corcoran's body, as Kitson himself had pointed out, was undoubtedly concealed beneath the canvas cover stretched over the back seat. All of this, of course, on the assumption that the fingerprints on the revolver were not Kitson's own! (Parenthetically, they were not. Though Dagobert had not yet had a chance to tell me, he had early this morning revisited Dr Perrault in Aze-les-Bains with Kitson's fingerprints and drawn a blank.)

Why, then, had Corcoran come to Andorra? Obviously not for the cuisine. Nor had he driven so far out of his way only to spend a pleasant hour or two in a picturesque inn alone with Naomi. Her irritation at the thought of Friday's luncheon betrayed that. It had left her with such a vivid and disagreeable memory that she told us all about it before she realized that

Dagobert's interest in the subject was, to say the least, rather peculiar.

'It was cold and dingy and not very clean,' she said. 'We were both in a filthy temper. We ate in about ten minutes and left. Of course, we knew we were going to arrive in Puig hours late.'

'Who did Corcoran talk to while you were there?'

'No one,' Naomi said bitterly. 'Including me.'

'No asides . . . to the waiter, or the manager?'

'No. I did what talking was done. Johnny didn't speak French.'

'Didn't he leave the table during luncheon? To wash his hands or anything?'

She shook her head. 'No, it wasn't that sort of place.'

'Where did you leave the car?'

'I don't remember. In a kind of courtyard, I think. Why on earth do you ask?'

'Background,' Dagobert said.

She bit her lip, smiled and looked at him with her large violet eyes. 'Background . . . to what?'

'To why Corcoran died.'

She continued for a moment to stare at him without expression. Then she lowered her eyes and half turned away. 'Does it matter?'

This point seemed new to Dagobert. He considered it and said cheerfully:

'No, probably it doesn't.'

'The only thing is,' I tried to explain, 'I write books and he has to keep probing into people's private lives to supply me with copy. Most people love it.'

'Yes, of course. How stupid of me!' she smiled quickly, having only the sketchiest notion of what I was talking about. 'Geoffrey's come to again, I see. Yes, your book. I must read it. Geoffrey was telling me all about it, about how, how . . .'

Her voice trailed off as she watched her husband stride towards us. She gave us such a look of mute supplication that I did not pursue the subject, nor remind her that she had already written me Geoffrey's impressions. Geoffrey had 'spotted my villain' at once, which still rankled.

As he approached us I wondered apprehensively if he had done so this time. . . .

Chapter 22

We fell into the clutches of a professional guide and wasted much more time in Andorre-la-Vieille than we had meant to. Naomi did her best to hustle us, but that day Naomi's skill in organization was continually frustrated. Geoffrey took an intelligent and tireless interest in everything, while Tyler took photographs left and right, mainly of Perdita standing on the steps of the ancient church, of Perdita leaning against the old bridge, of Perdita in front of the medieval dungeon.

The latter still contained a solitary prisoner – a man who had killed his wife's lover. The guide was very proud of him; he was his second cousin. Tyler said he'd have done the same thing, while Geoffrey said no, he personally would have killed the wife. The wife, we learned, was also the guide's second cousin.

During this slightly embarrassing discussion Dagobert escaped. We found him half an hour later in a shoddy café which – from Naomi's manner – I guessed to be the one where she and Johnny had had luncheon on Friday. He was buying Carmela cigarettes and trying in vain to engage the sullen *patron* in conversation. He rejoined us in haste. He had, he told me, learned nothing except that Johnny and Naomi had lunched there on Friday and left immediately afterwards. The *patron* had never seen Johnny before. He had become distinctly unfriendly when Dagobert asked him if the café counted many foreign agents among its clientele. He had heard about the English sense of humour, and didn't think much of it.

We all bought dozens of postcards and franked them with Andorran postage stamps, bringing most of them back into France with us, where, of course, the stamps are not valid. I still have one of the gaol, a fitting souvenir of that Sunday.

It was nearly five before we started home again. For the last hour Naomi had been drawing attention to the storm clouds which were piling up in the mountains behind us. Thunder was rumbling ominously when we got into the cars, and the storm broke before we'd gone half a mile. The narrow, dirt-surfaced road which led up to the pass on the border became a muddy torrent. The Renault stopped in the downpour, and the men got soaked putting on chains. Tyler and Perdita suggested that we might go back and stay the night in Andorra. Geoffrey, surprisingly, said, 'Yes, why not?' Naomi pointed out that we had no night clothes and that we'd be charged for our rooms in Puig whether we returned or not. Dagobert, too, wanted to go home.

'After all,' he argued, 'we've nothing to lose but our chains.'

Tyler and Perdita, comforted by the thought that we might get stuck in the mud and have to spend the night in a desolate mountain pass, proceeded. We splashed along behind them. Dagobert and Geoffrey, driving alternately, sat in the front seat while Naomi beside me in the back was unusually silent. It was Geoffrey who kept up the family's side of the small talk. Naomi contented herself with occasionally agreeing with him. Once she came out of her reverie to talk animatedly for a moment about the children's excitement on receiving the Andorran postage stamps she had sent them for their collections.

The mountain rain had lowered the temperature sharply. Luckily we had, on Naomi's insistence, brought coats, though she herself looked pinched with cold and shivered beneath her travelling rug.

Our meadow, where we had stretched out in the sunshine after the picnic, was now a sodden mass, the narcissus beaten down, the stream brown and swollen. Naomi pointed out the spot to me. I nodded.

'There's probably something symbolic about it,' I said, making conversation. 'The brevity of human . . .'

I stopped as she turned her head away. It was nearly dark, but I had the uncomfortable impression she was crying.

We reached the border a little after seven with nothing worse than a frightening skid or two – while, I regret to say, Dagobert was at the wheel. Again formalities were so nearly nonexistent that Naomi was sorry Geoffrey had brought only the single permitted bottle of untaxed brandy over the frontier.

'With a British number-plate they naturally assume you're honest,' she said regretfully.

Dagobert, who is always reliable in such lore, knew of a celebrated hostelry in the neighbourhood where the chef was an old pupil of Escoffier. His *Perdreau aux morilles* and *Fricandeau de mousserons* were famous, and Dagobert was interested in tasting such locally renowned wines as Clos Saint-Crescent and Château de Leverette. Though he was probably making up these names, he talked himself up to such a pitch of enthusiasm about them that he invited us all to dinner.

We were tired and hungry and on the map Dagobert's *relais gastronomique* looked much nearer than Puig d'Aze. It was – as the crow flies – and it took us only half an hour longer than it would have done to go home.

It was on the whole worth it, though it meant putting off certain plans I had entertained for my summer wardrobe. I tried not to look at the bill, and never afterwards hinted that we could have hired a car and stayed in a suite at the Alexandra for roughly the same sum.

Once or twice during dinner the thought struck me that such sumptuousness was an obscure result of Dagobert's guilty conscience, a kind of advance amends for possible suffering he might later have to inflict upon one or more of his guests. This was nonsense, of course, and merely indicates the state of my mind.

Not once during dinner did he steer the conversation in the direction of Squadron Leader Corcoran. He led Geoffrey on to discuss dry-fly fishing and the Stock Exchange, and encouraged Naomi to lay down the law about contemporary French literature.

We spent about two hours at table and decided that it was the pleasantest evening we'd had in years. Tyler, who had quite forgotten his engagement that evening with Vicki, said the 'chicken stew' (it was the *Perdreau aux morilles*) was the best thing he'd tasted since Dallas. Naomi, totally recovered from her temporary thoughtfulness of this afternoon, became with the *Meringue Chantilly* and Veuve Clicquot rather flirtatious and suggested that she and Dagobert drive back together in the Renault.

I alone was a damper on the party. My happy laughter did not mingle with the tinkle of the champagne glasses, and after dinner, when Dagobert drew me aside, my heart sank.

'There may be a little confusion about cars going home,' he murmured.

'And I'm not to worry.'

'No. I'll do that. I may be ten or fifteen minutes late – I want to get the recipe for that *Fricandeau de mousserons.*'

There was, as Dagobert had promised, a little confusion about cars going home, but it was less than half an hour's drive to Puig and Geoffrey invited everybody to the Alexandra for a night-cap. When we drove away Geoffrey was at the wheel of his Humber with Naomi safely beside him. Perdita and I were in the back seat. Dagobert and Tyler Sherman followed in the Renault.

The rain had stopped and the moon raced behind a jagged fringe of clouds. The night air was moist and fragrant. I felt physically exhausted and horribly wide awake. Geoffrey drove so fast that we lost the Renault long before we reached the Col d'Aze. Naomi told him to slow down. He said, rather brusquely: '*I'm* driving,' and Naomi said meekly: 'Yes, dear. I'm sorry,' which was practically all the conversation there was until we reached the Hôtel Alexandra.

It was after half past ten and Perdita and I, feeling that the festive spirit had evaporated, said we'd stroll back to our hotel. Geoffrey, whose post-prandial eagerness to continue the party had vanished, offered to drive us back. Naomi wouldn't hear of it.

'We're getting so stuffy,' she complained. 'It's only half past ten and this is supposed to be a holiday, Geoffrey. When the two men arrive I thought we might go and dance somewhere, the Casino at . . . well, there must be somewhere.'

'The Casino at Aze-les-Bains is excellent,' Perdita said without a moment's hesitation. 'Even Johnny commented on how good the band was.'

Naomi flashed her a look of gratitude and said: 'We shan't have to change, Geoffrey. Jane and Perdita can tidy up if they want to in my room. Let us know the moment the others arrive. The party,' she added recklessly, 'will, of course, be ours.'

She herded us into the lift, giving Geoffrey no time to argue. He returned without pleasure to the veranda to watch for Dagobert and Tyler. I didn't tell him he'd have ten or fifteen minutes to wait. Naomi chattered continuously, as though the champagne at dinner had had a delayed action. Even Perdita found her vitality a little overwhelming. I was exhausted after five minutes of it.

I don't know when the thought first crossed my mind that

there was something forced and unnatural about Naomi's relentless vivacity. I think it was when Geoffrey tapped on the door. At the sound of his voice Naomi went pale and said: 'You can't come in! We're dressing,' with much more emphasis than circumstances warranted.

Geoffrey had simply come up to report that Dagobert and Taylor still hadn't turned up.

'They've probably stopped on the way to have a drink,' Naomi said. 'Telephone us when they come.' And she slid the bolt of the door after his departing footsteps.

A bathroom connected Naomi's room with Geoffrey's, and the bathroom door leading into Geoffrey's room had, I noticed, already been bolted. Geoffrey's shaving kit and toothbrush, which on Friday were there on the shelf next to the bottle of Lanvin's Scandale and Dr Hervey's capsules, had been removed. The bathroom, then, was no longer shared, and if Naomi fell asleep again with her light on Geoffrey would not be able to come in and switch it off for her. I wondered if this were further evidence of the change in relationship between them I had noticed today.

'Did Geoffrey actually stroll around the village on Friday night?' I asked. 'Or was that only Fred Evans's idea?'

'Oh, yes, he did, as a matter of fact,' Naomi answered me in the same conversational tone. 'He couldn't sleep – I dare say the result of his nap at Kitson's! No, seriously, I'm afraid it was your fault, Perdita. You were supposed to come home by eleven, remember? And Geoffrey, who is old-fashioned in many ways, was worried when you didn't. I'm not *really* changing – just into this old afternoon dress – you don't mind, do you? You both look sweet as you are. Do help yourselves to Scandale. I'm wearing this new Caron stuff which costs the earth. Yes . . . so Geoffrey, the silly old dear, decided to wander around to the Commerce to look for you.'

'I was there,' Perdita pointed out.

'Yes, but he changed his mind – decided it was rather impertinent of him – and he came home again without going near the Commerce. I do think it's inconsiderate of Dagobert and Tyler to be so long! Still, the Casino stays open until . . . what time?'

'Four a.m., I'm afraid,' Perdita said ruefully.

'Oh, good!' Naomi exclaimed. 'We'll make a real night of it

and skip Kitson's concert tomorrow morning! I think your Tyler is rather sweet, Perdita.'

'He's not *my* Tyler!' Perdita protested, colouring. 'And I gather there's some rather keen competition.'

'The thing with the hennaed hair!' Naomi dismissed Vicki with contempt. 'Men don't marry that kind. And he is a gentleman,' she added disconnectedly, 'though it's so hard to tell with Americans. What fun it's been today. I wish you'd move to this hotel, Jane. Tomorrow, perhaps. The room across the hall is very nice and not having the view is half the price. Shall I wear this diamond clip, or does it look bitty?'

The bell of St Justin's struck eleven times. Perdita and I exchanged a glance in spite of ourselves. Naomi, misinterpreting, said quickly: 'It's not a bit too late, if that's why you're anxious. Casinos are never amusing before midnight.'

The telephone rang an instant afterwards and she said with relief: 'That will be them now. And high time, if I may say so.'

But it wasn't they. I answered the telephone. It was Geoffrey to say he was beginning to be slightly worried. I said I was sure there was nothing to worry about and immediately began to worry myself. Geoffrey said:

'Dagobert was driving, wasn't he? Not,' he added quickly, 'that he doesn't drive very well, but . . . or they could have had a flat tyre. I think I'll take the Humber and drive back over the road for a few miles just in case.'

'I'll come with you,' I said.

Naomi seized the telephone from my hand. 'Where?' she asked breathlessly. 'What's happened?'

I turned on her snappishly, thus betraying nerves that were nearly as frayed as her own. 'Nothing's happened! Geoffrey merely thinks they've had a flat tyre and we're going to look for them.'

'I'll come, too,' Perdita said.

Naomi looked at us so pathetically that I felt ashamed of myself. 'Why don't you come?'

She shook her head. 'Let Perdita go with Geoffrey. Jane – you stay. We'll wait for them here . . .' She smiled with bright reassurance. 'They won't be long.'

I nodded to Perdita. She unlocked the door and tactfully went. Naomi's bright smile remained fixed on her face like something she had put there and forgotten about. It was still there after I had mechanically rebolted the door, though it had begun to sag a little around the edges.

'It has been a good day, hasn't it?' she said in a curiously monotonous voice. 'That's why I don't want it to come to an end . . . not yet. It was so good of you, Jane, to stay with me. I didn't want to be alone – especially not tonight. Because, as a matter of fact, I may not be alive after tonight.'

Chapter 23

NAOMI'S voice, as she pronounced these outrageous words, was so flat and devoid of expression that I didn't take them in for a moment. I was still worrying about Dagobert. She said, and for the first time her lower lip began to quiver:

'*They'll* miss me.'

'Who?' I muttered absently.

'The brats. After I'm . . . gone.'

The quivering of her lower lip spread like an ague to her arms and shoulders. I seized her wrists roughly and shook her.

'Naomi! What *are* you talking about?'

She went limp when I released her and sank down on the chaise-longue. But she was on her feet again before I reached the telephone.

'I'm all right,' she said. 'Don't fuss. I get these giddy attacks occasionally. Dr Hervey says they're nothing to worry about. I'm supposed not to have emotional shocks! That's rather amusing, isn't it?'

'No,' I said, cutting short her attempt to laugh. 'I'm telephoning down to catch Geoffrey before he leaves.'

'No!'

I frowned. 'The doctor, then.'

'No,' she said, more calmly this time. 'Not the doctor, either. I'm afraid I've been a little hysterical. I'm quite all right again.'

I didn't point out that if she was, I wasn't. 'Why,' I asked bluntly, 'are you so frightened of Geoffrey?'

'Of Geoffrey?' she repeated, as though it was the first time she'd thought of him.

'Yes, of your husband.'

She looked at me steadily for a long moment before she lowered her eyes and whispered: 'But I'm not. . . . Why do you ask?'

'Naomi,' I said, 'you cannot make fantastic statements like . . . like the one you made a moment ago, and then simply change the subject. Emotional shocks are not good for me, either. Why did you say – what you said?'

'Don't you ever,' she murmured, 'get a kind of premonition . . . that you are going to die?'

'No.'

'How lucky! I do. Often.'

'I'm going now, Naomi,' I said coldly.

I got about half-way to the door when she stopped me. She said dramatically:

'Geoffrey knows . . .'

'Knows what?'

'Everything. . . . And so, I suppose,' she added dully, 'do you and Dagobert.'

I swallowed before replying, floundering mentally. I wasn't sure if by 'everything' we were thinking of the same thing. 'You mean,' I began, 'er, Friday . . .?'

I wanted to add 'night', but by this time I was as jittery as she was. I began half to wish I had made good my threat of leaving her.

'Yes, Friday afternoon in Andorra,' she said. 'And weeks, months before that, for that matter. I don't know how he does, but he does.'

I began to breathe again. 'In short, he suspects hanky-panky between you and Johnny Corcoran.'

'I was Johnny's mistress,' she announced.

The touch of the theatrical in her manner annoyed me. She had given me such a bad scare a moment ago that I was in no mood to sort out what was genuine in her suffering and what was self-dramatization. I said unsympathetically:

'I should imagine there is nothing especially unique in that position.'

'I gave *everything* to Johnny Corcoran,' she continued, ignoring my remark, 'my happiness, my peace of mind, my honour . . .'

'Was Corcoran the first skid you've ever had?'

The crudity of the question shook her momentarily from her perch. She said hastily:

'Well, there may have been one or two others . . . years ago. But they didn't count. I was a child, practically . . . and married to a kindly, indulgent older man whom I revered and respected . . . like a father. I may have, er, flirted and carried on occasionally like any scatter-brained girl who happens to be attractive to men. . . . But when Johnny came into my life two or three months ago it was *different*. I was a *woman*. A woman who suddenly realized just before it was too late that life was passing her by, that – oh! I know it sounds hackneyed, but it isn't – that this was her last opportunity. I shall soon be over thirty, you know.'

'Yes, I know,' I nodded briefly.

'Johnny gave me all this – the sense that I had not lived in vain. He is the only man I have ever loved. Except Geoffrey, of course. The others . . . they were less than nothing! Besides,' she added, 'Geoffrey didn't know about them.'

'What makes you think he knows about Johnny?' I asked, trying to get the conversation down to a more practical level. 'Has he said so?'

She shook her head. The slight chattering of her teeth at least was genuine. 'Have you noticed him today!' she whispered. 'How different he is? How much rougher, harder to argue with, determined to have his own way, not mine?'

I had and thought it a vast improvement, but said only: 'Men often enjoy pretending to be the head of the family.'

'And his saying at the dungeon in Andorra that he would have killed the guilty wife!'

'He was making conversation.'

'That's not the kind of conversation Geoffrey makes,' she shuddered. 'That's the dreadful part of it, Jane. The awful uncertainty. I'm not absolutely sure whether he knows or not.'

That, in a way, almost made sense. I remembered certain unfamiliar aspects of Naomi this afternoon – the wistful regret with which she had regarded her husband beside the mountain brook, the way she had spoken of their children, how she had fussed about Geoffrey's getting wet when he put on the chains. . . . I said suddenly:

'Why don't you tell him all about it?'

She clenched her teeth and shook her head again.

'You don't know Geoffrey.'

'I wonder if you do.'

'I've wondered that myself, once or twice . . . since Johnny's death. . . . Why, Jane, *why* did he go around to the Hôtel Commerce in the middle of the night? He's always asleep by eleven.'

'You said he went to see what had happened to Perdita.'

'I know I did. *He* told me that. But . . . but he looked at me in such a strange way when he said it. He *must* have known that *I* had arranged to meet Johnny in his room at half past twelve that night!'

'Oh, had you?' I gulped.

'Yes, naturally. It was a standing agreement. I came to his room every night at half past twelve. Sometimes it was a bit tricky.'

'And,' I said, fumbling in my handbag before I remembered that Dagobert had borrowed my cigarettes, 'and so you went round to the Commerce . . . as usual . . . that Friday night.'

She regarded me with her large violet eyes. I could read in them nothing but innocence and wonder. 'But you know I didn't,' she said. 'I took those sleeping things almost as soon as we came back from Kitson's private recital.'

'Yes, of course,' I nodded hastily. 'I thought perhaps you'd only said that for Geoffrey's benefit. Or, perhaps, that you'd taken them after you came back from the Commerce.'

'No, Friday night was exceptional.'

I agreed mutely. She continued with composure:

'In the first place, Geoffrey hadn't gone to bed as he normally does, in spite of yawns and hints from me. In the second place I wanted to teach Johnny a lesson! That I wasn't at his beck and call! I told you this afternoon that we'd had a miserable session over lunch in Andorra. I understated it. All the morning we'd had a ghastly row. We were supposed to make it up over luncheon and he had to choose that wretched café – probably to annoy me. I thought his insistence on going into Andorra was mad in the first place. But that's not the point. The row went on until he delivered me here at the Alexandra. The last thing I said to him was that in future he could get somebody else to spend the night with him. Not very dignified. And, naturally, I didn't mean it. But I thought – since Geoffrey hadn't gone to sleep anyway – I wouldn't turn up for once, and show him.'

'What was the row about? Not that it's any of my business.'

'Oddly enough, about Perdita. I said he was overdoing it a bit, the part about being more or less engaged to her. I pointed out that she was falling badly in love with him and that it was unfair to her. I really meant,' she added candidly, 'that it was unfair to me! That afternoon when you, Jane, suddenly asked me if Johnny was in love with Perdita it gave me a shock.

Though I'd been accusing him all day of just that, it never actually occurred to me that it could be true. Of course, it wasn't true.'

'What makes you think so?' I asked rather cruelly.

'It couldn't have been!' She flushed slightly. 'Not with that infant, pretty though she is, in an insipid way. And then, why do you think he took that crazy drive and killed himself?'

'Why do *you* think he did?'

She had been fidgeting around the room, while she related the history of why she had not kept her appointment that night at the Commerce. She paused now by the window, her back towards me. Again the dramatic note crept into her voice.

'Because,' she said brokenly, 'I didn't come to him as he'd hoped.'

I said incredulously: 'Are you suggesting he committed suicide because of disappointed love?'

She hadn't meant quite that, but she clearly liked the idea. 'I mean he drank too much and careered over the countryside in that Bugatti in order to cool down. But why not? How do we really know? He was so desperately in love with me.'

I stared at her with disgust. I think she would have almost enjoyed the thought that Corcoran had killed himself for love of her. A moment later I wasn't so sure. When she turned towards me her face was streaming with tears. She sobbed:

'Anyway I was . . . with him. I . . . *I'd* have killed *myself*. I tried to, you know.'

'No, I didn't know.'

Nor did I believe her; though Naomi herself – at least for the moment – may have. She said wildly: 'Driving back from Andorra that Friday afternoon I hoped I'd wreck the car and kill us both. Then that night when I took *two* of Dr Hervey's capsules! Don't you think I *knew* the result could be fatal!'

I controlled my exasperation. Naomi was trying to convince herself – not me – that she had tried to commit suicide. Since she seemed to derive perverse comfort from this I let her go on.

'I failed. I failed to kill myself – just as I've failed Geoffrey . . . and Johnny. Johnny wasn't in love with me. I lied when I said that, Jane. He was getting bored, screamingly bored. I've known it for weeks. I couldn't believe my ears when he proposed we drive to Puig d'Aze together. I felt like a condemned person who gets a last-minute reprieve. It was all going to be like the old days again – this spring when we first met.'

She sank down tragically on the chaise-longue and added in a broken whisper: 'Only it wasn't . . .'

I said: 'Am I supposed to feel sorry for you, Naomi?'

She smiled. It was that bright, glossy smile she had put on at the beginning of this unpleasant scene.

'No, of course not. I should hate anyone to feel sorry for me. . . . Besides, it probably won't last long.'

'What precisely do you mean by that?'

'Nothing! Nothing at all. Except that one can't *always* be a failure, can one?'

'This is where I came in,' I said, beginning to get angry. 'And it is also where I'm going to go out.'

'I'm sorry, Jane, if I bore you, too. You and Johnny . . . and probably Geoffrey. No, there isn't much to, er, retain one, is there?'

'There's everything in the world to "retain" one!' I said. 'Two children whom you obviously adore, an extremely nice husband who obviously adores you . . .'

'Who used to,' she corrected, 'before . . .'

I refused to be interrupted. 'You're rich and reasonably young. As far as Corcoran's concerned, you're very lucky to have got rid of him. And what's more – I think you know it.'

My impassioned speech did not hold her attention. She heard the tap on the door before I did. She was on her feet again, all sociability in an instant. In spite of tears and melodrama she looked considerably less raddled than I did myself.

'It's them!' she said gaily, going to the door. 'Who on earth bolted this? I should imagine young Tyler Sherman dances rather well. Husbands never do, do they?'

Chapter 24

THE last person either of us expected to find at the door was Vicki Stein. Vicki seemed to be almost equally astonished to find herself there.

She stopped biting her nails and stammered:

'I'm ever so sorry . . . but I tried to telephone you from downstairs and your telephone doesn't work. They are saying at the desk that you were here, and so . . .'

'Do come in,' I suggested, and Naomi, regaining her poise, repeated the invitation.

I introduced them – though each knew quite well who the other was – in order to give Vicki a moment in which to recover herself. She sat down on the edge of a straight chair on Naomi's insistence, but got up again immediately.

'It's about Mr Sherman,' she said. 'It is very wrong of me to come like this, and be asking. But I know he goes on a picnic with you today and . . . and so . . .'

'You're wondering,' I came to her rescue, 'where he is.'

'Yes,' she said. 'He asks me to dinner tonight and then he doesn't come and I wonder . . . well, yes, what happens to him.'

'So,' I murmured, 'do I.'

She went pale at my remark, and I added: 'We last saw him about two hours ago. He was with Dagobert, my husband.'

She sat down again. I thought she looked relieved. Perhaps she had been afraid he was with Perdita. But the more I weighed this theory, the less it convinced me. The distress in Vicki's eyes had not looked like jealousy, and the relief which followed it was of a deeper kind. It seemed to leave her momentarily exhausted. She closed her eyes and breathed:

'I am glad.'

'Have we such a thing as a drink?' I asked Naomi.

Naomi shook her head. 'We could telephone down. Brandy?'

I nodded and started for the telephone before I remembered that Vicki had said it didn't work. I tried it just the same. It was, in fact, out of order. I started for the door. Naomi joined me in the corridor.

'What's the matter with her?' she demanded. 'She looks as though she were going to faint.'

'I don't know.'

'I wonder why they haven't come back,' Naomi went on anxiously. 'They've been hours, now that I think of it. Surely, a flat tyre . . .'

I didn't answer her; her voice was beginning to grate on my nerves. I jabbed the lift button before I realized the lift was already there. I got inside, and to my annoyance Naomi got in with me.

The bar was closed, but the man behind the desk promised to send up brandy and cigarettes at once. It was, I noticed, twenty past twelve. The hotel lobby had a forlorn and forsaken look. My own appearance was not dissimilar. In one corner of it, behind a potted palm, I saw Perdita pretending to read a last year's copy of *Harper's Bazaar*. She rose and came across to me.

'But you went with Geoffrey!' I exclaimed. 'Where is he?'

'I – I don't know,' she stammered, taken aback by the unnecessary sharpness of my voice. 'I've been waiting down here. Wasn't that Vicki Stein who just went upstairs in the lift?'

'What do you mean, you don't know?' I didn't actually shake her, but she thought I was going to. 'You went with . . .'

'No, I didn't. That's what I'm trying to say. Geoffrey refused to take me along. He told me to wait here. He said he'd be back in half an hour. It hasn't been much . . .'

Her eyes strayed towards the clock over the desk and she gave up her half-hearted attempt to sound reassuring. Geoffrey had been looking for Dagobert and Tyler for nearly an hour and a half, and we both knew it.

'We could get a taxi, Jane.'

'What for?' I snapped. 'We're behaving like agitated hens.'

'Yes,' she agreed. 'Or if you think the police . . .'

That was exactly what I was thinking, but I said: 'Don't be absurd! And forgive me for biting your head off. If you want to be helpful, my dear, go home and go to bed.'

'I don't mind waiting.'

Naomi joined us. 'We've left that woman alone in my room,'

she reminded me. 'She'll probably have stolen half my jewellery by this time.'

'They could have gone straight to the Voyageurs themselves,' I said to Perdita. 'You go home and wait there.'

And I followed Naomi to the lift.

Vicki was still sitting where we had left her five minutes ago. She roused herself when we entered and began to apologize for her intrusion. It was just that she had been a little worried, and couldn't think of anywhere else to look. Tyler had been so insistent about meeting her tonight, but probably he had forgotten. It was quite unimportant, really it was.

She refused the brandy that arrived and excused herself. I slipped the packet of cigarettes from the waiter's tray into my handbag and said I'd walk back with her. She said please, don't bother; and Naomi said I simply *couldn't* leave her alone; besides, they'd be home soon and we could still go to the Casino, and in the meanwhile there was lots more she wanted to talk about.

I had had all the heart-to-heart conversations with my old school friend that I could stand for one evening, and there were other things on my mind. But I felt slightly conscience-stricken when I heard her bolt the door after us. I said to Vicki when we descended the hotel steps:

'We could go to the police.'

She shook her head sharply. 'No.' I was grateful to her for not hypocritically saying – as I had said to Perdita – 'what for?' I added:

'Has it occurred to you that I may be as worried about Dagobert as you are about Tyler? Why are you worried about Tyler, by the way?'

'But I have explained.'

'Yes,' I said, 'you ought to watch those explanations of yours. They grow less and less convincing.'

We continued across the gravel sweep and into the road without speaking. The Place de la République was deserted. We passed the police station without further reference to the police. What exactly had we to say if we went in and woke up the doubtless sleeping Brigadier Petitjean? That there ought to be a law against midnight motor-car jaunts in the neighbourhood of Puig d'Aze?

'Anyway, since they are together,' Vicki murmured, putting

in words what I was thinking myself. Her confidence in Dagobert was touching. I wished I felt an equal confidence in Tyler. The subject had no future and she changed it.

'I have seen this Mrs Gordon-Smith somewhere before. She is very chic.'

'You didn't, for instance, see her at the Hôtel Commerce?'

'No. It must have been at the concert. I don't like her.'

That subject also had no future and we dropped it. Vicki's thoughts had wandered even further than my own. She said in a small voice:

'I would have been liking America. It is so far away . . .'

'It's still there,' I pointed out, wondering whether she meant far away from the concentration camps of her childhood, or far away from Puig d'Aze.

She shook her head as though dismissing the vision she had summoned up.

'You mean,' I suggested, 'you'd like Dallas, Texas?'

She looked at me for an instant, began to protest, but finally looked away. 'Yes, I mean that. Mitzi would also be liking it. There is great chance for her in America and we have an uncle who lives very near in Brooklyn.'

'I don't think Brooklyn's *very* near, but you could start out by going there, couldn't you?'

'No. . . . There are reasons, many reasons.' She added a moment later in a conversational tone of voice: 'Your niece is very pretty, I think.'

'If,' I began in the interest of fair play, 'Perdita is one of your reasons . . . I should warn you that the betting is fifty-fifty. And I have it from an unimpeachable source, Tyler himself.'

'He has spoken about me?'

'I had you for breakfast,' I said. 'Both of you.'

'There are other reasons . . . family problems. It is very complicated. We are Jewish and these reasons mean much to us. We have a sister. Mitzi has been telling you.'

'Yes, Anna,' I nodded, wondering suddenly if family problems had not been brutally simplified by Anna's death. I resisted an impulse to tell her what Tyler had told me and said: 'There's also your brother, Rudolph, isn't there?'

'Yes, Rudolph,' she said quickly and, I thought, in a colder tone of voice: 'But he was always able to look after himself.'

'Was?' I said innocently. 'Isn't he still?'

'I suppose so. We have not heard from him for many years. . . . My hotel is here. I will say good night.'

'Walk along to my hotel and say good night there,' I said. 'You know quite well neither of us is going to go to sleep until Tyler and Dagobert turn up.'

To my surprise, she came without protest. Probably she didn't want to be left alone any more than I did. Puig d'Aze was full of edgy, deserted females tonight. Two of us received a salutary shock on reaching the Hôtel des Voyageurs. The Renault was calmly parked in front of the door!

We glanced at each other, giggled stupidly and tried not to feel light-headed. 'The important thing in these cases,' I said, 'is not to scratch their eyes out. Come in and help.'

She refused. She was satisfied that Tyler had returned safely and her anxiety to see him had vanished. I took her arm.

'I happen to know that Tyler especially wants to see you tonight. It's about Anna.'

I felt her arm stiffen in my grasp, but she came with me, walking like a wooden dummy. It was cruel, perhaps, to precipitate the scene which must inevitably follow, but the vagaries of Vicki's position in what had happened on Friday night at the Hôtel Commerce were becoming intolerable. The air needed clearing.

The front door was locked, but it opened automatically at a touch on the buzzer. The key to our room on the first floor was not hanging behind the desk and we tiptoed up the carpeted stairs. There was a light showing under our door and the key was in the lock. I turned the handle and pushed. The door was bolted on the inside. There was a slight scrabbling sound from the room, but no one rushed to let me in. I tried the bathroom next door. It had an entrance from the corridor as well as from our room. The corridor door ought to have been locked, but it wasn't. I opened it quickly and reached our room just in time to see someone hastily pushing my suitcase back under the bed. He straightened up as I entered, grinned foolishly and said:

'Oh, was that you just now at the door?'

'Yes, I live here. Did you find anything interesting in my suitcase? Try my hat-box. It's full of secret plans of romanesque abbeys.'

'Is that what they are?' Tyler said.

'Where's Dagobert?' I snapped.

'Dagobert? Oh, sure, Dagobert – he's fine. And you're not to worry if he comes home a bit late. That's what I dropped in to tell you.'

'Keep telling me!'

The grin disappeared, and the drawl became telegraphic. 'I left him at the cross-roads on the Col d'Aze. Said he'd walk home. Wanted the exercise and that you'd understand. Do you?'

'No. How does searching our room come into it?'

Tyler smiled again. It was the lazy disarming smile that used to disarm me. 'It seemed such a good opportunity.'

'It is,' Vicki appeared wrathfully from the bathroom door, 'because he is spying – as Mitzi is saying from the beginning.'

'Okay,' Tyler shrugged, 'if you're going to gang up on me. I'm spying; have it your own way. Only you've got to admit I'm about the lousiest spy that ever went into the business. A ten-year-old kid spots me right off. You two girls catch me red-handed.'

'What are you spying about?' I asked.

He sighed deeply. 'Vicki, as usual,' he said. 'Only I'm resigning here and now.'

'If you're spying on Vicki,' I persisted, 'why go through *my* belongings?'

'It's a long story.'

'Make it convincing.'

'I kind of figured,' he said, 'that since you and Dagobert went through Corcoran's room that night before Vicki got there, maybe you'd already found what she'd come in to look for. If you had found it, then maybe it would still be around somewhere – in this room, for instance. Is it?'

'No,' I said. 'Is what?'

'I don't know exactly. Dope about the Emerald Mark IV jet engine, I guess. Right, Vicki?'

Vicki had gone deathly white and, since her first outburst, deathly still. She seemed unaware that the question was addressed to her. Tyler had, until this moment, scrupulously avoided looking at her, and he had spoken exclusively to me. Seeing her now, he flinched and quickly averted his eyes again.

'Skip it,' he murmured. 'Dagobert, incidentally, assured me

that he found nothing in Corcoran's room. I was just checking up on him in case.'

'He is telling you that he found *me* in the Squadron Leader's bedroom!' Vicki rasped. She threw back her head suddenly and laughed. 'Now you are knowing what kind of girl I am!'

'Yes, I think so,' Tyler said quietly.

'And why cannot I go into whose bedroom I wish?' she continued scornfully. 'The Squadron Leader was a very attractive man. I shock the simple cowboy, yes?'

'Look, Vicki,' Tyler said, 'I've been to just as many movies as you, and honestly you don't play it very well. I know exactly why you went into Corcoran's room. So shall we stop beating about the bush?'

'Yes,' I said.

He turned to me again, glad to address his words to a third person.

'I've told you I've resigned,' he said. 'I mean it. My mission, as they say, is complete. It wasn't much, anyway. I was helping out a friend of mine, the one I told you I met in Paris. He knew – I don't know how – that Vicki was coming to Puig d'Aze. She was going to meet somebody here. I was supposed to find out who, and let my friend know. That's all. Well, I've found out. And I'll let him know, and to hell with everybody.'

He paced savagely up and down the room, staring at his own suède shoes. Vicki, during his words, had sat down rather abruptly. Her mouth had gone tight. Tyler repeated harshly:

'I told him I'd let him know, and I will. Only there's no particular hurry about it. . . .'

No one said anything and he stopped pacing. He looked tired suddenly. He sat down on the edge of the table with his back to Vicki and flicked cigarette ash into my bowl of jonquils.

'I'll tell you a rather corny story,' he said to me. 'I may have some of the details wrong and there are holes in it. Maybe it's better with holes in it. It's got a tragic beginning, and the end's pretty grim, too. Once upon a time a happy and united family of Jewish musicians lived in Warsaw. The father was a world-famous flautist. He was murdered by the Nazis. His wife was murdered the following year by the Communists. That left three daughters and a son. The son was considerably older than the other children. He was in the Polish Air Force. When Poland was overrun by the Germans and the Russians he flew his plane to England and joined the R.A.F. He was daring and did well. He spoke half a dozen languages, including English, like a native. He was dropped into Poland several times during the war, and on the last of these occasions he got two of his sisters out of a Russian concentration camp and back to England. Then he disappeared. No one knows quite how or where. The oldest sister stayed in Warsaw, where she became confidential secretary to a big shot in the Communist party. A couple of years ago, round the time of the Fuchs case, we – well, not me, but some friends of that friend of mind – decided that this girl – okay, let's call her Anna so as not to get too involved – decided that Anna had a contact in England. She was picking up odd bits of information that ought not to have been known in Warsaw. They checked on her sisters in London, but got nothing. Then they began to wonder about that brother who had disappeared. Who was he, where was he? No one knew. The obvious assumption was that he was dead. The only suspicious thing, when they came to look into it closer, was that his records at the Air Ministry had also disappeared. No details about him, not even a photograph. They watched the two sisters in Camden Town more closely. No suspicious visitors there. They decided that the two girls really had nothing to do with their brother, maybe didn't even know if he was alive. That is, they thought so until a month ago, when the two girls suddenly decided to spend lots more money than they can afford and come to – okay, let's say Puig d'Aze. That's when my friend gets this hunch. Maybe they're coming to meet this mysterious brother – call him Rudolph – who, my friend has reason to believe, is Anna's contact and, in a word, a Commie agent. Why, you'll ask, doesn't he meet her in London? Two reasons: one, he guessed that the girls in Camden Town are being watched; two, he has to get his information out of England anyway. What more innocent than a rendezvous at a musical festival? So he meets the two girls – or rather the older one. What happens . . .?'

He rolled the butt of his cigarette between his fingers, distributing the tobacco on the carpet, scratched his nose, leaving a smudge of ash across his sweating face, and muttered:

'I don't know. . . . And I don't even want to know. This is where those holes come into it, thank God. But I'll tell you what I think since I've started. This girl gets a nasty shock. She discovers for the first time what her brother is – a rotten agent for the people who murdered her mother. Probably – I'm only guessing now – probably he wants her to take certain information – details of the new Emerald jet engine – to someone who'll pass it on to Anna in Warsaw. He's afraid to do this himself because he's a fairly conspicuous and well-known person. Now, this girl has been brought up in England; it's where her kid sister has been given a decent chance and where they've been happy. She refuses bluntly to betray the country of her adoption – I warned you the story was corny. There is a quarrel. Maybe Rudolph gets tough and threatens her. Maybe he only tells her to go jump in the lake, he'll deliver the secret details himself. She says she's damned if he will. There's a gun around the room . . .'

He rose, shaking all over. He still looked only at me and there was an edge of anger in his voice as though I'd contradicted him.

'Do you know what *I'd* have done had I been in that girl's place?' he demanded aggressively. 'Okay, I'm only a simple Texan with a cowboy's morality. But I'd have shot the bastard!'

He groped for the door-knob. He didn't look at either of us again. He added flatly:

'Anyway, my report, if you're interested, says: "Man in question turns up, but drives over cliff. Get somebody else to do your dirty work in future ".'

He got the door open, grunted: 'So long, Vicki,' without turning round, and stumbled out. I murmured as his heavy footfall sounded on the stairs above:

'So Corcoran was Rudolph . . .'

I had to repeat it before Vicki heard me. She looked up and blinked at me as though coming round from an anaesthetic.

'Yes,' she said, and fainted.

Chapter 25

SHE lurched forward in her chair when she fainted, but I caught her before she slipped to the floor. She weighed nothing. I held her for an instant, trying to think what you were supposed to do in such cases, and resisted the temptation to shout for help. Inwardly I raged against Tyler; it was all very fine to accuse a girl of fratricide and then stalk out of the room, leaving the result to me. I clenched my teeth to stop them from chattering and remembered about thrusting the head between the knees. As I began to do this she revived.

'I must go home,' she murmured, struggling shakily to her feet.

'Yes, I'll take you.'

'Are you going to the police?'

'No – I'll leave that to you – if you think it's necessary.'

'You are thinking I shot him.'

'I'm not thinking at all,' I said truthfully. 'Did you?'

She avoided my eyes. 'Please can I go now?'

She edged towards the door, afraid I was going to stop her. Tyler had left the door ajar and when she reached it she fled. I caught up with her half-way down the stairs. She was clinging to the banisters, breathless after this burst of energy. I told her firmly I was going to walk as far as the Commerce with her; it was only a hundred yards up the street.

Tyler's Renault was still parked outside our hotel, where he frequently left it for the night. He had turned the lights out, but I noticed he'd forgotten to remove the keys. I seized Vicki's arm.

'I can't drive,' I said. 'Can you?'

She hesitated and shook her head. 'Mitzi can. You are wanting to look for your husband?'

'Yes.'

She made no comment, but, to my surprise, took my hand and squeezed it. I couldn't make out whether she was reassuring me, or whether I was reassuring her. We walked as far as the Hôtel Commerce without speaking. She said thank you and good night and turned towards the door. Then she hesitated.

'You said it was about Anna.'

'Anna?' I hedged, knowing quite well what she meant.

She looked at me candidly: 'That Mr Sherman wished to see me about.'

'You can ask him in the morning.'

She shook her head. 'I do not wish to see him in the morning – or ever again.' Her voice was level and there was no suggestion of tears in her eyes. It sounded like a flat statement of truth. 'Please tell me about our sister. Something has happened to her. He did not say all that he is knowing.'

'No, Vicki,' I said, making up my mind suddenly. 'Anna is dead. Tyler didn't like to tell you. They shot her while she was trying to escape.'

She said nothing for a moment, but her eyes filled gradually with tears. She was unconscious of them and they ran unheeded down her cheeks. 'Poor Anna,' she whispered gently. 'Poor, poor Anna . . .'

She drew a deep breath, became aware of my presence and attempted a smile. 'Thank you,' she said. 'It is better that Anna dies. I go now to see Mitzi.'

And she vanished into the hotel. I stood for a while in the street, trying not to think about the happy and united family of Jewish musicians who once upon a time had lived in Warsaw. I decided a brisk walk was what I needed. I reached the church square before my own apprehensions crowded back into my mind. It was long after one and I was at my wits' end. It was all very well for Dagobert to send me via Tyler that message not to worry! If – and the thought sent a chill down my spine – if he really *had* sent such a message! The trouble was I didn't quite trust Tyler. If only I knew how to drive the Renault! Perdita would, according to Tyler, make a driver in a few months; in the meanwhile I could go back to the hotel, wake her up and at least make her share my worries.

A café in the square was still open. It was the café where Dagobert and I had sat together that first night waiting for the Bugatti which had never returned. I entered it out of a kind of macabre sentimentality. There were three or four late customers playing *belote*, but Dagobert was not one of them. This did not surprise me, for I was certain by this time that he was lying by the roadside between here and the Col d'Aze shot or strangled.

There was a telephone in a corner of the café, and I found the number of the Alexandra. A sleepy night clerk answered me and I asked for Naomi's room. Her house phone was still out of order. I asked for Geoffrey's room, and at the end of several minutes' wait Naomi's voice answered. She'd heard the bell next door. Where on earth were we? We hadn't all gone to the Casino without her! I asked her if Geoffrey had come back and, when she said no, hung up.

Then I began flicking through the telephone directory until I found the number of the police station. I asked for Brigadier Petitjean and a pleasant voice told me in excellent English that Brigadier Petitjean was speaking.

'My husband,' I blurted out, 'hasn't come home and I am desperately worried and . . .'

There was a smothered noise at the other end of the line which sounded like a guffaw of mirth. Brigadier Petitjean suppressed it immediately.

'*Mais oui, Madame, parfaitement*. . . . And you saw him last?'

'After dinner tonight, but . . .'

'It is now only half past one. There was perhaps a little quarrel?'

'There wasn't,' I said, regaining my sanity. 'But I see what you mean.'

'Madame may rest assured that we shall do everything in our power. . . . If by morning Monsieur does not remember that a charming wife awaits so impatiently his return, perhaps Madame will do us the honour. . .'

'Yes,' I interrupted wearily, 'when I find his body I'll ring up to report it.'

'Patience, Madame . . . *dans le mariage toujours la patience*.'

'Do many women ring you up to report missing husbands?' I inquired curiously.

'Tonight Madame is only the third. *Mais que voulez-vous? Les hommes, vous savez*.'

'Yes, I know. Good night.'

'*À votre service, Madame*.'

'My husband's name,' I said, 'is Dagobert Brown, in case you need that little detail to assist you in your inquiries.'

He repeated the name sharply. 'Monsieur Brown . . . *Mais*... I wish to see Monsieur Brown.'

'So do I. Remember? That's what I originally telephoned about. Why do *you* want to see him?'

'But we have found his tandem bicycle!'

He sounded so pleased with himself that, instead of pointing out that we now owned two tandem bicycles, I congratulated him and asked him where he'd found it. This was the wrong question, for it forced him to admit that the missing tandem had been recovered not by the Puig d'Aze *gendarmerie*, but by his colleagues in Aze-les-Bains, ten miles down the valley. It had been found abandoned behind the Aze-les-Bains bus station. The thief or thieves had probably taken the bus on to Perpignan, where further investigations could be made if Monsieur Brown wished.

I hinted in a significant way that if further investigations were made they ought to be made *much* nearer home. I rang off, leaving him, I hope, uneasy and puzzled.

As I rang off I saw behind me, reflected in the wall mirror beside the telephone, Kitson's wild black beard.

'Yes,' he agreed as I started, 'it has that effect on me, too, when I come across it unexpectedly in the mirror. But without it I look like a rather fat stockbroker.'

'What are you doing here?'

'But I am always here,' he explained. 'Here or in the café next door or in the one across the square or the one down the street. What are you having to drink, my dear? You observe that I am much too polite to inquire what you are doing here. Besides, I heard you tell Petitjean. Very sad. . . . Gin?'

I said thank you, but it was late. He herded me towards a corner table and told the boy to leave the gin bottle.

'Some people put red wine in it,' he said, 'but I shouldn't advise that. Paulette used to telephone Petitjean in the middle of the night to report my absences. . . . Paulette is very possessive, which is a mistake – I trust you will not make it. Let us not look for Dagobert.'

'Have you a car?' I said suddenly.

He shook his head, removed a bit of broken comb from the pocket of his blue jeans and began to comb his beard. 'Only that bicycle Dagobert was so interested in last night.'

'Can you drive?'

'I imagine so.'

I shifted in my chair and rose distractedly. 'Mr Kitson ... this is a most peculiar request, I realize, but ...'

'Call me,' he murmured softly, 'call me ... *Maître*.'

'... there's a car in front of the Hôtel des Voyageurs with the keys in it. If you'd drive me ...'

'But of course, my dear,' he said warmly. 'Why didn't you say so! What fun! Where?'

He rose impetuously, seized the gin bottle and hastened to the door to hold it open for me. Though he was in point of fact fairly sober, I had half regretted my impulse before we reached the Voyageurs. Why I should have any confidence in Kitson when I had hesitated to trust Tyler Sherman is inexplicable. Some day I'll have to have my woman's intuition seen to.

There was a certain amount of excitement getting Kitson's paunch fitted in between the front seat and the steering wheel, and more when he started turning keys and pulling levers. We started forward with a jerk and a savage roar which ought to have woken up the car's owner two storeys above.

Kitson said with dismay: 'Do I have to turn it around? No – we'll take the back way. The one the gallant Squadron Leader took – isn't it thrilling?'

It was, in a way. For the next moment or two I quite forgot my anxiety about Dagobert. We bounced and rattled through the maze of alleys behind the church, coming out at the edge of the village into the road which led up towards the Col d'Aze. There was a sign which said: Col d'Aze Km. 4 – or rather there had been until we scraped it off its post.

'I knew all along it was child's play,' Kitson said.

'W-what?'

'Driving a car. I've always wanted to have a try. I wonder which one of these things you press to make it go slower.'

'Not that one!' I said as we shot up the road.

In front of us the headlights of another car suddenly loomed. For the next moment or two we both concentrated, clutching things. The car was upon us before I realized who it was. We swerved, it swerved – I closed my eyes and a second later there was a delicious sense of repose as we pursued our miraculous way.

'Must have been an English car,' Kitson remarked, delighted

with his skill. 'I passed him on the wrong side – rather intelligent of me, I thought.'

The car had been Geoffrey's Humber. I had, before shutting my eyes, caught a glimpse of Geoffrey himself at the wheel. He was apparently alone.

The apparition of the Humber sobered me. I remembered that the object of this excursion was not to give Kitson a driving lesson. I remembered something else suddenly. I had not said a word to Kitson about where Dagobert was, and yet he had started automatically for the Col d'Aze! I wet my lips and said:

'Why are we going . . . I mean, where are we going?'

'That is a very interesting query,' he said, 'and quite unanswerable. Theoretically the road leads to the Col d'Aze.'

'I m-mean you think we might find Dagobert there?'

'Either there,' he said heartily, 'or in the gorge beneath the cross-roads. . . . Does my driving make you nervous, my dear? Perhaps you'd like to have a go.'

He generously relinquished the steering wheel. I grabbed it before we went into the ditch. 'That's one way,' I admitted, 'of stopping a conversation. I merely wondered how you knew Dagobert was on the Col d'Aze.'

'Where else would he be?' he asked in surprise. 'Isn't he investigating Corcoran's death? I imagine it would occur to him to examine the wreckage. Heaven knows somebody ought to. Petitjean didn't.'

'Last night,' I said slowly, 'you warned us very solemnly to forget about Corcoran's death.'

'Yes, I know,' he shrugged amiably. 'Veiled threats and all. Wasn't it beastly of me? But I was afraid you'd find out I did it. And I had such a really splendid motive . . . don't you think?' he prompted me when I made no comment.

'Yes, of course,' I murmured, 'being the last to see him alive and everything. . . .'

'I was thinking more of the – er – defenestration of the wretched Sheila.'

Aware that he was watching me and not the road, I said: 'That sign means a hairpin bend.'

'Oh, is *that* what it means? I've always wondered. What do we *do*?'

He did, however, the right thing. That is, he negotiated the bend, and when we again had a straight climb of road ahead he said:

'I quite forgot to ask – have you found out who murdered Corcoran?'

The altitude must already have made me light-headed, for I replied: 'Yes.'

And remembered a second later that the answer could be true. Vicki had not said in so many words that she had shot her brother; but she had not denied it.

'Not me?'

'Not you what?'

'The murderer.'

I shook my head. I remembered with a certain remote comfort that at least the fingerprints on the revolver were not Kitson's. The road was climbing more steeply now and the cross-roads could only be a few minutes further on. The night was clear and it was distinctly colder than it had been in the village below.

'Don't tell me,' Kitson continued. 'Let me guess. Is it a man?'

I ignored the question and edged forward in my seat, my eyes searching the path of light cut by our headlights.

'A woman, then?' he persisted. 'Am I getting warm?'

'There are the cross-roads – just ahead of us.'

'I thought it must be a woman,' he sighed, 'but I was much too chivalrous to suggest such a thing.'

'There!' I breathed. 'That's the signpost. Not so fast.'

'Or there may even have been two people, to tell the truth. Though I shouldn't rely on that. Sad though it be, let's face it! I was seeing double at the time. That's why I could not recommend red wine in your gin just now. Where did we put the gin, by the way?'

I let my breath out slowly and sank back into my seat. I don't know quite what I had expected at the cross-roads; to see Dagobert leaning against the signpost, I suppose. I saw precisely – nothing.

Kitson stepped on the brakes and the clutch and the accelerator and stalled the engine a foot or two from the parapet. It was a second before I realized how near we had come to repeating the fatal leap which the Bugatti had made. I glanced at Kitson. He was sweating.

'These narrow escapes make consecutive conversation so difficult,' he said. 'Wasn't I talking about gin?'

He opened the door and eased himself through it, glad to be on terra firma again. I joined him breathlessly.

'No,' I remembered, 'you were talking about a woman! What woman?'

'The one I thought I saw in Corcoran's Bugatti that night,' he said. 'My dear, you must learn to pay attention.'

He had walked to the parapet and was peering gingerly over the edge. In spite of an almost full moon, the vast gorge below was filled with impenetrable shadow. He struck a match; the inadequacy of the tiny flame made us both laugh nervously. He tossed it over the edge; the feeble gloom was immediately swallowed up in the immensity below.

'By tipping our car half over the parapet,' he said, 'the headlights might light up the gorge. What do you think?'

'We'd probably lose the car in the process,' I said, 'but it's not our car.'

I glanced at the headlights, which he'd left full on. They played across the slope on our left, the embankment of the Andorra road beneath which Dagobert and I had taken shelter against gunfire that first afternoon. I could still see the rocks and bushes where he had torn the sleeve of his corduroy jacket when he climbed that slope to look for the bullet.

Then I saw something else which made my knees suddenly sag. I saw the very corduroy jacket Dagobert had worn that Friday afternoon. It was rolled in a ball and pushed under a bush not ten feet from the road. I put my fist in my mouth to stop myself from screaming.

He'd been wearing the same jacket today.

Chapter 26

THE jacket was in ribbons. The sleeves and pockets were slashed and the lining had been ripped out.

'Robbery,' Kitson said grimly, 'with, I'm afraid, violence. Was it his?'

I gulped and knelt down to recover a sock which had been flung a few feet farther on. It was a sock I knew; I had frequently darned it. Kitson moved with agility among the boulders, overgrown with shrubbery. I followed blindly, tearing my stockings and twisting my ankle. Once when I fell my hand encountered a metallic tube which turned out to be a U.S. Army torch. Its glass was smashed, but the bulb was intact; it still worked when I tried it. The initials T.S. were scratched on it. It was the torch Tyler Sherman had been using in the shed on the first occasion we had met him.

I found Dagobert's handkerchief caught in a thornbush a moment later. I recognized our old Hampstead laundry mark, an unsightly B in indelible ink in a triangle; for no particular reason this homely reminder made me start to snivel. I stopped abruptly. The handkerchief was freshly stained with blood. It was a moment before I realized that the bloodstains were my own. I had scratched my wrist on a thorn.

Kitson's muffled exclamation sent me scrambling after him. He had wandered off into the shadows to the right of the headlight beam where, a few yards from the cross-roads, was a low stone shelter of the kind Pyrenean shepherds build as a refuge against the weather. Kitson was on hands and knees before the narrow opening which served as a door.

'Something here,' he grunted, crawling in. 'Give me the torch.'

I crowded in beside him and in the process did something to the torch which put it out. It was dank and musty in the shelter and as still as death. We had both stopped breathing as I tried to get the torch working again. The shelter was either unoccupied or else its occupant had also stopped breathing. I thought I smelled Trumper's Isis Hair Tonic. Dagobert uses Trumper's Isis Hair Tonic. . . .

I was conscious of overwhelming claustrophobia and of lungs which were about to burst. My fingers were limp and without feeling; the torch slipped from them with a dull thud. It came on again and made a feeble yellow track across the straw-strewn floor. I saw Dagobert's shoe with its heel knocked off and the sole torn away. There was a path in the straw where a body had been dragged. The beam of the torch probed the corners of the shelter before I realized that neither Kitson nor I was holding it.

'What,' Dagobert asked in a puzzled voice, 'are we all supposed to be looking for?'

Kitson sat up so suddenly that he cracked his head against the stone roof. I squirmed round and crawled for the low opening which was blocked by Dagobert's head and bare shoulders. He tried to help me through and to my feet. I clung to him, sobbing weakly; there would be time to be furious later.

'Yes, of course.' He made an effort as though to concentrate. 'You were looking for me.'

He kissed me vaguely on the forehead, staggered and keeled over. His face was white in the moonlight and his lips twitched with pain. He was wearing only a pair of flannel trousers and his shoulders were scratched and bruised. He had been dragged, I learned later, into the shelter after having been knocked out a few feet away.

He was stirring again, even before Kitson ran back from the car with an army blanket and the gin bottle.

'How did you . . . Oh, yes, Tyler. Did he tell Vicki about Anna? Wasn't that Kitson, or am I light-headed?'

'Don't talk,' I whispered, and tried to stop crying.

He closed his eyes again, either to avoid this unattractive sight or because he was still too weak to keep them open. Kitson and I got the army blanket under and around him. We both noticed that his left fist was clenched and remained clenched even when I wrapped his arm in the blanket. Just as we had him comfortable he started up again.

'The tandem!' he said a little wildly. 'Did you notice it?'

'What a good thing I brought this along,' Kitson murmured, taking a deep draught from the gin bottle.

He glanced at me. I nodded and whispered: 'Doctor.' And to Dagobert: 'Yes, darling, the police have found our tandem. It's quite all right, and you're not to worry.'

'Where?' he said. 'In Aze-les-Bains?'

This time I started. 'Yes, as a matter of fact.'

He sighed with deep content and relaxed. 'In cases of concussion,' he said, 'you stretch the patient out in a quiet dark spot and loosen his clothes.' He opened a puzzled eye, shivered slightly and added: 'Somebody already seems to have done that.'

'Yes,' Kitson nodded thoughtfully, inspecting Dagobert's bare torso. 'I have rather repellent black hair all over my chest. I shave it with an electric razor. What do you suppose they were looking for?'

I felt Dagobert's left arm tighten; the fist beneath the blanket stirred. 'They didn't find it,' he said with satisfaction.

'That wasn't exactly my question,' Kitson said, 'but let it pass. Gin?'

'I'm not sure whether you give gin in cases of concussion or not,' Dagobert said. 'If I'm to go on getting knocked out, I'd better find out. Yes, you might leave me a drop.'

I took the gin bottle firmly from Kitson and put it under a bush. 'Get the car up as near as possible,' I said.

'I'm not sure I'm supposed to be moved,' Dagobert said. 'Besides, if you're thinking of *Couillon* . . .'

The doctor in Puig d'Aze is called Dupont and Kitson, not unnaturally, missed the reference. 'Extraordinary how these indelicate words always come to the surface when people are semi-conscious,' he muttered.

'We'll get Dr Perrault, of Aze-les-Bains,' I said.

'Thus killing two birds with one stone,' Dagobert agreed. 'I wonder who the other will be.'

I tried to make Kitson go, but he hesitated. 'In many ways I don't follow all this,' he admitted.

'Fingerprints,' Dagobert explained. 'I left about twenty sets with Perrault this morning – including yours. They weren't yours, by the way, on the revolver. But, then, yours may turn up somewhere else. Who knows?'

'Does he often talk like this?' Kitson asked me.

He does, of course, and it was this which partly reassured me. But I urged Kitson to get the car. Dagobert pointed out:

'Kitson likes to pretend he's asleep; I enjoy wandering in my mind. You can't hit me over the head with a – What did you hit me over the head with?'

'I didn't hit you over the head with anything.'

'No,' Dagobert said, discouraged. 'I was afraid it wasn't you.'

I whispered when Kitson had ambled off: 'I found the torch over there on the ground. It's Tyler's.'

'Yes,' he said. 'I borrowed it from him when he left me.'

'What *were* they looking for?'

'The same thing they were looking for the other day in our toothpaste and the guide book, I imagine. As Mitzi would say – "the secret papers".'

'Tyler was searching our room tonight when I came in.'

Dagobert sighed. 'I told him I didn't have them. People are so mistrustful.'

I stroked his forehead gently and made the blanket more comfortable around him. He took my fingers in his right hand and brushed them across his lips.

'So cool, so white,' he murmured, evidently delirious again.

'It's the moonlight.'

'No, it's French cigarettes,' he said unromantically. 'Unlike those you smoke at home they don't stain your fingers. They do other things, of course. . . . Would you have a spare one on you?'

I was watching Kitson trying to turn the Renault around, and I was suddenly attacked by that mistrustfulness Dagobert had just mentioned. I said before I thought:

'Kitson didn't know you were here! Tyler told me, but not Kitson. Why did he drive straight to the cross-roads?'

'Didn't you tell him to?'

'No. . . . Then, why did he immediately find this shelter and say he thought "something was there"?'

'Something had been. Me – until a few minutes previously, when I painfully regained consciousness and crept out for air. Yes, I see what you mean, Jane. . . . I think my headache's coming on again.'

I was stricken with remorse. This was hardly the moment to cast doubts on Kitson. Though I didn't for a minute believe that Dagobert was actually wandering in his mind, he was as weak as a kitten and we *had* to trust Kitson. I looked desperately around; the road to Andorra above us coiled like a sleeping serpent in the moonlight. The road that we had climbed so laboriously on the tandem plunged downwards towards the gorge, while the road to Puig d'Aze was hidden by folds in the hills. At two-thirty in the morning all were deserted, and would doubtless remain so.

'Did you mean it about Dr Perrault?' I asked.

'It can wait until the morning. I've never shared your faith in those fingerprints, anyway.'

'Whose did you give him?'

'Everybody's. Even ours. Not Corcoran's unfortunately, and they'll probably be his.'

'Dagobert!' I remembered suddenly. 'You know – who Corcoran really was . . .'

He nodded. 'Tyler and I had a chat driving back after dinner. . . . I see. He told you.'

'And Vicki.'

'What did Vicki do?'

'She fainted dead away.'

'That I can believe,' he said sympathetically. 'I wish I hadn't absolutely *proved* tonight that Corcoran was murdered . . .'

'I don't understand.'

'Then we could sell one of our tandems and take a long trip somewhere.'

'I mean, how have you *proved* it? Dagobert, it *could* have been an accident, couldn't it? And we could go for a trip – even on the tandem, if you insist. We could start tomorrow – anywhere you like. Even Andorra. Dagobert! You know what kind of life the Stein family have had. *Couldn't* it – please – have been an accident?'

'No,' he said unhappily, 'it couldn't.'

'Then why,' Kitson said softly, 'couldn't we leave it one of those fascinating unsolved mysteries? With, say, me, living out my days under a dark cloud of suspicion. I'm used to that, anyway.'

He had approached so quietly that I jumped at the sound of his voice. I wondered how much of our conversation he had overheard. He continued to eye Dagobert curiously, scratching his beard.

'Or if you absolutely insist on unmasking a villain,' he went on smoothly when neither of us said anything, 'why not make it Sebastian? Or you can have Paulette, if you wish. . . . *How* have you proved it?'

'Proved what?' Dagobert said groggily. 'I'm wandering in my head again.'

'Quite,' Kitson said dryly. 'Shall I tell you what has been worrying me?'

'Yes, do.'

'Why, dear boy, you are still alive.'

'There is that,' Dagobert said conversationally. I glanced from Kitson to Dagobert, feeling the hair at the back of my neck rise. Dagobert added: 'Frankly, it's been worrying me, too.'

'Perhaps they were merely trying to frighten you,' Kitson suggested helpfully. 'Have they?'

Dagobert didn't reply for an instant. His mouth was drawn as though with pain again and his eyes were suddenly lustreless. He turned his head away and said flatly:

'More than you realize . . .'

'We must,' I said quickly, 'get him into the car.'

Kitson stopped scratching his beard and became the man of action. 'How do we go about it?' he said tugging at the blanket.

'That's what I've been waiting to see,' Dagobert said, making no effort to be cooperative.

I tried to get an arm under his shoulders while Kitson puffed breathlessly with his legs.

'Yes, I see what you mean,' he grunted, after we'd struggled for a moment with the limp body. 'I'd have needed help, wouldn't I?'

'Still,' Dagobert said, 'with those peasant chums of yours, those rough but faithful Catalans you were telling us about, that shouldn't have been difficult.'

'True,' Kitson said. 'Then the Bugatti, being an open car, was easier to dump bodies into. Besides, Corcoran felt lighter than you.'

'Felt?' I repeated, swallowing.

'The last time I threw him out of the house,' Kitson nodded. 'Two years ago when he suggested putting up his price. Thought you'd caught me, didn't you? It would be easier to get him through this door if he'd relax his left arm for a change. Perhaps something's wrong with it.'

Dagobert groaned horribly and Kitson quickly dropped his end of our burden. Dagobert stopped groaning and, while

Kitson turned to fuss with the back door, winked at me and slipped something into his left trouser pocket. Kitson rummaged in the car for a moment, and then re-emerged. There was a revolver in his right hand. He pointed it at us tentatively.

'I've never tried using one of these things before,' he said, 'but I imagine it's quite simple.'

'Like,' I wet my lips with the tip of my tongue, 'driving a car?'

'Just so. . . . Would you mind letting me have whatever you've just slipped into your left pocket?'

'There's a car coming up the road from Puig d'Aze,' Dagobert said.

'Quite,' Kitson nodded. 'And probably this revolver isn't loaded. But in case there isn't a car and the revolver really is loaded, could you please give me whatever-it-is?'

Dagobert rose reluctantly to his feet. 'With concussion I ought not to be exposed to this kind of excitement,' he grumbled. 'Shall I stall until that car comes to the rescue?'

'If you like. I'm free until the concert at nine o'clock tomorrow morning.'

'Then you *did* know he was here!' I accused. 'How? Unless . . .'

'Somebody told him,' Dagobert supplied.

'I meant unless he knocked you out himself. Who could have told him?'

Dagobert glanced at Kitson hopefully. 'Any answer, Maestro?'

'How about a little bird?'

'Did he see any little birds, Jane, just before he joined you?'

'He came in from the church square while I was telephoning Brigadier Petitjean. He could have seen almost anybody.'

'It could be Tyler. Only we have his car.'

'Tyler went straight up to his room after leaving Vicki and me.'

'No, I mean driving the car which is now racing up from Puig d'Aze.'

Kitson broke in speculatively. 'D'you know, I've often wondered about these revolvers. One gets a kind of nervous tension when holding them. Most curious. One's hand begins to shake. I imagine they frequently go off, as it were, of their own accord.'

'You mean you'd like the thing I slipped in my pocket?' Dagobert said.

'On the whole, yes,' Kitson agreed. 'Then we can all hurry along to the doctor's.'

Dagobert shrugged good-naturedly and dug into his pocket. He opened his hand and produced a small shapeless blob of metal. He had been clutching this, it seemed, when he was knocked out. He had found it still gripped tight in his fist when he came to, hours later, in the stone shelter. Why his assailant, who had so thoroughly searched even the heels and soles of his shoes, should have overlooked it, remained obscure. For it was our sole material evidence that Squadron Leader Corcoran had been murdered.

Kitson took it between his left thumb and forefinger.

'The bullet that killed Corcoran?'

'Yes,' Dagobert said. 'It's been half melted, but Dr Perrault could doubtless establish what revolver fired it.'

'You found it in the wreckage of the Bugatti?'

'Yes. When the body burned it was left behind. Brigadier Petitjean ought to have found it.'

'But,' Kitson said smugly, 'he didn't. And now that I think of it, one only has your word for the fact that you found it.' He sighed, fingering the object thoughtfully. 'And,' he added sadly, 'you are admittedly wandering in your mind.'

'We have,' I reminded him grimly, 'the bullet itself.'

'We *had*,' Kitson corrected me.

He changed the revolver quickly to his left hand and flung the small lead pellet with surprising force over the black abyss which yawned for desolate miles behind us. A hundred men could search for years in that craggy wilderness and never find it again.

Chapter 27

'WHY did you do that?' I gasped.

'So that you can start out with clear consciences on your tandem trip tomorrow,' he smiled. 'Also I can now put away this ridiculous revolver that Paulette insists upon my carrying when I wander around at night.'

'Who,' Dagobert inquired, 'are you trying to spare? Besides us, of course.'

'Myself, dear boy!' Kitson exclaimed. 'Who else?'

Dagobert ran a shaky hand through his hair. 'I thought I'd said that,' he complained. 'This concussion . . .'

'Now, why *did* I throw the thing away?' Kitson asked blankly. 'I had it all worked out a minute ago. Oh, yes! Don't you see? If Petitjean got hold of this bullet and knew it was found in the wreckage, he would have to do something about it, poor chap. Even he would have to face certain depressing facts. One, that Corcoran was the only person who saw me, as it were, not pushing Sheila out of that window. Two, that Corcoran has touched me frequently since. Three, that I am the only one who *said* he actually saw Corcoran driving away from the hotel last Friday.'

'You said it wasn't Corcoran!' I interrupted. 'You said, half an hour ago, that it might have been a woman! Or that there might have been two people in the Bugatti!'

'Yes, my dear, I know. I never say the same thing twice. It's a most tiresome habit. But, please, don't interrupt. Now, as I was saying, Petitjean is very fond of me. It would be painful for him to be forced to draw obvious conclusions. So you see how my impulsive gesture has simplified life for everybody.' He broke off suddenly. 'How very odd!'

I, too, had been unaware of the approaching sound of the car climbing from the village below. Its headlights, appearing suddenly above the hill, swept the cross-roads.

'Someone to the rescue, after all!' Kitson exclaimed. 'How very thrilling!'

'That's what I've been trying to tell you,' Dagobert said,

thrusting his left hand into his pocket and grinning at me.

'Do you think I'd better get out my revolver again?' Kitson asked. 'Or would that look peculiar?'

Dagobert removed his hands from his pockets hastily and stopped grinning. Luckily, the car had reached us and Kitson did not notice. The car was unfamiliar to me and I did not recognize its sole occupant. Kitson and Dagobert apparently did; for both looked startled. The stranger looked startled, too, and a little annoyed. He muttered something about '*fumistes*', which, I believe, means 'practical jokers.' Then he took a look at Dagobert and changed his mind.

He was a small, vigorous and vociferous man in his sixties, who immediately leapt from the front seat with a small black bag. While he heaped what sounded like insults upon Kitson and me, he also very efficiently got Dagobert into the wide back seat of his car and piled blankets around him, ignoring Dagobert's protests. Everybody talked at once, but, unfortunately, in French, which left me out of things. The sudden thought flitted through my mind that I might be witnessing an abduction. I watched nervously while Kitson tried to draw me aside.

'Did you,' he asked, 'telephone Dr Perrault to come up here?'

'Why didn't somebody say so!' I said in relief. 'No, I should have, but I didn't think of it.'

'Then we must look elsewhere for our practical joker,' Kitson said gently, returning to the doctor's car.

I didn't realize how uneasy Kitson was until I heard him ask Dr Perrault at least five times who had telephoned him. The doctor was still too busy with Dagobert to do more than shrug impatiently and grumble because we hadn't kept the patient quiet until he arrived.

Finally, as Dr Perrault began to climb into the front seat again, he turned in exasperation on Kitson and said:

'I don't know who telephoned. She didn't give her name.'

'Oh, I see.' Kitson said quickly. 'That's very helpful. And you think our patient has a sporting chance of pulling through?'

Dr Perrault touched the self-starter. 'She spoke almost no French. It sounded like a child.'

'Quite. Mrs Brown and I will follow you in the Renault.'

It was, I think, the first time Dr Perrault had heard of the existence of a Mrs Brown, but then with Bertran de Born and fingerprints Dagobert and he had had other more interesting things to talk about. He said: '*Enchanté, Madame*,' but before he could close the front door of the car I jumped in beside him and closed it myself. As we moved forward I caught a glimpse of Kitson standing beside the signpost, thoughtfully scratching his beard. I said to Dagobert:

'What have you got in your left pocket?' but he pretended to be asleep and Dr Perrault asked me not to talk to him.

We drove through Puig d'Aze, past the Alexandra and on to the main road to Aze-les-Bains. I noticed that Naomi's light was still on; it was the only light in the hotel. It was after three when we reached Aze-les-Bains. Through the curtains of the Casino the wilting shapes of a few late dancers could still be seen and the orchestra which Squadron Leader Corcoran had once admired could be faintly heard as far away as Dr Perrault's house beyond the square.

Our conversation had been limited by the fact that Dagobert had dozed off while Dr Perrault's English was about as extensive as my French. He was unwilling to give an opinion on Dagobert's condition before thorough examination, but he was certain that he should not be moved again tonight. There was a room which he kept for his two daughters who lived in Paris where Dagobert could sleep. I could stay, too, if I promised not to talk.

Dr Perrault's housekeeper was up and the three of us got Dagobert into the surgery. The doctor had given him a shot and he was still groggy. While the doctor examined him the housekeeper prepared our room. I went out to the car to fetch in the remnants of Dagobert's clothes which he had insisted on our bringing. Luckily, they were beyond repair, but he would doubtless enjoy examining them in the morning. His passport had been with mine in my handbag, but his wallet was missing. Thanks to tonight's dinner party it had contained only a few hundred francs and a recipe, written in his own hieroglyphs, for *Fricandeau de mousserons*. I wondered who had got hold of this recipe and whether it would be forwarded, with suitable precautions, to Warsaw for deciphering.

While I was gathering the rags together the Renault drew up to the kerb behind me. It was Kitson to inquire how Dagobert was and if there was anything he could do. I told him Dagobert was going to stay the night. He opened the door of the car and said he would drive me home. I said I was going to stay the night, too. He said he thought that was very touching and added, solicitously:

'But I seem, my dear, somehow to have lost your confidence.'

'Yes.'

This seemed to sadden him. 'One tries so hard to do the right thing.'

'Such as pulling guns on people.'

'But it wasn't loaded!' he protested, beginning to fumble in the back seat. 'Would you like to see?'

'No, thanks.'

Aware that he was going to lose his audience, he stopped fumbling and said: 'It wasn't the same revolver that killed Corcoran, if that's what's embarrassing you. It's a different calibre – probably.'

'That will be easy to prove,' I said. '*If* we find that bullet you chucked away.'

'There is that,' he nodded with satisfaction. 'Then Dagobert was talking about fingerprints – I mean about fingerprints not being mine. I thought that was very reassuring, but I didn't quite grasp what he was talking about . . .'

'He was delirious,' I said.

Kitson leered at me cunningly. 'I remembered to bring the gin,' he whispered. 'Can I tempt you . . .?'

'You have a concert tomorrow at nine o'clock,' I reminded him.

'I have,' he began, 'a very startling idea about that concert which . . .'

But I was watching the lighted blinds of the surgery window where Dr Perrault's shadow moved above the long outstretched figure on the examination table. I started to shake slightly as I remembered stories of people with concussion who recover completely, only to relapse afterwards. I murmured: 'I wonder why they're taking so long.'

'Naturally, if you're not even interested . . .' Kitson sulked.

'Yes, of course.'

'No, you're not. You're not even listening!' he said petulantly. 'You're only interested in your husband, who is too tall and thin and has no black hair on his chest. I said I had a *startling* idea about tomorrow's recital.'

I nodded absently. 'You're going to call it off again.'

'And I am rather eager that there should be no hitch, no emotional scenes, if I make myself clear. The Maître will not appear at tomorrow's festival. Indeed,' he added, tragically, '*the Maître will never appear again!*'

'Don't be silly!'

'At least,' he said, 'I have your attention.'

'What are you talking about?'

'Mitzi Stein.'

'Would you mind starting over again?'

He handed me the gin bottle and, when I shook my head, took a deep swig himself. 'Mitzi Stein,' he said, 'is making her world début at the Puig d'Aze Musical Festival tomorrow morning at nine o'clock. She doesn't know it yet and that's why I warned you about emotional scenes or other hitches. She is going to play for the remainder of the festival according to the programmes which have been announced, plus a special programme of flute sonatas composed by her father and arranged for the harpsichord by me. In brief, Mitzi Stein is taking over where Kitson left off. You're the first person to hear this extremely important news, because I've just thought of it this minute.'

'Can she do it?'

'With me behind her, yes. She will live at The Abbaye, practise ten hours a day and, if I can keep Paulette out of the kitchen, be reasonably fed. At the end of a year or two I shall take her to London and then to New York. It will be interesting to see how two such remarkable personalities as Mitzi and I will get along together.'

'I was thinking of that,' I admitted. 'And when are you going to tell the Steins about it?'

'Vicki was with me this afternoon while you were all in Andorra. I telephoned the British Consul in Perpignan to find out about legal adoption. Vicki seems very enthusiastic about the idea. She thinks I have a heart of gold. I have, actually. I wanted to adopt Vicki, too, but Paulette seems to be against it. . . . Your husband appears to have revived.'

I looked round. The long shadow on the examination table was struggling into a sitting posture and trying to remove something from his trousers pocket. With his free hand he gesticulated, as he always does when he speaks French, a habit the French find puzzling. Dr Perrault was trying to calm him. We both watched the pantomime with curiosity. Kitson grasped its significance before I did. He said regretfully:

'It was very deceitful of Dagobert to give me that melted bullet when he obviously had two of them in his pocket. I suppose one should have frisked him. Still, one cannot think of everything. You might, however, give him the gist of what I've been saying before he goes to sleep tonight – especially the part about no hitches.'

'Yes,' I said. 'We'll wait until after the concert before asking Mitzi why she telephoned Dr Perrault and told him to drive up to the Col d'Aze.'

Chapter 28

KITSON thanked me gravely and suggested that we might wait until after the festival. Or even postpone the question indefinitely. We would discuss it tomorrow. Meanwhile I was doubtless eager to rush into the house and find out what the second bullet – if it was a bullet – could possibly signify. Did I not find all these bullets and fingerprints utterly confusing?

I said, yes, and ran into the house. He promised to send a suitcase down to us in the morning, waved to me with a friendly smile and drove off, scattering dustbins before the Renault.

I found Dr Perrault alone in his surgery. He had just put Dagobert to bed with something to make him sleep. It was at once apparent that Dr Perrault and I were the ones who needed the sedative. It was hard to say which of us was the more wrought-up.

Kitson's guess about the second bullet was correct. Dagobert had found two bullets on the Col d'Aze tonight. One – the half-melted bullet which had killed Corcoran – he had recovered from the ashes of the Bugatti and given to Kitson. It was irretrievably lost and, as Kitson had pointed out, we only had Dagobert's word for the fact that it had ever existed.

As this was clearly the crucial bullet I could not understand Dr Perrault's interest in the second one which I found him studying under his microscope. It was the bullet which had narrowly missed us on that Friday afternoon when we'd scrambled from the tandem. It had brought a boulder rolling down across the road. Dagobert had found it embedded in the embankment tonight a moment or two before he'd been knocked out.

It could (we had thought this even at the time), it *could* have been intended for the Bugatti. It could have been the first attempt on Corcoran's life. Since it was unsuccessful, I failed to see why it warranted microscopic inspection.

Dr Perrault was plainly of my opinion; for he at once abandoned his examination and I realized his excitement had another source. I had to remind him that I had a sick husband upstairs and was in no condition to think logically about bullets until I knew how he was.

There was, he explained, nothing wrong with Dagobert that a good night's sleep wouldn't put right. The blow on the base of his cranium had been skilfully administered, probably with a black-jack, and should leave no effect worse than a headache. It was, however, essential that he should not be agitated in any way and that was why he, Dr Perrault, was glad to have me to talk to instead. Did I know who was 'O.S.F.?'

I shook my head blankly and wondered if he, too, were wandering in his mind. He said it was very important and only professional delicacy had prevented him from asking Dagobert. I said, why was it important, and he started talking rapidly about '*le revolver*', translating the word for me as 'the revolver'. Our conversation was handicapped by this sort of thing. He said, then we must wait until tomorrow, which was a pity as he would have liked to awaken Dr Dupont and Brigadier Petitjean from their sleep at once.

By this time I was as breathless as he was. I exclaimed: 'Fingerprints!' which worried him, and then, with an immense effort at concentration, I remembered from the last Simenon novel I'd read the words: '*Empreinte digitale!*'

He nodded vigorously and took me over to a rolltop desk. He produced a photograph. It was a photograph of someone's fingerprints and across the photograph, also photographed, were the pencilled letters: 'O.S.F.' They were in Dagobert's handwriting.

Dr Perrault had placed a second photograph beside the first, a photograph of the fingerprints found on Corcoran's revolver. Though they were smudged, even I could see they were the same.

Dr Perrault had identified the fingerprints left on Corcoran's revolver.

And Dagobert, who alone knew who O.S.F. was, was in a drugged sleep. We were supposed to go calmly to bed and wait for him to wake up in the morning to tell us the answer!

I went upstairs not with any hope of sleep, but because I was too tired to remain upright any longer. I tiptoed into the room in order not to disturb Dagobert. I stumbled over the loose mat, which shot across the polished floor, but Dagobert continued to sleep tranquilly. My bed, which was across the room from his, had been turned down and a nightdress, a fluffy négligé and bedroom slippers belonging to one of Dr Perrault's daughters, were laid out for me. The linen sheets were fragrant with lavender, cool and slightly starched. There was a shelf of books over the bed and a reading-lamp.

There is no escape quite like a good book at such moments. I've never clearly grasped what they mean by 'escape fiction' – something which entirely engrosses you, I suppose, like the *Odyssey* or *Barchester Towers* or *The Murder of Roger Ackroyd.* I picked up a volume at random. It was a school prize awarded to Mademoiselle Françoise Perrault – *Théâtre Complet de Racine* – in nearly invisible print.

It fell open at *Phèdre.* I'd always meant to do something about *Phèdre,* anyway. We'd missed seeing *Phèdre* at the Comédie Française just before leaving Paris: the night we went to see the new Bob Hope.

Phèdre was easier than the way Dr Perrault talked, though the finer points – such as what it was all about – escaped me. O.S.F.... There wasn't anybody whose initials were vaguely O.S.F.

Very faintly in the distance I heard the sound of dance music from the Casino. That meant it wasn't four o'clock yet. I had hours in which to finish *Phèdre.* And then in the morning Dagobert would tell me who O.S.F. was and O.S.F. was Corcoran's murderer and I could go to sleep for a week.... It was beautifully simple. The thing to do was to keep quite calm and remember that *Thésée* was merely an odd way of spelling Theseus, who was of course *Phèdre*'s husband.

O.S.F.... I looked across at Dagobert. He *couldn't* go on sleeping like that indefinitely. It wasn't natural. Besides, sleeping on his back made him snore. He wasn't snoring, but probably he'd begin to. I could, of course, ease him gently over on to his side.

It seemed to me, somehow, that Theseus ought to be married to somebody else. Wasn't it Ariadne? Very well, if Dagobert refused to cooperate one could work the problem out for oneself, systematically.

O.S.F.... One could analyse this letter by letter, which seemed as fruitful a way of spending the night as any other. O. There was no one called Osbert, Oswald, Oliver or even Olga, connected with Corcoran's death! Unless . . . but of course! I didn't know Kitson's first name! Then Dagobert probably didn't either, and, besides, he'd already told me Kitson's fingerprints were not on the revolver.

O! *Phèdre* had a nurse called *Oenone*.

S! S was much better. One could spend many happy hours with S. Stretching it slightly, there were the Gordon-Smiths. Naomi couldn't have shot Corcoran unless she walked in her sleep; and she certainly could not have cracked Dagobert over the head with a black-jack tonight. Geoffrey could have, but why should he? It was odd that he had refused to take Perdita along with him tonight and had spent over two hours (unsuccessfully?) looking for Dagobert. But, knowing Geoffrey, was this really odd? Fearing an accident, he would naturally not want Perdita along; being thorough by nature, he would not come home again until he had searched everywhere.

Tyler's last name also began with S. But Tyler Sherman had left Dagobert at his own request on the Col d'Aze. That didn't mean that Tyler couldn't have parked the Renault somewhere, come back, sneaked up behind Dagobert, hit him over the head, searched his clothes for details of the Emerald jet engine and then, not finding them, driven home to go through our rooms once again! After all, we only had Tyler's word for which side he was on.

Why should Tyler kill Corcoran? He thought Vicki had done that. Or he pretended to think so. He had spoken tonight as though he had just discovered who Corcoran was and that Vicki had killed him. How could we be sure Tyler hadn't made his discovery on Friday night and had killed Rudolph himself? And dragged him down that ladder which he had explored that afternoon! Or – and my brain began to reel again – *found* Rudolph dead, *known* Vicki had shot him, and disposed of the body in order to prevent the murder from coming to light! In that case Tyler's fingerprints might well be found on the revolver. He could have put them there on purpose to obliterate Vicki's.

Vicki. . . . I sighed as I remembered that the entire Stein family started with S, and one of them – Mitzi – had very probably telephoned Dr Perrault tonight. Even Kitson had not argued with me when I had suggested it. Rudolph, however (as the victim), might logically be exempted as a suspect – unless he'd committed suicide! – and we could safely presume that Anna had not dropped in from Warsaw a week after her own death. . . .

There weren't any more S's that I could think of, but anyway the music had just stopped, which meant it was four o'clock and Dagobert was an early riser – at least, I'd see he was tomorrow.

F! It was staring me in the face. Fred! I hadn't thought of Fred Evans all day, which (at 4 a.m.) made him loom up most suspiciously in my mind. The very first time Fred had seen Dagobert he had been itching to crack him over the head and had said so. Fred had, to be sure, arrived the morning after Corcoran's murder, though his suède monk's shoes seemed rather mysteriously to have preceded him. But then Tyler Sherman also wore suède monk's shoes and what a vast number of enigmatic people there seemed to be around. . . . Somebody else's name began with an F. Yes, of course – Mademoiselle Françoise Perrault.

Cars were driving away from the Casino where it had all begun – Perdita's brutal discovery that Johnny was Naomi's lover – the quarrel – her shooting him and escape into our room – the gun that someone, the murderer, had found in Room 2 an hour later at midnight and used again to deadlier purpose. Someone who had murdered him because he was Johnny, the sexually successful bounder . . . Or because he was Corcoran, the occasional blackmailer. . . . Or because he was the test pilot who knew details of a highly secret jet engine. . . . Or because he was Rudolph Stein, who worked as an agent for the people who had killed Anna and Anna's mother. . . .

About this time I seem to remember recalling with a thrill of dawning intelligence that Sebastian Nevil's first name also began with an S. . . .

Chapter 29

I CONTINUED to analyse the situation along these lines until something (it seemed to be connected with the mongrel Fifi) made me start up frantically, battling with pillows and tightly tucked-in sheets. Quite unaccountably, Fifi himself leapt off my bed as I struggled for air. I heard him whimper reproachfully.

It was pitch dark. And I had not turned the light off!

'Geoffrey!' I said in a strangled voice and found I was running with sweat.

No, no, Geoffrey had switched out *Naomi's* light. . . . I began to breathe again, making a hoarse, panting sound which terrified Fifi.

'You went to sleep with the light on,' Dagobert said. 'I turned it out and tucked you in.'

'I was reading *Phèdre*. I must have dropped off for a second.'

'Yes, it's a quarter to ten.'

He pulled the curtains and threw back the shutters and crawled quickly back to bed. I collected myself slowly.

'What's Fifi doing here, or is it a relation?'

'He came with Tyler and Perdita about an hour ago when they brought my suitcase. I sent them off to the Casino Club to play tennis until you woke up. By an odd coincidence they were wearing tennis clothes and had racquets with them.'

'I hope they left the car.'

'No. I told them we had a spare tandem around at the police station.'

'There was,' I said, concentrating, 'something of vital importance I wanted to tell you.'

He looked interested, but when I went off into a long brood he returned to a large leather-bound volume he had propped across his knees. He stuck a thermometer in his mouth. Of course! It was to ask him how he felt. Before I could do this he removed the thermometer and said:

'What's retrograde amnesia?'

'Forgetting things. *Now* I remember!'

'That's what I was afraid,' he interrupted, turning a page and frowning. 'Here we are: "state of unconsciousness produced by violence applied to the skull and usually followed by retrograde amnesia. It may be a transient phenomenon from which the patient can recover completely . . ." We'll skip this part. "Death may occur without the patient regaining consciousness or he may partially recover and then – er – suddenly die . . ."'

He closed the book hastily and grabbed for the thermometer again. I got out of bed in alarm and put on Françoise Perrault's négligé.

'But last night,' I began anxiously, 'the doctor said . . .'

'Why don't we buy a négligé like that? Though, strictly speaking, I'm not supposed to be excited. . . .'

'Don't side-track the conversation.'

'Why not? Otherwise you'll begin asking questions that I don't know the answer to.'

'Yes,' I said, 'but here's an easy one you do know the answer to. Is O.S.F. Fred Evans?'

He looked so genuinely startled by the question that I believed him when he said blankly: 'Good heavens, no! Why do you ask? Oh, I see . . .'

'Then who *is* O.S.F.?'

He stuck the thermometer in his mouth and left it there this time. I repeated the question gently and he held out his medical dictionary, pointing out the words 'loss of memory' and 'headache'. I removed the thermometer firmly. He caught me in his arms and held me for a moment, and again I got side-tracked.

'Now what's my temperature?' he asked finally.

I read mechanically: 'Thirty-seven.'

'Then I must be dead.'

'Centigrade,' I added. 'Normal.'

He seemed disappointed. 'I thought I was feeling particularly well this morning,' he confessed. 'Of course, it's the first decent sleep I've had for days. From eleven-thirty, when someone knocked me out until half an hour ago. Ten hours – with negligible interruptions.'

He got out of bed. He fumbled in the suitcase Perdita and Tyler had brought from the hotel and removed a grey flannel suit, shoes and a shirt.

'I knew it was too good to last,' he sighed. And rambled on: 'They've forgotten socks. Shall we wait until after breakfast? The housekeeper once worked for a duchess, and she is dying to make a kedgeree for us and devilled kidneys – ."just like we have at home". I haven't seen Dr Perrault this morning. He was called out urgently just before I woke up. He didn't say anything to you about the bullet I gave him last night? No. Not that it matters really. It was just a far-fetched idea that crossed my mind, scarcely that. I don't think I'm hungry, anyway. But we'll have to eat the kedgeree and devilled kidneys whether we want to or not. . . .'

'Dagobert,' I interrupted him quietly, 'do you know who killed Corcoran . . .?'

He looked up from the shoe he was putting on his bare foot. His face was pale. 'No,' he said quickly. 'No, Jane. Really I don't. Though, I suppose, in view of everything, we'll have to . . . to *do* something at last. Unless you still think the tandem trip. It's downhill all the way from here to Perpignan, and we wouldn't have to climb back to Puig d'Aze. We could have our luggage sent on . . . if you think . . .'

He had made a hopeless knot in his shoe-lace, gave up trying to put it right and put on the other shoe. He said: 'Dr Perrault told you he'd identified the fingerprints on the revolver, I suppose . . .'

'Yes.'

'And they were O.S.F.'s.'

I nodded.

'I labelled the various fingerprints I gave him with silly initials because Dr Perrault has become extremely curious about the business, and, well, in case it turned out to be none of his business, I thought I'd leave him in the dark. Your initials, for instance, were H. M. "Helpmate". Not very good. I can smell breakfast. It's better than liquorice, but it makes me feel ill all the same. O.S.F. isn't much better, frankly. I suppose you'll want to know who it represents just the same.'

He mopped his forehead with the tail of his clean shirt and looked at me beseechingly. Fifi was watching me with a similar expression. I said nothing and Dagobert turned away.

'O.S.F. means "Old School Friend",' he said. He added with an unsuccessful smile: 'Not my old school friend Sebastian. Yours.'

'But . . .' I began.

'Yes, she was supposed to be asleep at the time. But unless Dr Perrault made a mistake, the fingerprints on the revolver are Naomi Gordon-Smith's.'

Chapter 30

DR PERRAULT had not made a mistake about the fingerprints. We found the photographs still in the rolltop desk. Dagobert verified them without triumph and my heart sank still further. I did not particularly admire Naomi. Did I even like her? The question had never arisen. She was simply a very old friend. She was why we had come to Puig d'Aze.

We had come because, in her own words, 'it was going to be such fun!' Because she was 'absolutely *relying* on us'.

And we had come to discover that she had committed murder.

Why had we interfered in the first place? Had we simply left that revolver in Room 2 beneath the window curtains where Naomi must have dropped it the problem would have been solved by normal police routine. Petitjean would have seen that the fingerprints were not Corcoran's and at once set about finding out whose they were.

The result would have been the same, only quicker and less painful.

But no! We had to take charge! We had to suppress vital information and work everything out for ourselves! We were now left with the choice of (*a*) personally confronting the Gordon-Smiths with what we knew, or (*b*) going, like loyal friends, behind their backs to the police and confessing that we had been clumsy busybodies. No, neither of us felt much self-satisfaction that Monday morning.

Meanwhile we faced the breakfast. Dr Perrault's housekeeper gave us porridge, kedgeree, devilled kidneys, English toast, butter and orange marmalade straight out of her Edwardian edition of Mrs Beeton's. Happily, Fifi was there and ate most of it.

We left the house before Dr Perrault himself returned. We were glad to escape inevitable explanations, though I wondered if we might not cravenly leave the whole business in his hands.

There were dozens of loose ends; but many of them probably had nothing to do with the murder of Squadron Leader Corcoran, and the police, if they wished, could tidy them up. We had lost our ambition to do so. Things like how Mitzi seemed to know or suspect that Dagobert had been knocked out on the Col d'Aze would doubtless fall into shape. The voice on the telephone had been feminine, not French. That was really all Dr Perrault could have been sure of. The telephone – especially the Puig d'Aze telephone – could easily distort such a voice so that it sounded like a child's. It could have distorted Naomi's voice. Naomi could have known that her husband had knocked out Dagobert, been filled with remorse and anonymously telephoned the doctor. ... Yes, it would all fall into place, probably.

At the moment neither Dagobert nor I cared.

We wandered out into the golden sunlight, feeling like pariahs in this mountain resort where everyone else was enjoying life. I tried to introduce a more pleasant note into our conjectures by telling Dagobert about Kitson's plans to launch Mitzi into the musical world. It was about eleven and Mitzi was, presumably, in the middle of her first public performance. We both prayed it would be a roaring success, which (as readers of musical periodicals already know) it was. Vicki's pride in her sister must at least partly compensate for the tragedy which had engulfed the rest of her family. The thought of the Kitson–Mitzi set-up cheered us up slightly.

Dagobert asked someone where the police station was and I wondered for a moment if he had decided to put the whole thing into the hands of the Aze-les-Bains police, who had proved themselves more efficient than Brigadier Petitjean in Puig d'Aze. But all he did was reclaim our tandem.

Physical exertion was not disagreeable, though Fifi, who had followed us, didn't care for it. After the breakfast Fifi had eaten this was understandable. He deserted us at the tennis courts, where we stopped for a moment to watch Tyler and Perdita playing, and returned later in the Renault with them.

They rushed over to us to ask if everything was all right and when we said yes, waited expectantly. Kitson had told them that Dagobert had been attacked, but had given no details. Dagobert was equally uncommunicative.

They offered to trade the car for the tandem, which Dagobert refused. I said we might all meet for luncheon and Tyler said swell, only there was a tea-dance at the Casino this afternoon, and they'd kind of thought of staying here for luncheon and dancing afterwards. Dagobert said: 'Do that,' and at Perdita's insistence promised rather evasively that we'd come back this afternoon and join them.

'Borrow the Humber,' Perdita suggested, 'but for heaven's sake don't bring the Gordon-Smiths.'

That we could promise with greater certainty.

I was glad that steering the tandem was entirely Dagobert's responsibility. Otherwise I think I should have given way to the temptation of taking the easier road which descended to Perpignan instead of the one which climbed towards Puig d'Aze. It was less than ten miles and actually the gradient was gentle. The sun was brilliant. This part of the Aze valley is green and in spring lush with fields of wild St Bruno lilies and pale blue flax. A breeze, cool from the high snowfields of the Pic des Quatre Vents, and full of nostalgic perfumes, stirred in the horse-chestnuts which lined the road. Nevertheless, those ten miles were the hardest of our Pyrenean journey.

I broke the silence after we had pedalled for about half an hour. 'I thought perhaps Kitson had seen Vicki in the Bugatti that night. But, of course, Vicki can't drive.'

He said a hundred yards or so farther on: 'She could have been a passenger. To handle Corcoran there must have been two of them.'

'Yes. Naomi and . . . but I *like* Geoffrey so much!'

This remark really didn't contribute very much to the subject and Dagobert made no reply. Ten minutes later I said:

People who threaten to commit suicide never do, I suppose.'

He avoided giving an opinion and asked: 'Has Naomi threatened to commit suicide?'

I'd forgotten that I'd told him nothing about that scene in Naomi's room last night. I gave him a detailed account of everything that had happened after we'd driven home after dinner last night – Naomi's morbid dread of being left alone, how we had waited and Geoffrey had finally gone in search of the Renault, Naomi's hysterical confession and Vicki's astonishing arrival, how we'd found Tyler searching our room and what he'd said to Vicki. I broke off at this point in my narrative.

'We'll have to tell Tyler at once!' I remembered. 'It's too unfair, too cruel to let him go on thinking that Vicki shot her brother.'

Dagobert made no comment, other than begging me to go on with what actually happened. I told him how Vicki had fainted and how before leaving her I'd suddenly broken the tragic news about her sister's death.

'Tyler should have done that days ago!' Dagobert said, nursing the back of his head. 'If he had, life would have been simpler.'

'Why do you say that?' I asked sharply.

'I'm dragging red herrings across the path again,' he apologized. 'I've been doing that unconsciously from the beginning, I'm afraid. As though . . . as though I didn't really want to find out who murdered Corcoran.'

But I refused to be led even further astray. 'How would it have made life simpler?'

'If Anna was, as Tyler tells us, a receiver of stolen information . . . and if Anna was dead, well, people might have stopped trying to steal information, going through our toothpaste, guide books and – er – me. I don't make myself very clear, do I?'

'No.'

'It may not be necessary in view of . . .'

'Naomi?'

'Yes. We got away from her for a moment, anyway.'

I nodded and we pedalled grimly on in silence. I tried to think of what a relief it was to know that Vicki Stein had not after all shot her brother. I said to myself that one great consolation in learning that X is the murderer is that it frees Y and Z from the shadows of doubt. At least one could now look Vicki and the others straight in the eyes.

But it was Naomi to whom every passing kilometre post brought us nearer. For a moment or two I clung to her alibi which had seemed so cast-iron. The two capsules she had taken at eleven that night – we had only her word for that. If the maid had found her in a drugged sleep the next morning it was because she had swallowed them after returning – *as arranged* – from Johnny's room. The light in her room at a quarter to two; how smoothly Geoffrey had explained the light away by saying he had come into her room at that hour to turn it out.

Geoffrey – Naomi had told me dramatically – '*knew everything*'. Geoffrey had been wandering in the village at midnight that Friday night. Yes, Geoffrey could know everything, and everything could well comprise much more than his wife's infidelity. Poor Geoffrey. . . .

For no reason I began to think of the two children staying with Geoffrey's parents in Kent and of the Andorran postage stamps that they would be receiving from their mother probably tomorrow. My eyes were so full of tears that I didn't see that we had reached the edge of the village.

I hoped Dagobert would ride straight to the police station. If alibis were to be cracked, it was now Brigadier Petitjean's job to do so. God knows we'd done enough on our own!

Dagobert turned left into the grounds of the Alexandra Hotel – as I'd known he would. We left the tandem with the liveried doorman.

I followed Dagobert into the lift and along the familiar corridor to Naomi's room. There was no answer to our knock and we tried Geoffrey's door. It opened at once. At the first sight of Geoffrey I realized that nothing we could say could give him a greater shock than the one he'd already had. He looked years older and I'd never before noticed how grey his hair was. He said come in mechanically and muttered:

'You've heard . . .'

Dagobert shook his head.

'. . . that Naomi's dead?'

Chapter 31

THE windows were closed and the room was stuffy. Geoffrey hadn't shaved. I smelt alcohol on his breath and noticed the bottle of duty-free brandy he had bought yesterday in Andorra half empty on the table. His hands were shaking so badly that he gave up trying to re-light his pipe. He jumped at the slightest sound.

When the telephone rang I jumped, too. I glanced at Dagobert as Geoffrey rushed to answer it. Dagobert was as ashen as Geoffrey.

Geoffrey said: 'Yes. Yes . . . yes,' several times into the telephone and finally let the instrument drop from his hands. He fumbled for several seconds before getting the receiver back into its cradle. It took a mental effort to realize that this nervous wreck was the same gentle, reliable Geoffrey Gordon-Smith we had known. He looked up, dull-eyed, as though trying to recognize us. He said vacantly:

'She just doesn't *want* to live. . . . She won't even try.'

'You said she was dead . . .'

Geoffrey nodded. 'She will be. There isn't a hope. They don't even pretend there's a hope. That was Dr Dupont from the hospital. There's a Dr Perrault there, too. And yet they won't let *me* see her.' He started up wildly and rasped: 'I've got to see her and tell her . . . something.'

He sank down on the edge of the bed and suddenly began to cry. I saw Dagobert turn away to study his feet. We both wondered if we could creep from the room unobserved.

'I've got to see her,' he repeated tonelessly, 'and tell her that I love her and always have.'

'She knows that, Geoffrey,' I said.

'Then why did she do . . . what she did?'

'Couldn't it have been an accident?' Dagobert said.

Geoffrey shook his head wearily; he had asked himself that question a hundred times and always received the same answer. 'No. She knew how dangerous those capsules were. We've discussed them often enough. Dr Dupont calls it an accident.

Dr Dupont is very kind and polite. Only . . . well, I know why she committed suicide.'

'*Tried* to commit suicide,' Dagobert corrected gruffly.

'Because of Corcoran,' he continued dully. 'She was in love with Corcoran. I've known it for months. I thought she'd get over it. She always has before. Only this time . . . well, she didn't.'

Neither of us said anything. Geoffrey continued to suck at his unlighted pipe, only dimly aware of our presence. He started for the telephone again, but gave it up half-way there. He'd been telephoning the hospital every five minutes and the staff was getting a little restive.

'The last time I telephoned a hospital like this,' he said, 'was in Ashford, when Mike was born.'

Michael, I remembered, was their youngest son. We'd sent him a silver mug.

'They both came through it with flying colours,' he added.

'She may again,' I said.

He stopped pacing the room. 'She doesn't want to. Because of him – of Corcoran.' His teeth clenched suddenly on the pipe-stem; it snapped in two. He must have caught sight of himself at that moment in the dressing-table mirror, for he stopped and stared, appalled at his own reflection. He said: 'Have you ever hated anyone?'

'Yes,' I said promptly, 'Johnny Corcoran.'

This seemed to please him and he gave me a look of gratitude. He began to straighten his necktie.

'I,' he stammered, 'I seem to have gone to pieces. I don't often. I never have, actually. I – I'm afraid I'm not very good at it. May I offer you something to drink? There's only whisky . . .' He examined the label of the half-empty bottle obviously for the first time. 'No, it seems to be brandy.'

We said 'No, thanks,' and asked him if there was anything we could possibly do. He said 'No, thank you very much'; then he suddenly remembered something.

'Yes!' He started for the bathroom door, jerked it open, then paused, flushing. 'I was going to ask you to take that bottle of Dr Hervey's capsules away and chuck them in the river or something.'

'With pleasure,' Dagobert said.

He hesitated, then strode through the bathroom into Naomi's

room. He returned with the bottle and handed it to Dagobert. He seemed relieved to get rid of it. Dagobert pocketed it without a glance. Geoffrey's face twitched.

He said shakily: 'I – thought of – finishing that bottle myself. I mean I didn't, not really. But I'd rather – not have it around. They promised to telephone again if she came out of her coma . . .'

He glanced towards the telephone, but sat down on the arm of a chair. He made an effort to control himself.

'I'm sorry about last night,' he said to Dagobert. 'What happened? I looked all over the place for you. I drove clear back to that hotel where we had dinner, but there wasn't a trace of you. Took another road home, I suppose. . . .' He shrugged, losing interest in the subject. 'Perhaps if Jane telephoned? The number's one-one-one.'

I telephoned the hospital to be told that Naomi's condition was grave and that that was all they were authorized to say at the moment. Perhaps if I telephoned later this afternoon, or this evening. Geoffrey read from my expression that there was no news. He thanked me politely and said that it was extremely kind of us to stay with him, but that if we had anything more important to do. . . . It was evident he wanted us to remain.

'Would you like to tell us what happened?' Dagobert said.

'Yes, yes – I would, if you don't mind listening. She took the things when I was out looking for you, we think. She must have done the same thing she did on Friday night – only this time – we don't know how many she swallowed – probably half a dozen. Anyway, enough to kill herself. Her light was on when I came back just before two, but I couldn't do anything about it this time because . . . well, she'd locked her door and the bathroom door, too. I don't know why. Yes, I do.'

He blew his nose once or twice and continued without looking at us. 'She thought I'd guessed about Corcoran and didn't want to see me. Poor little devil! If only I'd knocked in that door then and there! But . . . I didn't.'

'The doors are open now, aren't they?' Dagobert prompted.

He nodded indifferently. 'Yes, the hotel people unlocked them this morning. The maid found the door bolted and when she couldn't wake Naomi up she came running into me. I – well, we forced the door and sent for Dr Dupont. He brought a stomach pump. They took her to the hospital and called in a doctor from Aze-les-Bains who is supposed to be especially good, and . . . and that's all,' he concluded abruptly, as though astonished by the brevity of the story.

He tried to offer us brandy again, and when we refused he poured himself out half a tumbler. He began to drink it, but with a sudden grimace of distaste emptied it into a flower vase instead.

'She couldn't have really loved Corcoran,' he muttered.

'No, I think she'd got over it,' I said, not entirely convinced.

'Then why . . .' he began.

I thought I knew the reason why. But I didn't say that a woman who has shot her lover might almost reasonably commit suicide afterwards. Besides, Geoffrey must know what Naomi had done. Who else could have helped her get rid of the body? But if Naomi died and Geoffrey wished to maintain the fiction that his children's mother had not been a murderess – that was really none of our business. If Naomi recovered. . . . Then we'd have to think again. Meanwhile I interrupted quickly:

'She told me last night that it was you she'd always loved.'

This was only half true – she'd said Geoffrey *and* Johnny, but it seemed to comfort him. He sighed.

'You probably didn't think very highly of Naomi. She was affected and silly in many ways. I know, I know. I was quite aware of the fact that what she said about art, literature and music was largely nonsense when it wasn't plain wrong. But it amused me. I used to see other people wincing when she made howlers, but to me she was like a child playing grown-up games. I found it endearing. Then she was a bully, if you like. She arranged everything for everybody. Do you know why? Because she actually wanted everyone to be happy. And most of the time what she arranged was exactly what people wanted. Perhaps she was not always faithful to me. But she never flaunted it, never humiliated me. And she always came back. Above everything – and no one ever realized it – Naomi was a mother. I have two sons at home who know that she was the kindest and most unselfish person on earth. When you think of her, I wish you'd remember this.' His voice dropped to a murmur. 'It's all I shall remember of my wife . . . her goodness. The rest does not matter.'

He didn't seem to hear the telephone ringing and I answered it. It was the hospital. Naomi, Dr Dupont told me, had come out of her coma but was sinking. It would be advisable for her husband to come at once.

Chapter 32

We went to the hospital with Geoffrey and waited downstairs for news. It was long past lunch time, but we were as unaware of this as Geoffrey himself. I had seen him follow the nurse, shuffling along the polished corridor like a broken old man, his lips moving as though in prayer. I wondered if he were praying what I was praying: that Naomi would die swiftly and in peace.

Dr Perrault caught us in the waiting-room before we could escape. We were in no mood to discuss things with him. His eyes lighted up as he spotted us and Dagobert's face went blank. I cut him short in the midst of fingerprints and O.S.F.s by asking him about Naomi. He immediately became professional.

'Mrs Gordon-Smith is Dr Dupont's patient,' he explained, 'and you must ask him. *Dr Dupont* – I may say – takes a very grave view.'

He didn't exactly say that Dr Dupont was an ignorant fusspot, that Dr Dupont knew nothing about his *métier*, that Dr Dupont lived on encouraging foolish foreigners to imagine they were iller than they were – but his tone and manner implied it. My heart sank, though I remembered that Dr Perrault disliked Dr Dupont and disagreed automatically with his opinions. Dr Dupont could be right. Dr Dupont *had* to be right.

Dagobert changed the subject. 'Have you examined the bullet I gave you last night?'

'Yes – it's the same.'

Though they spoke in French, I followed this much.

'The same as what?' I said.

'The same,' he told me, 'as the one your husband gave me the other day.'

'The one I dug out of the wall of Corcoran's room,' Dagobert explained.

'Both were fired from Corcoran's revolver,' Dr Perrault said. 'But the essential,' he continued, getting excited again, 'is the fingerprints!'

'Yes,' Dagobert agreed evasively. He stared with astonishment at his wrist-watch. 'I mustn't keep you from Mrs Gordon-Smith,' he apologized. 'Meanwhile, I've something – rather important.'

And he bolted for the door. Dr Perrault stared after him, shaken in his diagnosis that Dagobert had completely recovered from last night's blow on the head. I caught up with Dagobert in the street. He has long legs and I had to run to keep pace with him.

'What have you to do that's so important?'

He slowed down at once. 'That's true. What, indeed?'

'Those two bullets couldn't have been fired from the same gun!' I said suddenly. 'It doesn't make sense.'

'No,' he said. 'Dr Perrault could be wrong. The science of ballistics is still in its infancy.' He broke off, then added miserably: 'Nothing makes sense, Jane. Nothing . . .'

A thought so dreadful crossed my mind that I refused to think about it. Had we only told Dr Perrault frankly whose fingerprints we had found on the revolver – Naomi might *not* recover. A slight miscalculation, a mistaken diagnosis . . . doctors can presumably make such errors. I shivered as Dagobert suddenly stopped and said – almost as though the same thought had occurred to him:

'I'm going back to have a word with Perrault. You might wait for me in the café in the square.'

I waited for him in the café, but he didn't come. I waited two hours over a small cup of lukewarm black coffee before I realized I was faint with something – doubtless hunger – and ate one stale *croissant*. Fred Evans found me there and insisted on giving me a glass of beer. What he really wanted was help for an article he was writing for *Workers' Playtime* about the 'New Star who had blazed into the Musical Firmament'. The Stein kid had, everyone said, given a smashing performance of something called the Goldstein (or maybe it was Goldwyn) Variations, and Kitson had said he'd run Fred out of the community if he failed to give her a rave notice. Fred was quite willing to rave, but he wondered if I could help him get it into technical language.

I wasn't much help and the beer and the sunshine made me sleepy. I decided to walk back to the hospital. I ran into Mitzi and Kitson coming out of Ann's Pantry. They were having a violent argument about the interpretation of a 'fugal passage in D Minor', which I interrupted in order to congratulate Mitzi on her triumph. Kitson said she had played indifferently, but might improve. Irritable, because no one seemed in the least concerned about Naomi, I said:

'Perhaps Mitzi would improve if she got to bed at a reasonable hour.'

'Er, yes, I seize your point,' Kitson said hastily.

'And have you yet thought of why she telephoned Dr Perrault last night to say that Dagobert had been attacked?'

'Because Dr Dupont didn't reply?' Kitson suggested.

Mitzi looked me straight in the eye. 'I guess Jane might as well know,' she said. 'Kitson hired one of his local toughs to knock out Dagobert – wanted to put the wind up him. Kitson told me just before he picked you up last night, so I went out and telephoned the doctor.' She added innocently: 'I've not got anything against Dagobert, especially.'

'What an infant prodigy she is!' Kitson sighed admiringly.

'Yes,' I agreed, 'if she can play the harpsichord as prodigiously as she lies . . .'

I continued on my way to the hospital. There I learned that Dr Perrault had driven off with Dagobert nearly two hours ago. Naomi's condition was neither worse nor better. Geoffrey was still with her. I went back to the hotel. I tried to buy a copy of the Continental *Daily Mail*, but it only arrived in Puig d'Aze at five o'clock in the afternoon. I wrote a long and extremely dull letter to mother about the weather and the St Bruno lilies and had tea sent up to my room.

Dagobert telephoned me a few minutes before six. He was at Dr Perrault's in Aze-les-Bains and he thought I might be worried. I did not reply to that and he said he'd be back shortly. Tyler and Perdita would give him a lift in the Renault.

I interrupted him finally. 'What is it, Dagobert?'

He stopped talking and for a moment I thought the line had been disconnected. Then he said:

'You were the last person to see Naomi last night, weren't you?'

'As far as I know Vicki and I were, yes.'

'You heard Naomi bolt the door after you. And the door through the bathroom into Geoffrey's room was, you told me, also bolted?'

'Yes. I noticed it particularly. She seemed very nervous at the thought of being alone with him. He's told us why.'

'Quite. I've checked up with the manager of the Alexandra, who says it was still bolted when the maid found Naomi this morning.'

'Does it matter?' I asked anxiously.

'Probably not,' he said. 'It was a point Dr Perrault raised. He's taking this business seriously.'

'Have you told him that the fingerprints were Naomi's?'

'No, I've told him they were mine. That's why he thinks we have to tackle the problem from the Naomi angle.'

'But there isn't any Naomi angle! I mean, no one could have tried to kill Naomi – except herself.'

He agreed. Something in the way he agreed made me uncomfortable. 'Just to satisfy Dr Perrault,' he continued, 'you telephoned Naomi at half past one, didn't you? So that we can say she was alive and well and safely locked in her own room at that hour?'

I didn't answer him for a second, and during that second my heart stopped beating. I thought I had given Dagobert a complete version of last night, but I had forgotten one small detail.

'Can't we?' he prompted.

'No, we can't,' I said. 'Not that it can possibly make any difference. Naomi's telephone wasn't working when I called her. So I tried Geoffrey's room. She answered me eventually from there. She had to come through the bathroom to get there. So she must have unbolted the bathroom door herself.'

'I see.'

He added, after a moment's reflection: 'I think we'll suppress this little detail, too. As you say, it cannot possibly make any difference, and she probably rebolted the door when she went back to bed. We'll ask her when she recovers.'

'Dagobert! Is she going to recover?'

'Of course.'

'And is that . . . a good thing?'

I heard him inhale sharply and let out his breath slowly before he answered: 'Nothing's any good. I suppose I ought to come home. . . . The lovebirds are waiting outside in the Renault for me.'

'You don't sound very enthusiastic.'

'No . . .'

But he didn't ring off. I said, half-dreading to receive an answer: 'Why does Dr Perrault wish to tackle the Naomi angle?'

'Because of the sodium ethyl iso-methylbutyl.'

'That Naomi took?'

'Yes. He's not very happy about it.'

'You're not, either?'

'Not very. You remember the capsules. The stuff's packed loosely in them; normally they're about half full. Only some of the capsules in the bottle I have are nearly empty while others are packed to twice their ordinary capacity. These are at the top – the ones Naomi would get hold of first. Dr Perrault doesn't think this could be the chemist's fault. He says that if Naomi should die it will be his duty to inform the police that the capsules have been tampered with.'

He rang off. I held the receiver in my hand for several minutes before I remembered to put it back again.

Chapter 33

TYLER and Perdita knocked at my door about half an hour later. They had left Dagobert at the hospital and had just heard about Naomi. Perdita was upset and obviously wanting to talk to me privately about it. As I didn't want to talk about it I sent her upstairs to change her tennis clothes. Tyler lingered. He clearly had something to say and didn't know how to begin. Finally, he said:

'I don't think Dagobert approves of me. Is it because of Perdita?'

'Is what because of Perdita?' I said impatiently.

Tyler coloured, but persisted. 'I haven't exactly proposed marriage yet, but everybody – except, maybe, Perdita herself – can see I'm working up to it.'

'Would you mind if we put off the problems of young love until a more suitable occasion?'

His flush deepened. 'I guess you're right,' he admitted. 'Do you happen to know why Dagobert has asked me to meet him in about half an hour at the Hôtel Commerce?'

'It's the first I've heard of it. Perhaps he's not satisfied with your alibi for last Friday night.'

Tyler achieved a faint grin. 'You may have something there. That would certainly account for his not approving of me. You know what? I think he half suspects me of having bumped off Rudolph Stein myself!'

I made no comment and Tyler awkwardly withdrew. I felt suddenly cooped up in the room and went out. It wasn't seven yet and the streets were busy. I passed the Hôtel Commerce, followed by Fifi, who had arrived in the Renault. In the church square the usual loafers were watching the seven o'clock bus, which was about to leave for Perpignan. I watched, too.

Then I recognized the furtive figure in the shabby mackintosh and beret standing in the bus queue. It was Vicki. She was carrying a large fibre suitcase. She kept glancing round uneasily, as though afraid of being seen. I looked in vain for Mitzi.

While I watched a tall man swiftly crossed the square and joined her. He took her suitcase. It was Dagobert.

Vicki jumped as he touched her and began to bite her fingernails. The bus doors closed and the bus nosed its way across the square. Vicki watched its departure with resignation, as though she had never really expected to find herself safely installed inside. Dagobert spoke to her quietly and took her arm. I saw them take a narrow street behind the church and disappear into the Hôtel Commerce.

A moment later Tyler Sherman parked his Renault in front of the Commerce and entered. I hesitated, my curiosity struggling against a reluctance to probe further into what was clearly not my business. The struggle was brief, and I walked into the Commerce, followed by Fifi, who theoretically lived there.

There was no one in the downstairs café except the landlady, who was serving drinks to two workmen. She glanced at me without surprise and indicated the stairs behind her.

'Room 2,' she said.

I must have looked thunderstruck, for she added, as though in explanation: 'He said you were all to be sent up to Room 2.'

'All? He?' I began, but as it was plain that she was no wiser than I was, I murmured: 'Yes, of course,' and started for the stairs. He, presumably, was Dagobert, and I wondered what Fred Evans would think of his room being used as a place of rendezvous.

Fred, however, was not there. But Vicki was, and Tyler and Dagobert. They looked at me blankly and Dagobert said:

'Strictly speaking, you weren't invited, Jane. Do you mind if she stays?'

Vicki and Tyler, who occupied opposite corners of the room and were studiously avoiding each other's eyes, both shook their heads indifferently. Dagobert closed the door behind me and said to Vicki:

'Jane also has a right to hear about your brother Rudolph. After all, you fainted on her last night when Tyler accused you of shooting him.'

Neither of them said anything and Dagobert added, quietly:

'May I suggest why Vicki fainted? She fainted from sheer relief. Because, you see, Vicki did not shoot her brother.'

Vicki for the first time stopped biting her fingernails. She shot a glance of supplication at Dagobert, which he pretended not to see. Tyler, flushing, growled:

'I don't care whether she did or not. I said so last night. He was a son of a bitch and deserved it.'

Vicki flared up at the word. 'What are you knowing about it?'

Dagobert grinned slightly. 'Not much. Tell him.'

Vicki's red hair glinted in the dusk which invaded the room and her breast was heaving. She made a last effort to control herself, but luckily Tyler himself upset it. He muttered, defensively:

'Well, anyway – I loathed his guts.'

'You!' she said witheringly. 'You're not worthy to speak of my brother. He is saving me and Mitzi from the concentration camp and risking his life ...'

'Sure, sure,' Tyler placated her, 'but that's a long time ago. Since then ...'

'Since then he is still risking his life. For Anna.'

'And making a good thing out of it, too.'

'I hate you! You are knowing nothing. Three times Rudolph has been in Warsaw to smuggle away Anna. Twice he is being tortured and saving himself by saying he is a Communist spy who brings information to Anna. This is information that he and Anna are concocting from papers she is stealing from the safe of the Minister she works for. You think Rudolph and Anna will work for the pigs who murdered our mother! Since five years Anna is trying to escape. Since five years Rudolph is working to help her to escape. Last week my sister is caught and murdered by the Communists. Why? Do you think it is because she is working for them?'

'That's true,' Tyler said. 'But ...'

'But Anna is dead,' Vicki said mechanically. She turned towards the open window, where, over the rooftops, the last rays of the sunset lingered among the grey tiles. She seemed to have forgotten there was anyone else in the room. She murmured: 'Anna is dead and I am glad because she suffered much and Rudolph suffered for her and must suffer no more ...'

'That's true,' Tyler repeated unhappily, 'and I guess there's no use going into it any further. Okay. Rudolph was a swell guy ...' He spoiled it by adding: 'He wasn't going to sell out the specifications of the Emerald jet engine, I suppose ...'

'No,' Vicki said dully. 'They would have been altered before they reached Warsaw. With them he would be saving Anna maybe. Maybe not.'

'We only have his word for that,' Tyler remarked sceptically. 'We haven't even got that, since he's dead. . . . By the way, how do you work into it, Vicki? Why did he come all the way from London to Puig d'Aze to meet you? Were you supposed to take the specifications on to Warsaw or what?'

Vicki came back from a private reverie of her own. She glanced at Tyler contemptuously. 'You are knowing so much. Last night you have it all worked out. Now you ask me.'

'Yeah,' Tyler muttered doubtfully, 'I didn't like it much at the time. As Corcoran, the famous test pilot, he was too conspicuous to do his dirty work – I beg your pardon, his mission of salvation – for himself. He had to get his little sister to do it, huh?'

Vicki continued to regard him with scorn. I thought there was almost an air of smugness about her, as though she held a trump card Tyler didn't suspect. She glanced beyond Tyler to Dagobert in the background and the smugness went. Tyler said suddenly:

'Okay. You loved and admired him. You didn't shoot him. Who did?'

Vicki shook herself slightly and said: 'Pardon?'

'You heard me. Who killed him?'

'I don't know.' Her lips went tight. 'Maybe *you* did!'

It was nearly dark in the room by this time and Dagobert, stirring from the shadows in the corner, switched on the light. The bulb behind the moth-filled alabaster bowl gave a sickly yellow glow. Beneath it Vicki and Tyler faced each other.

'I don't seem to have restored confidence between you two,' Dagobert remarked.

He opened the door. The rest of us had not heard the footstep outside. Fred Evans stood gaping at us in astonishment.

'What's the big idea?' he began aggressively.

'We're reconstructing that crime you wanted to write up for *Workers' Playtime*,' Dagobert said dryly.

'Why do you have to do it in my room?'

'Because that's where it took place. We've got to the state where we're all accusing each other.' He glanced uneasily at his wrist-watch. 'Other possibly important witnesses will be arriving shortly,' he said. 'So we'd better clear away certain – er – domestic points before they come.'

'Don't mind me, old boy,' Fred said with heavy sarcasm. 'I only live here.' He reached for a packet of Players. 'Would there be any objection if I smoke a cigarette?'

'Remind me about those cigarettes later, will you?' Dagobert said.

'I don't get it, laddie. What have cigarettes to do with it?'

'Just a small detail which might interest readers of *Workers' Playtime*. You know, Sherlock Holmes stuff.'

Fred stuck the cigarette between his lips and began to crack the joints of his fingers. 'No, I don't know.'

He continued to crack his finger-joints methodically. He became aware that both Dagobert and I were watching the process curiously. He stopped and glanced at his own fingers. I don't know whether he, too, noticed that they had become stained with nicotine during these last three days.

'You ought to go back to Carmelas,' Dagobert said helpfully. 'They don't stain the fingers. But let's not wander. It's complicated enough without that. We were,' he said inaccurately, 'just going back to that moment – about five past twelve on Friday night – when Vicki said she saw Corcoran. Where were you at that moment?'

'You know damn well where I was. In Perpignan. I thought you said let's not wander.'

'Your shoes were under Vicki's bed. I thought you might have been under there with them.'

Tyler started, stared at Vicki and then looked suddenly away. Vicki giggled. Fred laughed.

'Only wish I had been, old boy.'

'Possibly you were still in the box-room next door,' Dagobert conceded.

Fred began to get angry. 'If you're trying to suggest I was in Puig the night of the murder. . . . What about the crowd of people who saw me get off the Perpignan bus at eleven o'clock on Saturday morning?'

'What about the crowd of people in Aze-les-Bains who saw you get on that bus at half past ten that Saturday morning?' Dagobert asked mildly. 'You know, Fred, you should have gone farther down the line. Though, in a way, I sympathize with you. Riding a tandem alone is hot work, even in the middle of the night. We've recovered the tandem, by the way, in case that's been worrying you. Or is something else worrying you?'

'Yes,' Fred said, 'you. Whether to crack you over the head or . . .'

'Not again, Fred,' Dagobert protested. 'I've hardly recovered from last night. Luckily, Vicki sent the doctor up to my rescue. It was Mitzi who telephoned, but I'm sure the idea was Vicki's.'

Vicki had gone white, but she returned Dagobert's interrogative glance without flinching. I remembered how nervous and worried she had been last night when Dagobert and Tyler had not turned up. Even then she knew (or suspected?) that the danger which threatened them was real. She said:

'No, it wasn't my idea to send the doctor. It was Fred's idea.'

She continued earnestly: 'Fred didn't mean to hurt you. He – he just happened to be there – looking around – when you came. So, so . . .'

'So he cracked me over the head – and continued to look around.'

'Yes,' she nodded. 'And ran home and told me. And Fred – he was worried – and said we'd better telephone a doctor in case he'd really hurt you . . .'

Dagobert smiled. 'I like to think that's true. Perhaps it is.'

Fred said impatiently: 'Get on with it, chum. You can't prove any of this, but I like to hear you talk. So I was here in Puig d'Aze all along – sez you.'

'Not all along,' Dagobert corrected. 'Only since late Friday afternoon, when you arrived from Andorra.'

'By bus, I suppose?'

'No, there aren't any buses. You came in Corcoran's Bugatti. You entered this hotel in exactly the same way that Corcoran left it. Except that you were alive, and he wasn't. I mean, you arrived via the shed, ladder and box-room, after travelling from Andorra under the canvas cover over the Bugatti's back seat. It must have been stuffy, especially as you smoked a Carmela cigarette during the journey.'

'You know everything, don't you!' Fred sneered.

'Yes,' Dagobert said without pleasure. He sat down, borrowed a cigarette from Fred and, when no one spoke, continued:

'Corcoran had instructions to pick you up at a certain café in Andorra, where he parked his car. While he had luncheon you made yourself snug under the luggage cover. He was to smuggle you into France and into this hotel, where, at his leisure, he would give you the specifications of the Emerald jet engine. Luckily, he never had the chance, or you wouldn't have kept on looking for them.'

'*I* looked for them!' Vicki interrupted. 'I don't want them – now.'

'No,' Dagobert said. 'If Tyler had only told you sooner that Anna was no longer alive . . . we'd all have been spared . . . things like rifling rooms and knocking me over the head.'

'It was a pleasure knocking you over the head,' Fred said.

Dagobert nodded. He looked as though he wished Fred had done a better job of it. Last night, I remembered, the fact that he was still alive had seemed to depress him. He glanced again at his wrist-watch and said:

'The others ought to be along in a minute, so we'd better finish this part first. . . . Vicki, who paid for your trip to Puig and made reservations at the Hôtel Commerce for you?'

She glanced at Fred and began: 'But I paid myself and . . . and . . .'

'If somebody from *Workers' Playtime* made the arrangements,' Dagobert cut in impatiently, 'your loyalty is misplaced! This evening's Continental *Daily Mail* contains a paragraph saying that *Workers' Playtime* has been suspended, pending an inquiry into subversive activities. I may be partly responsible. After reading Fred's credentials, I telegraphed a friend of mine in the Home Office and asked him to look into *Workers' Playtime*. I also gave him the number of Fred's passport – so that's probably no good any longer.'

'Yes,' Vicki said, 'it was someone from *Workers' Playtime*. I don't know his name . . .'

'He also, I suppose, gave you Fred's passport, suitcase full of dashing new clothes, credentials as a Special Correspondent and, of course, those very fetching suède shoes – which, by the way, I'll accept in exchange for the ones he ripped to pieces last night.'

Vicki nodded. 'Yes, he did.'

Tyler stirred uncomfortably and ran a hand across his fair-cropped head.

'So Fred was brother Rudolph's contact,' he murmured.

'No,' Dagobert said, 'Fred *is* brother Rudolph.'

Chapter 34

'Now that's all cleared up,' Fred said, mopping his brow, 'I wish I had a drink.'

'It isn't quite cleared up.'

Fred sighed. 'I see what you mean, old boy.'

He wandered across the room, paused beside Vicki to give her hand a reassuring squeeze and pounced on the bottle of Highland Fling, which was the last relic of Corcoran in the room. He shook the bottle hopefully. It still contained the modest single we had left in it the night we had found the revolver. Fred measured it carefully into a tooth-mug, murmuring:

'I don't know who needs this most.'

'You probably,' Dagobert said, 'when you tell us how you disposed of Corcoran's body.'

Fred dropped the tooth-mug and the bottle. Both shattered as they struck the stone floor. 'Don't say things like that, old boy – suddenly,' he complained, regarding the pieces sadly, 'my nerves aren't good.'

'Tell him, Rudolph,' Vicki said quickly.

'You tell him. He knows all about it, anyway.'

'The rest of us don't,' Tyler said.

Vicki began to stammer and Dagobert came to her rescue.

'Vicki saw Corcoran for the first time at five past twelve, just as she's told us. Though not in the corridor – and not alive. She knocked at Corcoran's door to find out whether her brother could safely come in. He hadn't seen Corcoran yet. He had stayed in Vicki's room after the drive from Andorra. There was no answer, but the key was in the door and Vicki entered. She found Corcoran dead. She ran back into her own room for Rudolph – or shall we continue to say Fred? There was a rapid council of war. If Corcoran were found murdered there would be a full police inquiry. Fred would be discovered, and how he got to Puig d'Aze and who he was. There would also be no chance of finding the specifications Corcoran had come to deiver. They acted hastily. Of course they knew about the box-room next door and the ladder which leads down to the shed. Between them they got the body into the Bugatti and fixed the canvas cover over it. They also put our tandem on the luggage rack. They drove to the Col d'Aze, got out, removed the tandem and the spare petrol tin and let the Bugatti plunge into the gorge. I imagine Fred then climbed down, poured petrol over the wreck and set it alight. Am I right, Fred?'

'Quite right, old boy,' Fred murmured, scraping up the mess on the floor. He sucked the spilled whisky from his finger-tips with regret and appeared to be only half-listening.

'Then they came back to Puig on the tandem, up the ladder again and into Vicki's room. This was about five o'clock. I happened to stroll down to the courtyard shortly afterwards and our tandem had returned. Vicki crept into this room with the key they had taken when they turned out the light and locked up after removing Corcoran's body. They were going to search the room thoroughly, but Vicki found Jane and me here. She put up a most unconvincing story about an amorous appointment with Corcoran. Jane and I retired and afterwards, I suppose, they did search the room. Fred, just before dawn, left the hotel, this time alone on the tandem which he rode as far as Aze-les-Bains, where he abandoned it. He jumped on the ten-thirty morning bus from Perpignan and arrived back in Puig at eleven. He came to the Commerce, where he was lucky enough to get Room 2. That was handy, as it would give him a chance to search the room thoroughly. He had to find Corcoran's notes. Or rather, not knowing that his sister Anna was beyond help, he *thought* he had to find them. As we know, he didn't . . .'

Fred looked up with a grin. 'How do you know?' he asked, with a broad display of protuberant teeth. 'As it happens, chum, I have found them.'

Dagobert, fiddling with the door-knob, did not at once register this. 'There's somebody at the door,' he said. 'What!'

'You heard me, old boy,' Fred said. His smile became wistful. 'I'm losing my grip, taking you all into my confidence like this. There might be a couple of thousand quid in it if I didn't. Maybe I'm just big-hearted.'

'The whisky label!' Vicki exclaimed.

Fred nodded. 'Yeah, cute, isn't it?'

We all stared at the soaked Highland Fling label Fred had

absentmindedly peeled from the broken bottle. The glass was opaque, and this had hidden the fact that the reverse side of the label was covered with minutely drawn diagrams and mathematical symbols. We gaped at them with interest, but without enlightenment. Fred struck a match. The damp label spluttered and burned. Even Fred looked relieved as he scrunched the remaining ashes beneath the sole of his suède shoe.

'I may,' he murmured, 'have to fly one of those engines one day – on the same side I flew for last time.'

Tyler stammered: 'I've called you a lot of names in the past. I'd like to say . . .'

'Skip it, pal,' Fred said. 'You called Corcoran those names. You put it mildly.'

'Anyway, I'd like to say . . .' He turned to Vicki, who watched him coolly. 'Damn it all,' he blurted out, 'won't anybody let me apologize? Your brother's a . . .'

'Swell guy?' Vicki mocked. She relented an instant later and added gently: 'I know, Ty.'

Dagobert cleared his throat. 'Before we all get too matey,' he frowned, 'there's the matter of Corcoran's murder.'

'You said someone was listening at the door!' I suddenly remembered.

He opened the door, but Mitzi had already removed her eye from the keyhole and with Fifi strolled nonchalantly in. She called back over her shoulder:

'It's okay, Perdita. They're expecting us.'

'We are not,' Dagobert said sharply. 'But have you seen . . .'

'Kitson?' Mitzi supplied. 'Yes, he's downstairs at the bar, he says, "fortifying himself for the ordeal." He told us to run on up. What was Rudolph burning just now?'

'None of your business!' Vicki snapped.

Kitson himself peeked shyly in, pushing Perdita before him. 'Courage, my dear,' he murmured, letting his hand linger affectionately on Perdita's bare arm.

He caught my eye and removed it. 'Where?' he said briskly, 'is Gordon-Smith and that flighty wife of his? Dr Dupont tells me he's performed a miraculous cure and she'll be with us again in no time. These inefficient women who try to commit suicide!'

Dagobert said: 'Naomi didn't try to commit suicide. Someone made a very clumsy attempt to poison her.'

Kitson sat down suddenly on the bed beside Tyler. 'Oh,' he muttered.

Fred broke the ensuing silence by saying:

'I'd still like a drink. Did the same person who shot Corcoran also try to poison Naomi?'

Dagobert seemed not to hear the question; he was listening for the final footstep in the corridor which would complete the company assembled in the room. I saw that the cigarette Fred had given him had become a glowing stub between his fingers. He was not, apparently, conscious that it was burning them. There was a knock on the door.

It opened and Geoffrey entered. He glanced at Dagobert, nodded and retreated into a corner. Dagobert said:

'Yes, Fred, the same person,' and went slightly green.

He went on more quickly, addressing Geoffrey, though he didn't look at him: 'You missed the part about the disposal of Corcoran's body,' he said. 'Fred and Vicki got rid of it for reasons of their own. Kitson, as a matter of fact, saw them driving away in the Bugatti, or rather he saw a man and a woman. I thought for a while he'd seen you and Naomi. This unforeseen disposal of the body confused us all because it seemed reasonable to suppose that the person who'd shot Corcoran had also got rid of his body in a way to make it appear like an accident. It must have confused the murderer most of all. For the murderer had planned things very differently.'

He stopped pacing the room and sat down on the edge of a straight chair under the light. His face was drawn; he looked like a prisoner who has been kept awake for days under a brutal crossfire of questions until a confession is at last forced from him. He slumped forward and stroked Fifi's ears mechanically.

'I don't know why I asked you all to come here,' he stammered. 'It's really nothing to do with you. I thought you might help in getting certain points straight, but they don't matter any more. If anyone would like to go . . .'

No one stirred. Tyler said quietly: 'It does matter, Dagobert, because some of us are under suspicion of murder.'

Dagobert agreed wearily. He looked at Geoffrey, as though begging for help. Geoffrey said tonelessly:

'My wife had arranged to come to this room after midnight on Friday when Corcoran was shot. Brown found Corcoran's revolver over there under the curtains. Two shots had been fired from it. The fingerprints on it were my wife's.'

He stopped. Fred stared at him with disbelief. 'You mean to say that Naomi . . .' he began.

Geoffrey's face became a mask and Dagobert said: 'No. Naomi did not shoot Corcoran. Naomi did not keep her appointment. Naomi took a sleeping draught exactly as she has told us and was asleep from ten-thirty to eight o'clock the next morning. But the murderer thought she was coming. Corcoran had said so. And the murderer knew that Naomi's fingerprints were on that revolver.'

'How could they have been?' Tyler asked.

'That afternoon, driving back from Andorra, Naomi had stopped the Bugatti and fired Corcoran's revolver – four times. I don't quite know why. Target practice? Trying to frighten him?'

'She says target practice,' Geoffrey said quickly.

'In any case she frightened us,' Dagobert said wryly. 'The third bullet missed us by a couple of yards. That was the bullet I didn't give you last night, Kitson. Dr Perrault says that it was fired from Corcoran's gun, not that it now needs establishing.'

'Is *that* what was going on?' Fred exclaimed. 'Being battened down in the back seat, I couldn't imagine. It scared the pants off me.'

'And you think the murderer knew that Naomi's fingerprints were on the revolver,' Tyler mused. 'How? Oh, you mean Corcoran told . . . told him.'

Dagobert nodded.

'Hey, wait a minute!' Tyler said. 'There were only two shots fired when you found that revolver. What about the other four? I mean the four Naomi had fired that afternoon?'

Dagobert shrugged indifferently, as though he had suddenly lost interest. 'It's those missing cartridges which prove that the murder was carefully thought out. And premeditated. They and Naomi's intact fingerprints.'

'He used gloves? So as not to obliterate her fingerprints?'

'Something like it,' Dagobert nodded. 'And carefully removed the four spent cartridges, replacing them with fresh ones.'

'Where did he get the fresh ones?'

'There were dozens in the holster.'

'What did he do with the empty shells?'

'Got rid of them,' Dagobert said dully. 'When you searched the room, Fred, you didn't by any chance find them – say, among the debris in the electric light bowl?'

'I never looked there,' Fred admitted foolishly.

As though glad of an excuse to do something, Fred climbed quickly on to Dagobert's chair and reached in among the dead moths. We all – all except Dagobert – watched him stupidly. He climbed down again, looking badly shaken. There were four spent cartridges in his hand.

'I still need that drink,' he said earnestly. 'Maybe we all do. Oi! Mitzi! Run downstairs and do something about it. And get a move on!'

Perdita said suddenly: 'I'll go.'

I glanced at Dagobert. He remained remote and expressionless as he continued to stroke Fifi's ears. Mitzi, abashed into unfamiliar silence, continued to clutch Vicki's hand. Perdita, receiving no answer, went. She closed the door so quietly behind her that we were almost unaware that she had gone. Dagobert said:

'She didn't use gloves. She used that crimson scarf. She shot him at eleven o'clock, not at twelve. She fled to our room, but while she lay on our bed she began to think. She would frankly confess that she had shot at him. But the police would decide she had missed. They would find a bullet in the wall well above the bed. And they would discover Naomi's fingerprints. But of course there had to be two shots fired. She waited until nearly midnight and came back into this room. It must have taken nerve. While midnight was striking she shot wild above the bed where the calendar now hangs. She carefully put the revolver beside the curtains where an intruder from the window might have dropped it. She knew it was covered with Naomi's fingerprints – Corcoran had described the shooting incident of the afternoon and told her that Naomi would be arriving at half past twelve. In brief, Naomi must be accused of the crime. We know that she had reason to loathe Naomi almost as much as she hated Corcoran. She went back to our room and waited for us. She was hysterical when we arrived at a quarter to one. She had a right to be, for more reasons than one. In the first place, why hadn't Naomi come, screamed on finding Corcoran dead – and, of course, roused the whole hotel? She opened our door once or twice to find out what was going on – or rather why nothing was going on. And this is where,' he said, rising and straying over towards the window, 'I owe you all a deep apology. There was something the first night which ought to have given the show away. I overlooked it. I think I must have overlooked it on purpose – because, I suppose, I was so blindly determined to prove that it was somebody else – one of you – who had murdered Corcoran. . . .'

He glanced down from the window into the courtyard and turned miserably to me.

'You may remember, Jane. Perdita suddenly started with fright when she was telling us about it that first night. She thought she had left her scarf in Corcoran's room. You pointed out that Fifi had it, and she quickly dropped the subject. I think she *had* left the scarf in this room when she fired the second shot into the wall at midnight. Only – and she didn't notice it – Fifi had followed her and brought the scarf back into our room. It was there, in a limp ball, where Fifi had dropped it when we came into our room. *But Fifi wasn't. Fifi was outside the door, waiting for us.* When I asked Perdita repeatedly whether she had even once left our room after eleven she denied it. The proof that she was lying about this was staring at me all the time. Fifi had brought the scarf into our room, but Fifi wasn't in our room. Yet Perdita insisted that she had never opened our door.'

He glanced from the window again and slowly drew the curtains. He heard the car starting. Tyler recognized its motor and jumped to his feet.

'But she doesn't know the first thing about . . .' He bit his lips and stopped.

Eight o'clock struck from the tower of St-Justin-d'Aze, and in the throbbing silence which followed it I heard Vicki and Mitzi sobbing quietly in each other's arms.

The wreckage of Tyler's Renault was found only a few yards away from the remains of the Bugatti. It had not caught fire, but its driver was dead.

Chapter 35

We have often wondered what happened to Rudolph Stein. He had, we understood, about two thousand pounds in various currencies which he was supposed to turn over to Corcoran. The money, strictly speaking, was not his own, though Kitson felt he had earned it. When we last saw Rudolph he was brooding over a glass of beer, nervously cracking the joint of his little finger. Dagobert sold him our spare tandem, so perhaps he got away on that.

We had luncheon at Claridges' the other day with Dagobert's friend in the Home Office, and I suddenly mentioned Fred Evans. Dagobert's friend was studiedly vague. Fred had, he understood, come into a couple of thousand pounds somehow and started a small but respectable business somewhere – in South America, probably. The subject was rather pointedly dropped.

Vicki's last letter is equally uninformative. It does not mention her brother, though it is mainly about someone called 'Rudi Sherman'. The letter was postmarked 'Dallas, Texas', and was full of snapshots of a very fat, jolly baby, presumably Rudi. Tyler had added a note saying that his son Rudi was, at the age of six months, already astonishingly musical and that he hoped to make a great violinist out of him. Vicki had scribbled across this: 'No! My Rudi is going to be a cowboy!' Time will doubtless tell.

Naomi's latest letter (forwarded to us by Thomas Cook's in Paris to Soho Square, where we are temporarily living in order 'to be near Dagobert's work', the nature of which I still have not fathomed) is full of new clothes, new art exhibitions and Mitzi's Wigmore Hall debut. 'Kitson,' she says, 'was as charming and witty as ever when we went around to congratulate Mitzi afterwards and was delighted with my criticisms which he said were most valuable.' She goes on about parties every evening, amusing new night clubs and new restaurants. She raves so much about Federico's in Greek Street ('nothing approaching it in Paris') that we tried it last night. It's just around the corner.

It really justifies Naomi's eulogy. Federico himself is a fiery Spaniard with sleek black hair and a butterfly moustache. He has a flashing smile of welcome, set off by white prominent teeth. He speaks Spanish and French volubly, but almost no English, which pleased Dagobert, as it allowed him to practise. The dinner, as Naomi had promised, was 'a dream'; we were particularly struck by the *Fricandeau de mousserons* – the best dish we have tasted since the little inn near Andorra. I imagine the recipe was the same. Federico bowed and scraped when we congratulated him on it. He rubbed his hands together with unction and once, absentmindedly, cracked the joint of his little finger.

Naomi's letter is, as usual, a series of postscripts. In one she wonders 'vaguely whatever happened to that black afternoon dress I once lent you? I've found a little woman in Bruton Street who is so clever with alterations.'

The postscript immediately below this reads:

But of course! You can give it back to me next week! I'd totally forgotten what I meant to say. For some reason Geoffrey insists on taking me to Paris for the autumn dress openings. We're bringing the new Daimler, of course, so afterwards we can all drive down to Monte Carlo together! We can split the petrol bill if you like. The Daimler is vast and there will be plenty of room for us all. Dagobert and Geoffrey can sit in the front and drive, while you and I and Eric can easily squeeze into the back seat. Won't it be fun!

There is no final postscript to explain who Eric is. I haven't yet written to ask her.

THE PERENNIAL LIBRARY MYSTERY SERIES

Delano Ames

FOR OLD CRIME'S SAKE	P 629, $2.84
MURDER, MAESTRO, PLEASE	P 630, $2.84

E. C. Bentley

TRENT'S LAST CASE	P 440, $2.50
TRENT'S OWN CASE	P 516, $2.25

Gavin Black

A DRAGON FOR CHRISTMAS	P 473, $1.95
THE EYES AROUND ME	P 485, $1.95
YOU WANT TO DIE, JOHNNY?	P 472, $1.95

Nicholas Blake

THE CORPSE IN THE SNOWMAN	P 427, $1.95
THE DREADFUL HOLLOW	P 493, $1.95
END OF CHAPTER	P 397, $1.95
HEAD OF A TRAVELER	P 398, $2.25
MINUTE FOR MURDER	P 419, $1.95
THE MORNING AFTER DEATH	P 520, $1.95
A PENKNIFE IN MY HEART	P 521, $2.25
THE PRIVATE WOUND	P 531, $2.25
A QUESTION OF PROOF	P 494, $1.95
THE SAD VARIETY	P 495, $2.25
THERE'S TROUBLE BREWING	P 569, $3.37
THOU SHELL OF DEATH	P 428, $1.95
THE WIDOW'S CRUISE	P 399, $2.25
THE WORM OF DEATH	P 400, $2.25

Andrew Garve

THE ASHES OF LODA P 430, $1.50

THE CUCKOO LINE AFFAIR P 451, $1.95

A HERO FOR LEANDA P 429, $1.50

MURDER THROUGH THE LOOKING GLASS P 449, $1.95

NO TEARS FOR HILDA P 441, $1.95

THE RIDDLE OF SAMSON P 450, $1.95

Michael Gilbert

BLOOD AND JUDGMENT P 446, $1.95

THE BODY OF A GIRL P 459, $1.95

THE DANGER WITHIN P 448, $1.95

FEAR TO TREAD P 458, $1.95

Joe Gores

HAMMETT P 631, $2.84

C. W. Grafton

BEYOND A REASONABLE DOUBT P 519, $1.95

Edward Grierson

THE SECOND MAN P 528, $2.25

Cyril Hare

DEATH IS NO SPORTSMAN P 555, $2.40

DEATH WALKS THE WOODS P 556, $2.40

AN ENGLISH MURDER P 455, $2.50

TENANT FOR DEATH P 570, $2.84

TRAGEDY AT LAW P 522, $2.25

UNTIMELY DEATH P 514, $2.25

THE WIND BLOWS DEATH P 589, $2.84

WITH A BARE BODKIN P 523, $2.25

Robert Harling

THE ENORMOUS SHADOW P 545, $2.50

Matthew Head

THE CABINDA AFFAIR P 541, $2.25

THE CONGO VENUS P 597, $2.84

MURDER AT THE FLEA CLUB P 542, $2.50

M. V. Heberden

ENGAGED TO MURDER P 533, $2.25

James Hilton

WAS IT MURDER? P 501, $1.95

P. M. Hubbard

HIGH TIDE P 571, $2.40

Elspeth Huxley

THE AFRICAN POISON MURDERS P 540, $2.25

MURDER ON SAFARI P 587, $2.84

Francis Iles

BEFORE THE FACT P 517, $2.50

MALICE AFORETHOUGHT P 532, $1.95

Michael Innes

DEATH BY WATER P 574, $2.40

HARE SITTING UP P 590, $2.84

THE LONG FAREWELL P 575, $2.40

THE MAN FROM THE SEA P 591, $2.84

THE SECRET VANGUARD P 584, $2.84

Mary Kelly

THE SPOILT KILL — P 565, $2.40

Lange Lewis

THE BIRTHDAY MURDER — P 518, $1.95

Allan MacKinnon

HOUSE OF DARKNESS — P 582, $2.84

Arthur Maling

LUCKY DEVIL — P 482, $1.95

RIPOFF — P 483, $1.95

SCHROEDER'S GAME — P 484, $1.95

Austin Ripley

MINUTE MYSTERIES — P 387, $2.50

Thomas Sterling

THE EVIL OF THE DAY — P 529, $2.50

Julian Symons

THE BELTING INHERITANCE — P 468, $1.95

BLAND BEGINNING — P 469, $1.95

BOGUE'S FORTUNE — P 481, $1.95

THE BROKEN PENNY — P 480, $1.95

THE COLOR OF MURDER — P 461, $1.95

Dorothy Stockbridge Tillet
(John Stephen Strange)

THE MAN WHO KILLED FORTESCUE — P 536, $2.25

Simon Troy

THE ROAD TO RHUINE	P 583, $2.84
SWIFT TO ITS CLOSE	P 546, $2.40

Henry Wade

THE DUKE OF YORK'S STEPS	P 588, $2.84
A DYING FALL	P 543, $2.50
THE HANGING CAPTAIN	P 548, $2.50

Hillary Waugh

LAST SEEN WEARING . . .	P 552, $2.40
THE MISSING MAN	P 553, $2.40

Henry Kitchell Webster

WHO IS THE NEXT?	P 539, $2.25

Anna Mary Wells

MURDERER'S CHOICE	P 534, $2.50
A TALENT FOR MURDER	P 535, $2.25

Edward Young

THE FIFTH PASSENGER	P 544, $2.25